‖‖‖ ‖ ‖ ‖‖ ‖ ‖‖‖‖‖ ‖ ‖‖
☞ **W9-BSE-897**

THE HOMECOMING

It was his aunt's voice that broke the painful stillness of his dark room. "Dick, dear," she called softly, "may I come in just a minute?"

He made a muffled sound in his pillow. To be caught crying by his aunt this first night of his arrival! This was too much!

"I couldn't go to sleep without kissing you good-night, Dick. I always used to kiss my brother Dick good-night. It's been so many years now, and you are so like him!"

There was a sob in her voice. Why, she was crying, too!

Then somehow Dick didn't mind anymore. He put up his young, strong arms, flung them about her neck, and held her tightly in a fierce boy grip.

"Thanks, awfully!" he blundered out. "I'm glad I came. I—guess we'll—get on—all right."

It was a great deal for a boy like him to say. It was equivalent to a hundred loyal speeches and kisses thrown in, and it meant entire surrender . . .

Bantam Books by Grace Livingston Hill
Ask your bookseller for the books you have missed

The Obsession of Victoria Gracen

Grace Livingston Hill

BANTAM BOOKS
TORONTO · NEW YORK · LONDON

THE OBSESSION OF VICTORIA GRACEN
*A Bantam Book / published by arrangement with
J. B. Lippincott Company*

PRINTING HISTORY
First published 1927
Bantam edition / February 1979

*Bantam Books are published by Bantam Books, Inc. Its trade-
mark, consisting of the words "Bantam Books" and the por-
trayal of a bantam, is Registered in U.S. Patent and Trademark
Office and in other countries. Marca Registrada. Bantam
Books, Inc., 666 Fifth Avenue, New York, New York 10019.*

PRINTED IN THE UNITED STATES OF AMERICA

Chapter I

THE carriage turned the corner at a cheerful trot, and drew up before the door of a smart brick house in a row of new houses on a little new street. The occupants, one by one, alighted on the sidewalk with an air of relief and of duty well done.

Mr. Miller, tall and heavy, with a thick, red neck and a coarse, red face, got out first, followed by his sharp-faced aspiring wife in borrowed mourning,—because of course one wouldn't want to wear mourning after the funeral for a mere sister-in-law who left nothing behind but a mortgage and a good-for-nothing son.

The three little Millers, Elsa, Carlotta, and Alexander, in black hair-ribbons and black hat-bands, who had gone along solely for the ride to the cemetery, spilled joyfully out, glad to be back home again; and finally the only mourner the carriage contained, Richard, the son of the dead woman, stepped awkwardly forth from his cramped position, and looked gloomily about him.

The setting sun was sending long, red rays across the pavement. It was good to the Millers to be back in every-day life again with thoughts to death put aside, and little, common, *alive* things going on everywhere—children calling to one another in the street, wagons and carts hurrying home after the day's work, the clang of the crowded trolley, the weak light of the street-lamps suddenly blinking ineffectually into the ruby light of the setting sun. It was good to see one's own house standing safe and homely in shining varnish and glowing painted brick, and to know that life could now go on in its regular pleasant monotony, which had been interrupted solemnly for four days by the sudden death of one who had been near without being particularly dear. The sister who had married above her station into a family who never

1

received her or took any notice of her child; whose husband had the ill grace to die young and leave her to struggle on alone with their house only half paid for and a handsome, lazy boy whom she had allowed to grow up to have his own way, was not deeply mourned by any of them. They looked upon her son as almost irretrievably spoiled, but they intended to do their sensible best to make a man of him in their own way, though they felt that for his good his mother should have died ten years earlier.

They marshalled their forces on the sidewalk in front of the house, and looked closely at him now with a strange, new, possessive glance.

"Supper'll be ready t'woncet," said his aunt pointedly; "so don't you go to goin' off."

Richard regarded her defiantly, but said nothing. He was not hungry, but he had no relish for an argument with his aunt. He had always kept out of her way as much as possible. She knew he disliked her. He had once come upon her while she was in the midst of giving his mother some wholesome advice about his upbringing; and he had loomed darkly in the doorway and told her to go about her business, that his mother knew how to manage her own affairs. He had looked so big and fierce, with his fine, black brows drawn and his dark eyes blazing, that she had gone away, deferring her further advice until a more convenient season when he should not be by, but she knew that since then he had never liked her.

Richard looked furtively down the street; but his uncle's heavy hand was upon his shoulder, and there was that in his uncle's eye that made it apparent that the thing to do was to go into the house. The boy had no desire to make a scene. He wished to do all that was necessary to show respect to his mother, but his soul was raging at the necessity which made him a part of this group of unloved relatives. His uncle had once told a man in his presence that Richard resembled his father's family, with an adjective describing that family which was anything but complimentary, and that if he had his way with the boy he would be taken

from school and made to work to get the foolishness
out of him. He had said that it usually took two generations at least to get the "fine-gentleman" strain
out of a family, but he'd take it out of Richard in one if
he had half a chance. Since then Richard had hated his
uncle.

Entering the house, they found supper all ready; a
good roast of beef with vegetables and three kinds of
pie in honor of the occasion. The family ate with zest;
for they felt the hard part of the day to be over, and
they might now enjoy the gala part, which consisted
mainly in eating the things prepared as for a wedding-
feast. This was a funeral-feast. Mrs. Miller had invited her two sisters to share it with them. It helped
to pay a long-standing score of invitations, besides
looking well to the neighbors that she went to so much
trouble for just a sister-in-law.

The two sisters had brought their respective husbands and children, and arrived from the cemetery
almost immediately, laughing and talking with discreetly crescendo voices. Altogether it was a jolly company that sat down to the table; and Richard, frowning,
silent, was the only one out of accord. He ate little, and before the rest were half through, sat back
with sullen gaze. His uncle talked much, with his
mouth full of beef, to the two brothers-in-law, and
laughed heartily. The funeral aspect was fast disap-
pearing from the group. His uncle rallied the boy on
his solemnity.

"It's no more than natural," said one of the aunt's
sisters, peering at him not unkindly with curious, mild
eyes. "Of course the boy feels it. But then it ain't as
if he was all alone in the world. Richard, you'd really
ought to be thankful you've got such a good home and
such kind relatives to take care of you."

Richard's face flushed angrily. He was not in the
least thankful, and he had no idea whatever of being
taken care of by any of his kind relatives. He did not
care for even the kindness in the eyes of this woman
who was not a relative, for which latter fact he was
very thankful. He wanted to tell her to attend to her

own affairs, but it did not seem a wise remark to make just then. He was one against many. He knew he could not knock them all down.

"Have another piece of pie, Richard," invited his aunt magnanimously, as if the second piece of pie were a panacea for all troubles. "His ma always let him have the second helping," she explained portentously to her sisters, as if it had been a habit of the dead woman much to be deplored. Richard declined the piece of pie curtly. The soul within him was at the boiling-point. He had never been outwardly a very loving son to his mother, but it frenzied him to hear her spoken of in his aunt's contemptuous tone.

"Richard goes to work at the slaughter-house tomorrow morning," stated his uncle to the brothers-in-law, as if it were something quite understood between the uncle and nephew. "Work'll take his mind off his loss. There's nothing like work to make a man of a fellow."

"That's so!" declared the other two men, heartily, "that's so! Right well do I remember when I first started out to work."

"So you're going to work in the slaughter-house, Richard," said the mild sister, again turning her curious eyes on him approvingly. "That's right. Your mother would 'a' been real pleased at that. She was always awful troubled about your idle ways, your not getting on in school, nor hunting a job——"

But Richard interrupted her further remarks.

"Not much I ain't going to work at the slaughter-house," he blazed in a low angry tone that sounded like a rumble of thunder.

He shoved his chair back sharply, and rose to his feet. He would stand this thing no longer.

"You sure are going to work at the slaughter-house, Richard," declared his uncle; "and you're going tomorrow morning. I got a job for you just yesterday, and told 'em you'd be on hand. It's a good job with reasonable pay right at the start, and you'll be able to pay your board to your aunt like any young fellow that earns his own living. Of course you couldn't get

board that low anywheres else; but it's a start, and
when you get a raise we'll expect you to pay more.
It's only reasonable. You'll have a chance to rise and
learn the whole business, and some day you may
have a business of your own."

"No, thanks!" said Richard curtly in the tone that
offended because it was so like his fine-gentleman father's manner.

"None of your airs, young man! I'm your guardian
now. You'll do as I say, and I don't intend to have
you loafing about the streets smoking cigarettes and
learning to drink. You've got a *man* to deal with now.
You're not mamma's pet any longer. You've got to go
to work to-morrow morning, and you might just as
well understand it right now."

Richard was too angry to speak. His throat seemed
to close over the furious words that rushed to his lips.
He stood facing his great, red-faced, beefy uncle,
whose work had been in the slaughter-house since he
was a mere boy, who had early learned to drink the
hot blood of the creatures he killed, and who looked
like one of his own great oxen ready for slaughter.
There was contempt and scorn in the fine, young face
of the boy, fine in spite of the lines of self-indulgence
which his dead mother had helped him to grave upon
it. He was white and cool with anger. It was a part of
his aristocratic heritage that he could control his manner and voice when he was angry, and it always made
his tempestuous uncle still more furious that he could
not break this youthful, contemptuous calm; therefore
Richard had the advantage of him in an argument.

The boy looked his uncle defiantly in the eyes
for a full minute, while the relatives watched in mingled surprise, interest, and disapproval the audacity of
the youth; then he turned on his heel, and without a
word walked toward the door.

"Where you goin', Richard?" called out his cousin
Elsa, disappointed that the interesting scene should be
suddenly brought to a close by the disappearance of
the hero. Elsa frequented moving-picture shows, and
liked to have her tragedies well worked out.

Richard had never really disliked Elsa. She had but too lately emerged from babyhood to have been in the least annoying to him. Her question was merely the question of a child.

"I'm going home," he answered briefly, and his hand was on the door-knob; but his progress was stopped by the thundering voice of his uncle.

"Stop, you young jackanapes!" he roared. "Do you mean to defy me in my own house? Just come back to your seat at the table, and we'll have it out. Now is as good as any time. You've got to understand that I'm your master, if it is the day of your mother's funeral."

"And your mother scarcely cold in her grave yet!" whimpered his aunt. "You're going to run around town and disgrace us all, you know you are."

"I am only going home, Aunt Sophia," said Richard with the calm dignity that was like a red rag to the fury of his irate uncle.

"Home!" thundered the uncle. "You have no home but this. Don't you know that the old house you called home was mortgaged to more than its worth, and that I hold the mortgage? Your mother was deep in debt to me when she died, and there wasn't even enough left to pay her funeral expenses. It's high time you understood how matters stand, young man. You *have* no home! You will have to come down off your high horse now, and get right down to business. A boy that can't even pay his mother's funeral expenses has no room to walk around like a fine gentleman and talk about going home."

Richard looked his uncle in the eyes again, a cold fury stealing over him, a desperate, lonely, heart-sinking horror taking possession of him. He felt that he could not and would not stay here another minute. He wanted to fly at his uncle and thrash him. He wanted to stop all their ugly, gloating voices, and show himself master of the situation; but he was only a lonely, homeless boy, penniless—so his uncle said—and without a friend in the world. But at least he would not stay here to give them the satisfaction of bullying him.

Suddenly he turned with a quick movement, and bolted from the room and the house.

It was all done so quickly that they could not have stopped him. His uncle had not thought he would go after he heard the truth. His aunt began to cry over the disgrace she said he would bring upon the family, running around town the night of his mother's funeral, and perhaps getting drunk and getting his name in the paper. She reproached her husband tearfully for not having used more tact in his dealings with the boy this first night.

The two visiting brothers-in-law advised not worrying, and said the boy would be all right. He was just worked up over his loss. He would willingly come to terms next day when he was hungry and found he had no home. Just let him alone to-night. Elsa said she shouldn't think Richard would want to go to his home. She should think he'd be afraid. She said she'd stay by the window and watch for him, and thus she stole out of the uncomfortable family debate.

Richard, meanwhile, was breathlessly running block after block toward his old home. It might be true or not that the house was mortgaged to his uncle. It probably was true, for he remembered his mother worrying about expenses when the boarders began to leave because the table was getting so poor they couldn't stand it, and she got sick, and the cook left; but, true or not, they could not take him away from the house to-night. It was his refuge from the world by all that was decent. He would go back to his home, crawl in at a window, and think out what he would do with himself. His uncle would not pursue him there to-night, he was sure; and, if he did, it would be easy to hide. His uncle would never think to look on the roof, which had been his refuge more than once in a childish scrape.

He stole in through the little side-alley entrance to the tiny kitchen-yard where his mother's ragged dish-cloth still fluttered disconsolately in the chill air of the evening. He was thankful it was too cold for the neighbors to be out on their front steps, and thus he had been able to slip in undetected.

It was quite dark now, and the distant flickering arc-light on the next street gave little assistance to climbing in at the window; but Richard had been in the same situation hundreds of times before, and found no difficulty in turning the latch of the kitchen window and climbing in over the sink. Many times in the small hours of the morning after a jolly time with the fellows he had stolen in softly this way; while his anxious mother kept fitful vigil at the front window, weak tears stealing down her cheeks, to be mildly and pleasantly surprised an hour or so later on visiting his room at finding him innocently asleep.

Richard always assured her the next morning that it had not been very late when he came in, and joined in her wonder that she had not heard him; so she continued to have faith in him and to believe that she had been mistaken about thinking he was not in when she went upstairs from her nightly toil in the kitchen.

Oh, he had not been a model son by any means, but neither had she been a model mother. She was well-meaning and loving, but weak and inefficient; and the boy, loving her in his brusque way, while he half despised her weakness, had "guarded" her from a lot of what he considered "unnecessary worry" about himself. He was all right, he reasoned, and none of the dreadful things, like drowning, or getting drunk, or being arrested, that his mother feared, were going to happen to him. He would look out for that. He could take care of himself, but he was not going to be tied to her apron-string. There was something wild in him that called to be satisfied, and only by going out with the boys on their lawless good times could he satisfy it. There was nothing at home to satisfy. Women didn't understand boys; boys had to go, and to know a lot of things that women did not dream about. He did not intend to do any dreadful thing, of course, but there was no need for her to bother about him the way she did; so he kept her politely blinded, and went on his careless free-and-easy way, deceiving her, yet loving her more than he knew.

As for his gentleman father, the boy worshipped his dim memory, the more, perhaps, because his mother's family lost no occasion to cast scorn upon it.

But, as Richard climbed softly in over the sink, a kind of shame stole over him, and his cheeks grew hot in the darkness. He let down the window noiselessly, and fastened it. There was no need to be so quiet now, for no mother waited up-stairs at the front window for his coming. It was wholly unnecessary for him to remove his shoes before he went up the stairs; for the ear that had listened for his steps through the years of his boyhood was dull in death, and would listen no more for his coming.

But habit held him, and his heart beat with a new and painful remorse to think that he had ever deceived her. For the first time in his life his own actions seemed most reprehensible. Before this his deception had been to him only a sort of virtue, just a manly shielding of his mother from any unnecessary worry. It had never occurred to him that he might have denied himself some of the midnight revels.

They had been comparatively harmless revels, in a way. Temptations, of course, had beset him thickly, and to some he had yielded; but those of the baser sort had not appealed to him. The finer feelings of his nature had so far shielded him; a sense that his father would not have yielded to such things had held him. But he was young, and had not felt the fulness of temptations that were to come. His character was yet in the balance, and might turn one way or another, though most people would have said the probabilities were heavily in favor of the evil. He had taken a few steps in the downward course, and knew it, but was in no wise sure that he intended to keep on. He did not consider himself the bad boy that his mother's relatives branded him, though he was defiantly aware of the bad reputation he bore, and haughtily declined to do anything to prove that it was much exaggerated.

He crept stealthily through the silent rooms, now so strangely in order, the rooms that he never remembered to have seen quite in order before. The chairs stood stiff and straight around the walls, shoved back by alien hands after the funeral. He shuddered as he passed the doorway of the dingy little parlor. He knew his mother's casket was no longer there. He had stood by and seen them lower it into the grave; but somehow in his vision the still form, and white, strangely young, and miraculously pretty face of his dead mother seemed still to lie there. Quickly turning his head away from the doorway, he hurried up the stairs as though he might have been pursued.

He wondered about the youth and beauty that death had brought to his mother, of which he had never caught even a glimpse before. Now he understood how his father had picked her out from her uncomely family, and been willing to alienate his own people for her sake. He felt a passing thrill of pride in his father that he had stuck to her for the two years until his death, in spite of the many temptations of his wealthy relatives, though it meant complete alienation from all he had before held dear.

"Father was 'game' all right, if he *was* used to different things," he said to himself softly as he opened the door of his own room, and avoided the creaking board in his floor, as was his wont. "Pretty punk family they must have been, though, to let him!"

He stood looking about his own room by the light of the street-lamp that shone dimly in at the window. It looked unfamiliar. Some one had evidently been up here clearing up also. The baseball pictures from magazines, and the pennants that came as prizes with a certain number of cigarette packages, which had clumsily decorated the ugly little place, had been ruthlessly disposed of. He suspected that this had been done by his aunt's orders; for she had once severely scored him for having such disreputable things about, and had told his mother that she was to blame if he went wrong, if she allowed things like that on his wall. He frowned now in the darkness, and wished he might find some way of

getting even with his aunt. He resolved once more
never to get within her power again—no, not if he had
to run away before morning.

But his own room had an unfriendly look; his heart
was sore, and his mind distressed. With a strange yearn-
ing that he could not understand he went out, closed
the door quietly after him, and stole softly down the
hall to his mother's room.

This was cleared up, too; but still there were a number of things about that suggested her presence, and
with a queer, choking feeling in his throat he suddenly
turned the key in the lock of this door, flung himself
full length upon his mother's bed, and buried his face
in her pillow. There was something about the old,
woollen patchwork quilt with which the bed was covered—it being the back room, and consequently not
on exhibition, there had been no necessity for a white
spread—that touched his heart and took him back to
his babyhood; and here he found that what he wanted
was his mother.

The mother that he had grieved so sorely, deceived,
neglected, disappointed, and worried into her grave!
But she was all he had had in the world. He knew that
she had loved him; and it was the loss of that love that
made him feel so terribly alone in the world now that
she had been taken from him.

Tears! Unmanly though they were, they stung their
way into his eyes, and sobs such as never had been
allowed to take possession of him since babyhood now
shook his strong young frame. For a time his desolation
rolled over him like the darkness of the bottomless pit.

Then suddenly, when he grew quieter, a loud peal
from the door-bell sounded through the empty house
and echoed up to him.

Chapter II

MISS VICTORIA GRACEN sat before the open fire in
her pleasant library, under the light of a softly-shaded

reading-lamp, with the latest magazine in her lap, ready for a luxurious evening alone.

Miss Gracen, always a pleasant picture to look upon, was especially lovely against the setting of this room. The walls were an indescribable color like atmosphere, with a dreamy border of soft oak-trees framing a distant, hazy sky and mountains. Against this background a few fine pictures stood out to catch the eye.

The floor was polished and strewn over with small moss-brown and green rugs, and the furniture was all green willow with soft green velvet cushions; even the luxurious couch with its pillows of bronze, old gold, and russet, and one scarlet one like a flaming berry in the woods. Every piece of furniture stood turning naturally toward the hearth as though that were the sun; the dancing flames of the bright wood fire played fitfully over the whole room, lighting up the long rows of inviting books behind the glass doors of the low, built-in bookcases.

Miss Gracen herself, in her soft lavender challis frock, with the glow of the lamplight on her abundant white hair, seemed like a violet on a mossy bank, a lovely, lovable human violet. Her face was beautiful as a girl's, in spite of her years; and the brown eyes under the fine dark brows were large, luminous, and interested.

People said she lived an ideal life, with her fine, old house full of rare mahogany furniture, priceless pictures, and china; her carriage and horses; three old family servants—of whom the kind is now almost extinct —to keep all in order and wait upon her; and plenty of money to do what she would. She had nothing in the world to trouble her, and everything for which to be thankful.

Yet, as she settled herself to the reading of the latest chapter of her favorite serial, she was conscious of a sense of restless dissatisfaction and of an almost unreasonable longing to have a companion to enjoy with her the story she was about to read.

She looked up with a welcoming smile for old Hiram, who tapped and entered with the evening mail. It was a relief to speak even to the old servant when she was in this mood. A fleeting whim that perhaps, after all, she would run in and see some neighbor instead of reading just now passed through her mind as she held out her hand for the mail; but when Hiram said it had begun to rain a little, she put the thought aside and settled down to open her letters and enjoy the evening beside her own bright fire.

There were bills for putting the furnace in order for the winter, and for mending the slates on the roof where the big tree fell during a summer storm. There was the winter's calendar for the Women's Club; a notice of the next Ladies' Aid meeting, with a reminder that Miss Gracen was chairman of the refreshment committee; a request from the president of the missionary society that Miss Gracen would read a paper on "The New China" at the next monthly meeting; a request for a donation from a noted charity in the near-by city; and a letter from an old college-mate whom she had invited to take a three months' trip abroad with her, saying that she could not possibly be spared from her family this winter.

There was also a single newspaper.

Miss Gracen went through them all hastily, keeping the letter from her friend till the last to enjoy; but she laid it down with a disappointed look. Somehow the letter was not what she had expected from her old chum. It expressed gratitude, of course, for the royal invitation; but it seemed by the answer that the possibility of accepting it had scarcely been considered; the mother's heart was so full of her children that she had not even *wanted* to go with her old friend for three short months. The rest, the delight of travel, and the reunion with her friend, were as nothing to her compared with losing three whole months of care and toil and love out of her home life. Well, it was natural, of course. It must be great to have folks of one's own; but then, they were also a care. One could not do as one pleased; still— and the wistful look lingered around Miss Gracen's mouth as she reached out her hand for the newspaper in a soiled wrapper, wondering idly what it could be. It was not the night for either of the weekly papers she took regularly, and the daily evening paper from the city came to her door-step by the hand of a small boy at five o'clock in the afternoon.

"Marked Copy" was scrawled in the corner of the wrapper. What could it be? Some notice of her last paper at the club that had crept into a city paper and some one had sent to her? No, it was a Chicago paper. She had no intimate friends in Chicago. How strange! It must have got into her box by mistake.

She looked at the wrapper again, but her name was written quite plainly in a scrawling, cramped hand. There could be no mistake.

She hastily turned the crumpled pages to find a mark; and her heart gave one quick throb out of its natural course as she saw the black marking around a tiny notice in the column of deaths. Yet why should she be agitated? There could be no near friend in that locality. It was nearly fourteen years since the telegram had come telling of her brother Dick's death, and since then Chicago had held no vital interest for her.

Yet there it was, her own name, Gracen, with the ink-scrawls about it; and something tightened around her heart with a nameless fear she could not understand. Yet of course Dick's wife,—that wife that her father had not been willing to recognize because the family was a common one, and beneath his son socially, educationally, intellectually, every way—she was there. If Miss Gracen had thought anything at all about her, it had been with relief that the tie that bound the unknown girl to them was broken by her brother's death. It would have been no more than natural for her to marry again, and the name of Gracen did not seem in any wise to belong to her.

There had been a child. After the death of her father and stricken mother, Victoria Gracen had written, offering to take the child and have him educated as befitted his father's son; but the offer had been ungraciously declined. The illiterate scrawl of the mother had reminded Miss Gracen of the low growl of a mother lion she had once heard in the Zoölogical Gardens when another lion came near the cub. She could remember yet the wave of mortification that had rolled crimsonly over her face as she read, and resented the name signed to that refusal. That woman had no right to that name, no right to her handsome young brother, whose face they had never seen after he went from them in anger the day his father refused to recognize his marriage with the foolish, pretty girl.

Yet there the name stood in clear print, with all the dignity of death about it. Death, the leveller of all ranks and stations:

Lilly Miller Gracen, widow of the late Richard Pierson Gracen. Relatives and friends are invited to attend the funeral on Thursday at 2.30 from her late residence, 3452 Bristol Street. Interment in Laurel Cemetery.

It was a simple enough statement, in the time-worn terms of such notices; but it strangely stirred the soul of the woman who read. The very name "Lilly" in connection with the family name of Gracen was an offence. It brought to remembrance the photograph of the silly, pretty girl-bride that Dick, her brother, had sent home to them when he had written to tell them he was to be married. The name "Lilly," with all its pretense and lack of dignity, seemed to express in a single word the sharpness of the sorrow of those bitter days.

Miss Gracen had come out from under the cloud of sorrow, and had made her own life sweet and calm again; but she had never quite forgotten the beloved brother who had gone so suddenly out of it, nor had she ever forgiven the woman for whose sake that brother had left father and mother and sister.

And now the woman herself, it seemed, was gone! And what had become of the child, the child that was Dick's as well as hers?

As if to answer her question, she noticed a rude hand pointing to another column, where a brief paragraph was also marked:

Mrs. Lilly Miller Gracen, widow of the late Richard Pierson Gracen, died on Wednesday at her home on Bristol Street after a brief illness. Mrs. Gracen was a sister of Peter Miller, of 18 Maple Street, head foreman in the slaughter-house of Haste Brothers, and had since her husband's death kept a lodging house on Bristol Street. She leaves one son, Richard.

It was a strange item to creep into a great city paper when one considered it to be about an obscure lodging-house keeper, but it never occurred to Miss Gracen that it might have been put into the paper and paid for by the obnoxious family of the dead woman just that it might reach her eyes. If Peter Miller had been well acquainted with Miss Gracen, he could not have well planned a paragraph which would have been more mortifying to her family pride. A slaughter-house! A lodging-house! And in connection with the historic name of Gracen. The haughty pride wounded, the blood mounted in rich waves to the roots of Miss Gracen's white hair, and receded, leaving her pale and trembling, almost breathless.

For a few minutes she was filled with a strange weakness, as though she had been publicly brought to shame; for so bitter had her father been against the woman who had unwittingly come between him and his beloved son, that he had succeeded in making his whole family feel it more or less, although, as Miss Gracen in the silence of her thoughts had often owned, it was an utterly unfair prejudice; for she had never even seen the face of her sister-in-law, except in a photograph.

But now the woman was dead, and a strange sadness came into the heart of her patrician sister-in-law. False shame receded, and pity took its place. After all, the woman had been proud and had maintained a certain courageous attitude, not allowing them to give her money nor to take her child from her after the death of her husband. A boarding-house keeper! Miss Gracen in her sheltered home shuddered at the thought. It had surely been a hard life; and death had probably brought blessed relief.

And that child, a boy of sixteen now! What must he be? What was to become of him now? Would he go to live with that uncle who was foreman in a slaughter-house,—horrible, brutal creature!—and sink back to the level of his mother's family—if, indeed, he had ever been above it? Yet he was Dick's child, Dick's only son, and bore Dick's name in full, the honored name of his ancestors for generations back,—Richard Pierson Gracen. How dreadful to have Dick's son grow up to be manager or something in a slaughter-house! There were even worse depths, of course, than that, to which he might descend.

Well, what could she do? It was dreadful, of course; but they had not accepted her offer of help when he was a little child and she might have really done something toward bringing him up rightly. Now he was probably impossible from every point of view. She couldn't, of course, have him come to her now.

She looked around upon her pleasant room, the immaculate furniture, the spotless peace that reigned, and found it quite impossible to imagine a boy at home there. It seemed to be an invasion of her rights that she could not bring herself to endure.

And yet—her eye travelled back to the printed notice in the paper. "She leaves one son," it spoke to her in reproachful tones from the coarse ink of the paper. "One son!" Left! And suddenly the boy seemed to have taken on the form and feature of his father as he was, bright-faced and happy, bidding her good-bye so long ago; and tears filled her eyes. Dear Dick! How she had loved him, and how much he and she had always been to each other until that strange girl-wife had come between them! How Dick would feel to have his boy grow up with such surroundings! Ought she not for her dead brother's sake to try to do something for this orphaned boy of his?

But how? In that old, conservative town of her father how could she bring an alien grandson, who might, perhaps,—very likely would,—disgrace his memory and name? There were the servants, too, to consider; for they were getting old and had been faithful.

And there was her own life. She had a right to live it in peace, for had she not been faithful to her father and mother and given up bright hopes for their sakes? Now at least she had a right to enjoy herself as she

chose. There was her trip to Europe. She would have
to give that up, too, for of course she never could go
off and leave a strange boy on the place with only the
servants. No, that was entirely out of the question.

With a tightening of her sweet lips she folded the
Chicago paper quite determinedly, put it on the under
part of the table, and settled herself to her magazine
serial.

She must have read fully half a column without letting her thoughts really stray from the story, when
the pleading eyes of her brother Dick finally conquered,
and made her look around the room again, as if she
almost felt his presence there. She seemed to see a boy
sitting across the table from her; and his eyes were the
eyes of her brother, and somehow it suddenly seemed to
be a very pleasant thing to have a boy there, and not
nearly so incongruous as she at first had thought. With
a warmer feeling at her heart she turned her mind back
again to her story.

She had not finished the first page when she finally
abandoned the magazine entirely, and closed her eyes
for serious thinking.

The little clock on the mantel was striking eight
when Miss Gracen got up with decision, and went over
to her telephone to send a telegram, pausing on her
way to reach under the table for the Chicago paper and
search out the marked notice.

After a moment's thought she first called up her local
banker, who was also a personal friend, and told him
she wanted to send some money to a friend in Chicago; could he advise her where and how to place it?

He gave her the name of a Chicago banker who was
his friend, and gave her all necessary directions for the
sending. She thanked him, and hung up the receiver
with interested face. The first step in her project was
now perfectly plain before her.

The telegraph office in Roslyn was closed for the
night, but she could telephone a message to the city
twenty-five miles away and have it sent through at once.
Her mind had worked swiftly, and she knew just what
she meant to say. Her voice was calm, almost eager, as

she gave the call and waited for the operator to take her dictation for two telegrams.

When she hung up the receiver after the messages were taken, her hand was trembling; but her eyes were shining, and her lips had a sweet line of pleasant decision that was most charming.

She started over toward her chair and magazine once more, but paused with a look of indecision. Somehow her chair and her magazine no longer fitted her present mood. She must do something to get used to her new arrangements. Her eyes travelled quickly about the room. How could she make that room look inviting to a boy? Suppose he came, and did not like it? It would be worse than if she had never brought him home at all. Was it possible for her now, at the age of forty-five, to take in a boy, any boy, even if he were a model, and assimilate him with her present life? And especially a boy against whom she was prejudiced; could she possibly be any kind of a guardian to him? Would it not have been better, after all, to have left him to his mother's relatives?

But no; she could not, would not, retract now. What she had done, she had done. She realized that it had been the hasty action of an impulse; but she would stand by it to the best of her ability, come what would. Perhaps, after all, the boy would elect not to come, and settle the matter for her. Then she could feel that at least she had done her duty. But with this thought came one of anxiety. Was it possible that she really desired to have Dick's boy come to her, invade her home, and fill her life with new cares and perplexities? A kind of pleasant wonder over herself began to dawn in her face.

With her eyes full of happy excitement she went quickly about the room, moving the chairs, drawing a big easy Morris-chair up to the light, throwing down a magazine open to a picture of a baseball field, as if a boy had left it for a moment; gathering the russet and green and crimson pillows out of their prim stiffness, and throwing them in pleasant confusion. But still she was not quite satisfied that it looked like a room where a young boy could live. She was trying to imagine how it would seem to him, and was wondering whether he would like it.

She was too restless to sit down again, and with a look of quiet enthusiasm she went out to the hall and up-stairs, turning on the electric light in advance. Into each bed-room she went on her tour of inspection, looking at the house from a different viewpoint, the viewpoint of a boy of sixteen. The guest-rooms, with their fine old furniture and solemn air of rich gravity; he would never feel at home there. Her father's and mother's room. Not there! They had hated him. They would not have wanted him to come to their house, though of course they must feel differently now. There was but one other room on that floor besides the servants' rooms; and that was the room next to her own, the room that had belonged to her brother Dick.

It was just as he had left it; his fishing-rods, books, balls, and pictures were there. All the things that a boy of twenty years before had cared for, the bird's nest with three eggs that he had brought in when the old birds had been frightened away by the workmen when the house was repaired; the wasps' nest from the east gable! She could remember the day when Dick rigged up a pole, and cautiously detached it from the house while she stood in the yard below and watched and gave advice. She could not give the stranger boy that room, Dick's room! And yet he was Dick's boy, and that was just what Dick would have wanted, she knew.

With one of her swift looks of determination she gave a glance of surrender around the room, and, turning, went down-stairs. Just an instant she paused in the wide doorway of the great, stately parlor, swept her glance about, and wondered whether that, too, would have to be sacrificed, then went on to her own library, and, pulling the cord that was still connected with the old-fashioned bell of the servants' part of the house, she sat down with the magazine in her lap, but a sparkle of expectancy in her eyes.

In a moment old Hiram limped up to the door, and opened it.

"Hiram," she said with a pleasant smile, just as if she were going to ask him to put another stick on the fire, "I'm expecting my nephew to visit me. I wish you would tell Molly and Rebecca that I'd like my brother's room got ready for him to-morrow. He may be here very soon; I am not sure yet—in a day or so, I think."

There was nothing in Miss Gracen's voice to indicate that she was saying an unusual thing, save the suppressed excitement in her eyes; and the old servant bowed quietly enough, and turned to go, though one might have noticed that his hand trembled as it touched the door-knob. But just as he was about to close the door he opened it a trifle wider, and, putting in his respectful gray head, said reverently, "Is it Mr. Dick's child you're expectin', Miss Vic?"

"Yes, Hiram," and Miss Gracen answered his look with a smile of indulgence. He and she had suffered together in the days of the elder Dick's banishment; but it was not a matter to be discussed, both knew.

"The Lord be praised, Miss Vic," said the old man again, reverently. "I knowed you'd do it sometime, Miss Vic; I knowed you'd do it."

Miss Gracen looked earnestly at her servant.

"His mother is dead now, Hiram. She would not give him up before. I have sent him word to come. I do not know yet what he will say, but we are going to get ready for him. Tell Molly and Rebecca."

The servant bowed, and went with shining eyes to tell his fellow-servants, while Miss Gracen lay back in her chair, and felt as if she had done a hard day's work. Would it pay, she wondered, or was it possible that she might be sorry for what she had done?

Chapter III

THE peal of the bell startled Richard into attention. Could it be that his uncle had really followed him, and meant to carry out his threat of compelling him to

work in that loathsome slaughter-house? His whole
soul revolted in horror. Of course he must work somewhere now, he supposed, but not there!

He arose quickly, and stole through the hall to the
front window where his mother had so often watched
for his late home-coming. He must find out at once
who was ringing that bell.

Softly pushing up the window and looking out, he
saw a messenger boy in brass buttons, with a book and
a pencil in his hand, impatiently looking up at him.

"What do you want down there?" he called out in-
hospitably.

"Telegram," answered the boy tersely.

"Guess you've made a mistake. There's no telegram
coming here," answered Richard decidedly, preparing
to shut the window.

"It's the number all right," said the boy with bold
assurance.

"Well, it's a mistake. What's the name?"

"Richard Pierson Gracen," drawled the boy, getting
close to the street-light to see.

Richard thumped the window down, and hurried
wonderingly to the door. Could it be that his uncle had
resorted to a telegram? Surely he would never spend a
quarter unnecessarily. Or was this a ruse to get him out
of the house, and was his uncle in hiding behind the
corner ready to seize him?

He opened the door warily, kept his foot braced
against it and his ears alert, while he signed his name
with the stubby pencil against the door-frame, and drew
a sigh of relief when the door closed on the impatient
messenger boy.

He stole softly back up-stairs to his mother's room
again with the telegram in his hand, wondering who in
the world could have sent it. It very likely was something about a bill, and wouldn't be worth lighting the
gas to see. However, no one from the street could see
the light in that room, and perhaps it would be as well
to read it.

He closed the door, drew the wooden shutters close,

lighted the gas, and with a curious apathy sat down on the edge of the bed to tear open his first telegram.

"Dear Dick," it read, "I wonder if you and I don't need each other. Suppose you come and make me a visit, and perhaps we can find out. Come as soon as you can, and telegraph me when you will arrive. I have only just heard of your loss, and am deeply sorry for you. Of course you will have expenses to meet, and I know it is not always easy to get money immediately at such a time; so I am placing five hundred dollars in your name in the Dearborn Trust Company Bank for you to use in whatever way you may need it. It will be there for your use by to-morrow morning. If you need more, just let me know. Buy a through ticket and a sleeper, and check your baggage to Roslyn. I hope you can come at once."

"Your aunt,
VICTORIA GRACEN."

Richard felt his senses reeling as he read, so that at first he scarcely took in the sense of the words. He had to read it over again before he grasped the full meaning of this marvellous telegram, about which the most marvellous thing, after all, was its length and the fact that it had been prepaid. How could any one have the temerity to send a telegram of that length when the prescribed number of words was ten?

"Gosh!" he ejaculated softly to himself.

The boy sat quite still, and stared blankly at the paper in his hand, while the dim gas-light from the worn-out burner flickered fitfully in the room, and the steady ticking of his mother's clock sounded loudly through the empty old house.

But the boy heard it not, for he was undergoing a change, and chief among his sensations was a desire to tell his mother what had happened.

True, his mother had always felt bitterly toward this aunt, who now invited him to visit her and hinted that perhaps they needed one another. True, his mother had always declined any help or suggestion from one who had scorned her as a sister-in-law, and he was proud of his mother for having done so. It was the one fine quality besides her love for him and for his father which linked her with aristocracy in his vague and unformed mind, this pride of hers that had caused her to work so hard to keep her child rather than to give him up, or to accept any help from those who had always despised her.

But she was gone now, and his situation was indeed desperate. His mother's family were not at all to his mind, nor the situation they were trying to force upon him. His mother had never seemed to want him to be with his uncle, even though he was her brother. He had an instinctive feeling that she would not want him to go with his uncle now. She had once sighed that she was unable to send him to college, as his father would surely have wished. He hadn't cared much about college himself, at least not for the sake of the education; but he remembered now that his mother had always wanted better things for him than just a mere place in the world to earn his living. Would his mother, now that she was gone, want him to hold out against his father's family? He thought not. Besides, it was a choice between going to work in the slaughter-house and running away if he did not accept this invitation of his aunt's.

Richard found himself longing inexpressibly for the sympathy, the thoughtfulness, the understanding, that seemed to breathe itself into the words of this telegram, though boylike he did not realize it.

"I wonder if you and I don't need each other."

When had anybody ever needed him before. Not even his poor, toil-worn, worried mother. The telegram implied that the writer was lonely, and his own lonely heart went out in quick response to the appeal.

Then there was another great thing. She had anticipated his penniless state, and had known how he would feel about paying expenses and things. She hadn't said a word about it, but had spoken just as if this money was his own, right from his father. She had conveyed that soothing impression to his queer, proud boy-heart. He wouldn't be accepting charity; it was *his,* placed in the bank without waiting to see whether he would do as she had asked, and plenty more if he needed it.

He could now pay the undertaker's bill; he could get a stone for his mother's grave, and could pay the long-standing grocery bill which had secretly mortified him beyond any of his childish troubles. He fairly hated the sneer on that grocer's face as he came and went by the store daily. The man had refused to let him have a chicken for broth for his mother the day before she died, and had said that he never expected to get a cent for all that she owed him. Richard hadn't blamed him so much for not giving him the chicken, but for the cold contempt in his face as he gave the denial he hated him. It gave him great comfort now to think that he could pay that bill. It was something more than a hundred dollars, but it should be paid, every cent of it.

His heart went out with gratitude toward his unknown aunt who had made it possible for him to hold up his head and pay his debts. There were other debts, too, debts of "honor" he called them, for sodas and cigarettes and games that his mother did not know how to play, and his instinct taught him that his aunt would not approve; but she had said he was to use the money for what he needed, and he could not go away without making it right with the boys. It wasn't much. A few dollars would cover it, and he must treat them all handsomely to ice-cream and maybe a supper before he left. They had been loyal friends of his always, even when he hadn't a cent in his pocket and could not get a chance anywhere to earn anything. His mother had worried about his friendship with them, and his uncle had openly told him he was on the highway to destruction by associating with them; but they had been good friends to him through all sorts of scrapes, and they were all the friends he had left unless perhaps this unknown aunt was going to prove to be one.

A sudden wave of curiosity and gratitude made him read the telegram again, just to be sure it was all true. It sounded like what the fellows would call "pipe dreams." Yet there it was, all perfectly clear and plain. He knew where the big stone bank was, in the heart of the city, and the next morning he could go and present his claim and put it to a test.

He liked the thoughtfulness of his aunt in suggesting a sleeper. A sleeper for a boy! His uncle would sneer at that, and call it extravagance. But he would take a sleeper. He would have the experience; it was what his whole soul had been hungering for all his life, experience. He would have experience, he would accept the invitation, and then if he didn't like it there he could go away. His aunt suggested that it was an experiment, and it suited him well to take it just as she put it. He thought her a rather jolly good fellow for having put it just that way. It laid no obligations upon either of them, and yet gave him a chance to like her if he chose. That she might not like him never occurred to him, so egotistical is youth; and, indeed, at that time it is doubtful whether he would have cared.

After a brief deliberation over the telegram Richard arose, accepting his new situation calmly, and went about making his plans.

He searched out a small trunk in the attic, which some bankrupt boarder had left for his board; and into this he put the few articles that he cared for in the house. He found the hiding-place of his despised pictures and pennants, and put them in first; he examined his clothing, and decided that he would need two new suits if he was to make a visit, and he would see about those in the morning if the money was on hand; he put in his mother's old Bible and a small, faded photograph of his father; and his packing was done.

He then lay down to sleep.

His first waking thoughts were dazed, and filled with the sudden remembrance of the shadow of death, and the sickening horror with which the realization of loss always comes after sleep. Gradually remembrance came to him. For a minute he felt sure that telegram had been a figment of his imagination, a dream of the night, but on turning over he felt the rattle of the paper; and, springing up quickly, he threw open the shutters, letting in the morning sun; and there were the words just as he remembered them. A strange glow of pleasure filled him at the thought that his aunt needed him, and his answering heart told him that he needed her—or some one—most mightily.

He dressed quickly, and hurried down-stairs, hauling his trunk to the front door that it might be ready for the expressman when he came for it. With a glance of almost pathetic loneliness around him at the only home he had ever known he hurried out of the front door, and slammed it behind him, going straight down the street to the little corner grocery.

The grocer frowned as he looked up from weighing out sugar and saw him coming in, but Richard walked straight up to him with a new dignity in his face.

"Mr. Bitzer," he said in a clear voice, "I want to pay my bill here this morning. Can you have it itemized for me when I come back in about an hour?"

The insolent snarl on the man's face melted into a look of astonishment.

"*You* want to pay the bill?" he said incredulously. "You ain't got any money to pay any bill. Where'll you git the money?"

"I will be back to pay the bill in about an hour if you will have it ready for me," said Richard haughtily, and, turning on his heel, went out of the store. His heart was boiling with rage that a man had ever the chance to think of him with such contempt for lack of a little money. He felt again that strange thrill of something— was it gratitude? love?—toward the woman who had understood and who had made it possible for him to hold up his head before this man who had always despised his hard-working mother because she was poor.

His first goal was the bank, and with no thought of breakfast he spent his last nickel to take a trolley down-town. It suddenly seemed to him that he had a great deal to do, and he was seized with a wild desire to get it over with and be off before his uncle tried to stop him.

Arriving at the bank, he found a lot of other people

ahead of him, and himself obliged to stand in line. He
felt himself grow small as he saw business men cashing
large checks for hundreds of dollars, and rolling the
bills together as carelessly as if they might have been
ones instead of fifties.

He was within two of the window when a new
difficulty presented itself to his mind. The young man
ahead of him was evidently a foreigner who spoke little
English, and was having trouble to get what he wanted.
"You must be identified," the cashier was explaining;
and finally, after numerous shakings of the head, the
poor fellow had to turn away with his check uncashed.

That was something Richard had not thought of,
identification. What should he do? His uncle could, of
course, identify him or get some one else to do so; but
Richard did not want to ask this favor of him. He had
a strong feeling that his uncle, if he knew of it, would
find a way to get that five hundred dollars into his own
possession under the plea that he would pay the bills
himself and take care of the rest for his nephew.

Richard resolved that until he was safely out of the
city his uncle should know nothing about that money. He set his lips more firmly, and decided to find some
other way out of his difficulty. Would the telegram, he
wondered, be sufficient identification?

With fear and trembling he put on a calm face, and
took his turn in the line at the window, the open telegram in his shaking hand.

"Will I have to be identified?" he asked, quietly
handing the telegram to the cashier. "I want to draw
some of that money."

The cashier looked at him sharply and then at the
telegram, and just at that moment another man walked
breezily up to the window behind him, and in a pleasant voice said: "Why, good morning, Richard. What
are you doing way down-town this morning? Do you
have a situation down here now?"

The cashier looked up quickly, and greeted the new-
comer as if he were well known, as indeed he was, being
a prominent business man as well as one of the stock-

holders of the bank. His home was near to Richard's home, though in quite a different neighborhood.

Richard in his little-boy days had run errands occasionally for him, and had for a time delivered his morning paper. The charm of the man was that he never forgot the boy, and had always had a smile and a pleasant word for him, though it had been at least three years since Richard had done anything for him.

The boy felt a glow of pleasure now at the recognition, and he was just turning it over in his mind whether he dared ask the man to identify him, when the cashier saved him the trouble.

"You know this young man, Mr. Minturn?" he asked. "He's Richard P. Gracen, is he?"

"Sure!" said the big man heartily. "I've known him since he was a little chap so high. We're old friends. Anything I can do for you, Richard?"

"That's all right then, my boy," said the cashier, nodding assurance to the lad. "We have some money deposited here for Richard P. Gracen, and we didn't know him; but of course, if you can identify him, it will be all right, Mr. Minturn."

"Yes, I can identify him," said Mr. Minturn heartily. "Got some money coming to you, have you, Richard? That's good news. Take care of it, and use it wisely. I guess you will, all right."

Then he turned to speak to another new-comer, leaving the boy with a glow of pleasure in his face and immense relief at his heart.

Five minutes later he walked out of the bank with more money in his possession than he had ever handled in his life before, and a brand-new bank-book and check-book in his pocket.

He had thought it all out before he went to sleep the night before, and decided to pay the big bills in checks. He enjoyed the thought that he had a bank-account and could pay in checks like any man.

He had drawn out only money enough to use for his immediate needs; but they included his ticket and berth, some new clothes, food for the day, and enough to pay his little outstanding debts to the boys; so the sum he carried made him feel exceedingly rich.

He went first to the station to buy his ticket and sleeper berth and send his telegram. Until those things were attended to he had no thought for breakfast. It was a wonderful experience to be buying a ticket for a long-distance journey for himself. He watched with awe the ticket-agent stamping the long strip of paper, and took it almost reverently into his own hands, proudly handing out the crisp new bank-bills in exchange.

He got the best berth in the first section of the through train, and with his tickets safely in his breast-pocket he went thoughtfully over to the telegraph office. The telegram he must send was the hardest part of his day's work. He had not been able to think what to say last night before he went to sleep. He felt a shyness coming over him at the thought of addressing the great personage who had so easily provided him with money and a way of escape from his uncle's espionage. No words seemed quite fitting, at least not the words that were familiar to him. But after getting a time-table and inquiring most minutely about arrivals and departures of trains he finally produced the following message with infinitely greater labor than any school composition had ever cost him:

Miss Victoria Gracen,
        Roslyn, Penn.
Leave Chicago 10.30 to-night. Reach Roslyn 5.30 P.M., Wednesday.

Here he had paused with puckered brow, and deliberated. It seemed as though the occasion demanded some recognition of his aunt's friendly overtures after the years of coolness between the families. His boyish vocabulary was hard put to it for anything along this line; but at last with desperation he dashed off the rest, and sent his message before he would have opportunity for further hesitation.

Hope we will get along all right. Thanks for the cash.
                                            DICK.

He reflected afterward that it would have sounded
a great deal more friendly if he had said "dough" or
"tin" instead of "cash," but perhaps an aunt might not
understand. He had never signed his name Dick before
nor been called that,—the fellows had other and varied
appellations for him,—but he gladly accepted her attempt at intimacy by taking up the new name. He had
a suspicion, which afterward proved to be correct, that
she maybe used to call his father "Dick"; and in that
case the boy welcomed it as a heritage hitherto unknown.

The telegram and ticket off his mind, he began to
realize that he was hungry; and, as he was passing the
station restaurant, the lure of coffee and the palm-
guarded entrance summoned him with all the power
that that elegant and mysterious realm had held for
him from childhood. He decided that for once in his life
he would eat in the station restaurant and have what
he wanted from the bill of fare. He had money of his
own in his pocket, enough and to spare; why should he
not?

His wants were sensible, however. He ordered a beefsteak with fried potatoes, buckwheat cakes and maple-
syrup, and a glass of cream. Cream was five cents more
than milk, and he might have had coffee instead; but
he had never had enough cream in his life; in fact, he
had scarcely ever had any, and he wanted to see now
what it would really be like to *drink* cream.

Refreshed in body and spirit, he went out to pay his
bills. He was just boarding an up-town car when he
caught a vanishing glimpse of his uncle getting out of
another car. He could not be sure whether or not his
uncle had seen him, and he kept watching furtively
from the back window, but saw no sign of pursuit.

It was queer for his uncle to be down-town so far
from his place of business at that time of day. Could
he have been tracking him? The fear made him feel that
he must make all possible haste, for he did not wish
to be interfered with until all his plans were carefully
made. He must get that trunk out of the house im-

mediately, or his uncle might put a stop to his taking it at all.

He stopped at the corner grocery to get the bill paid, and took much pleasure in the look of astonishment and disappointment on the countenance of Mr. Bitzer when he took out his new check-book and wrote a check for the amount of the bill.

"I don't like to bother with checks," said the man crossly. "I thought you'd pay the money. How do I know you've got money in that there bank?"

He took the check slowly, hesitatingly, and looked it over incredulously.

"Just call up the bank on the telephone," said Richard loftily. "Ask for the cashier. I'll wait till you get your answer."

Reluctantly the grocer went to the telephone, and in a few minutes came back with a sheepish look on his face and the check in his hand.

"It's all right," he admitted, and then, again reluctantly, "Thank you."

Richard nodded gravely and went out saying softly to himself, "Stung!" But even as his tongue finished the word there came a queer choking sensation in his throat, and he found himself wishing that he could tell his mother that the troublesome bill was paid at last. Did she know, he wondered, in that strange, far-off place to which she had taken her journey; or might it be that she didn't care any more about bills over there?

Well, he was glad to have it paid, anyway. It seemed like making good his mother's honor, for something in his uncle's taunt the night before had strangely stirred the dormant manliness of the boy.

The choking feeling was still in his throat when he unlocked the door of his home for the expressman to take out his trunk; and something like tears were near to his eyes as he gave a final glance back at the dingy, dismal rooms he had known so long, and would perhaps never see again. A great sense of loneliness swept over him as he slammed the door shut and jumped up beside the expressman to ride with him down to check his trunk.

There was one more disagreeable duty to be done before he could feel quite free. He must go to his uncle, get the undertaker's bill, and pay it. He wished that after that he need never see his uncle again.

As soon as the trunk was checked, he turned his face resolutely toward the office where he would be likely to find his uncle.

Chapter IV

WHEN Richard opened the door of the room his uncle called his "office," there were two men talking business with Mr. Miller.

That gentleman looked sharply toward the door, and frowned at his nephew.

"So you've concluded to come back have you, you young jackanapes?" he said when the two men turned away to discuss some matter together. "This is a pretty time of day to turn up. What do you think of yourself coming to work at two o'clock in the afternoon? It's a wonder your job isn't gone already. You sit down over there, and wait till I'm done here, and I'll tend to you."

"I didn't come to work," said Richard haughtily. "I came to get that undertaker's bill. Have you got it here? I want to see how much it is. I'm going to pay it."

"You're going to pay it!" roared his uncle derisively. "A lot you are! It'll be a long while before you save up enough money to pay that. I guess you don't know how much it costs to die. See there!"

He opened his wallet and took out the bill, flinging it at the boy triumphantly. His harsh, coarse voice made Richard shiver. It seemed as though it were trailing over his raw nerves.

The two men had come to some conclusion, and his uncle turned his attention to them once more. Richard, taking advantage of his uncle's turned back, pocketed the bill, and quietly slipped out of the door into the street. In a moment more he had boarded a downtown car and was safe from pursuit. When his uncle realized that he was gone, it would be too late to do anything about it.

Richard went straight to the undertaker's, made out a check for the amount of the bill, and asked for a duplicate receipt. He desired his uncle to know that the bill was paid, but he did not intend to let the receipt go out of his own possession. He did not realize that the check would be a sufficient receipt.

The undertaker took the precaution to call up the bank and ask whether the check was good, and then gave him the receipts as requested. Richard went straight to the waiting-room of a department store, and wrote a letter.

It ran thus:

Uncle Miller:
   I am sending you a duplicate copy of the receipted bill, to let you know I have paid it. I have the original. I had some money my aunt, Miss Gracen, gave me, and I have paid all bills I know anything about.
   I leave Chicago to-night; so you needn't bother any more about me. My address will be Roslyn, Penn., in case you need to ask me anything about the house.
                                          Yours truly,
                                             R. P. GRACEN.

It took him a long time to write the letter, because there were so many things he would have liked to say which he knew for his mother's sake he ought not to say, and there were so many things he did not want to say that his uncle would naturally expect him to say, that it was pretty hard work. When it was written, he discovered that it was almost four o'clock, and he had had no dinner. He addressed the letter and put it into his pocket. His plan was to mail it in the station just as he took the train.

He decided that he would do the one other thing that he had always been longing to do and never had

had the money for—take a meal in the great tea-room up-stairs. It might be extravagant for a person whose entire fortune was well under five hundred dollars; but it couldn't do any harm just once, and, besides, this was a day of great things. He might perhaps never come this way again and then the experience would be impossible. He took the elevator to the tenth floor, and dined in state amid polished floors, hot-house flowers, and orchestral music; but somehow he felt lonelier than he dreamed he could feel in that stateliness, and was glad when the meal was over.

It was when he was going down in the elevator that he remembered his plan to purchase some new clothes. He must hurry, or the store would be closing. But, boy-like, he did not take long to make his selections. He chose a dark-blue suit and a rich leafy-brown with a Norfolk jacket, and decided to put the brown suit on for his journey; so his old clothes went into the suitcase, and a half-hour later, to all appearances, he came forth from the clothing department a new boy. It was because of the glimpse he caught of himself in the great mirror by the elevator that he decided on new tan shoes and a soft brown felt hat. Before he was through he had purchased socks, neckties, collars and cuffs, and a lot of other little necessities; and the suitcase was being taxed to its utmost to hold them all.

It was just as he was passing out of the store, and nearly closing-time, that the darkness of the sky sent him back to purchase a raincoat; and at the glove-counter he saw a young fellow about his own age buying a pair of kid gloves. He had never had a pair of gloves in his life that he remembered, and it suddenly occurred to him that he would like to have some; so they were added to his outfit. All together, when he came out of the store in the gathering twilight, he was a well-dressed fellow.

He took the suitcase over to the station and checked it, reserving the raincoat for a refuge in case the threatened storm came, and started out to find the "fellows." But again, as his startled eyes caught sight of his new self in the window of a great candy-store, in passing, he stopped astonished and looked himself over. He really was a nice-looking boy. Why hadn't he known it before? It would have been a great comfort to him, helping him through innumerable embarrassing places, if he had only known it was in him to look as well as that. How he wished his aunt and uncle and his little cousins could get a glimpse of him! Wouldn't they be astonished? It would give his wounded pride a decided healing turn if he could only appear before them for a minute dressed in this way.

But he had too clear a remembrance of his uncle's face and the grip of his hand to risk any such meeting. His uncle hated the very thought of the Gracen family, hated him because he bore the name, and would never allow him to get away to any member of the family to be pampered and petted and made to hate his mother's family. There was no telling to what lengths his uncle might go if he knew what Richard was planning to do.

However, there would be no harm in letting Elsa see him. His uncle would hardly be at home yet; or, if he were, he would be in the house washing up for supper. He could easily whistle for Elsa. He had done it before when sent on errands by his mother. Elsa would keep his secret. She was the only one of the family he had ever tolerated. As he thought it over now, she was the only person in the whole city who would miss his going very much; and she was a giddy little thing, and would soon forget him. However, for the sake of the times when she had taken his part and helped to screen him from his uncle's wrath, he would go and say good-bye to her. She was very fond of chocolates; why shouldn't he take her some?

He stopped at a large candy-store, and purchased a two-pound box of chocolates, tied with a pink ribbon. As he did so he felt like a millionaire; this was truly the crowning-touch.

His uncle's house was not far out of the way he meant to take in his search for his friends; and, dropping off the trolley-car at the corner, he walked rapidly around the corner of the new street toward it. The sun was just setting, the lights appearing as they had appeared the night before when the carriages drove up to the door. The scene brought back his own desolation so strongly that he almost made up his mind to leave the candy on the side window-sill and slip away without being seen; but just at that moment Elsa came out of the front door with her red sweater over her shoulders, and ran toward the corner bakery.

She stared hard at Richard in his new clothes, but did not appear to recognize him until he spoke; and even to himself his voice sounded constrained and queer.

"Hello, Elsa!" he said embarrassedly.

Elsa paused, and stared hard.

"Why, Richard! Is that you all dolled up so? Ain't you got the togs, though? Where'd you get 'em?" Her face expressed unbounded admiration, and Richard's pride rose. He was pleased to have produced so favorable an impression.

"I bought 'em," said the boy with a proud lift of his chin.

A shade of anxiety came over the girl's stolid little face.

"Say, Richard, you ain't been stealing, have you? Mother has been awful worried lest you'll get into jail, and disgrace us all. She says if Aunt Lilly hadn't just died it wouldn't be so bad; but it's such a disgrace to have you acting this way just after the funeral, when everybody's noticing everything."

The boy's face hardened, and a steely glitter came into his eyes.

"No, I haven't been stealing, and I don't ever mean to do any such low-down thing in my life. Whatever put that into your mother's head, I'd like to know? She always thinks the worst she can of everybody. Did you think that about me, Elsa? Say, tell me honest; did you?"

He caught her by the arm, and glared at her in the softening twilight of the street till the child seemed almost frightened.

"No, course not; honest I didn't, Richard. I told 'em

I knew you'd come back all right. I knew you wouldn't steal."

The boy's face softened again.

"Well, I brought you something," he said in a less harsh tone; "but, if you were going to believe things like that about me, I would rather throw every bit of it in the gutter than give it to you."

The girl's eyes turned longingly toward the big, white box of bonbons.

"You know I never thought such a thing, Richard," she pleaded.

"Well, look here; I'm going to tell you something if you'll promise not to tell a word of it till to-morrow morning. Promise?"

"Mayn't I tell I saw you, and what you gave me?" she asked with gloating eyes on the box; "and mayn't I tell about your new clo'es? You look awful swell. I wish they all could see you."

"Yes; you can tell them you saw me and I don't care about the clothes or anything; but you mustn't tell where I got the money, nor where I'm going, until to-morrow morning. Do you promise?"

"Sure, I promise," said Elsa, jumping up and down delightedly and holding out her hands eagerly for the beautiful box.

"Well, I'm going to my aunt, Miss Gracen. She's sent for me, and she gave me a lot of money to pay the bills; and I've paid everything, and bought these clothes. Now don't you forget, Elsa; you're not to tell a living soul till to-morrow morning."

"All right," said Elsa, already beginning to untie the gold cord that held the paper. "But why can't I tell till to-morrow morning?"

"Elsa! Elsa!" called her mother from the front door; and then, wrapping her apron around her head (for she had come straight from the hot kitchen), she stopped and stared. To whom could Elsa be talking? No one who lived in that neighborhood, and yet there was a very familiar look about him.

"Elsa, did you get that loaf of bread yet? Hurry in here with it."

"O my goodness!" said Elsa. "What'll ma say? I've got to hurry. Good-bye, I won't forget!" And she was off down to the bakery while her excited mother alternately called and stared at the strange boy with whom her child had been talking.

He was walking unconcernedly down the street and taking a trolley right before her face and eyes, and could it be? Yes no—it could not be; it *was*—Richard!

Alarmed, she rushed down the steps; but the trolley was under way now, and the motorman could not see her. Richard, smiling scornfully, stood on the lower step of the trolley, and actually had the impudence to tip his beautiful new brown hat to her as he vanished out of sight around the corner! Of all things! Her wrath boiled high; and she stood staring after the departing trolley and wondering what her husband would do now to that boy. The upstart! Dressed up like that and riding on trolleys like any dude; when his poor mother was just buried!

Elsa, hurrying back with her loaf of bread and trying to peer into her candy-box, almost ran into her mother, and was greeted with a volley of questions, which she answered by opening the wonderful box of bonbons in her astonished mother's presence and announcing that Richard had given them to her. All that evening she smiled serenely to herself over her chocolates, and answered not a word to their angry questioning. She would reserve her announcement till the morrow, and she felt it would lose none of its dramatic features by waiting. She was a keen child in many ways, and Richard had managed to impart to her somewhat of the spirit of the "gang" in being loyal to him. Moreover, she had an eye to other possible chocolates. That last was in the blood, and she could scarcely help it.

Richard, as they rounded the corner, caught sight of his uncle coming up the street, and quickly vanished inside the car, thankful that he had escaped, and very soon he changed cars, which made pursuit impossible.

He was not long in finding his gang, who duly admired his clothes, but were a little inclined to be jealous and sulky until he proceeded to hand them out the money he owed them, to the last penny, when everybody grew exceedingly happy; and the leader of the group proposed a supper in honor of the occasion. Richard declared that was just what he had come to invite them to; and, as most of them had not overeaten at their evening meal, they were ready to go with him immediately.

Richard himself was not hungry. Somehow, now that the time had almost come for him to leave his native haunts, he began to feel a strange shrinking and loneliness. The day had been filled with excitement and unusual occurrences; and, when he came to sit down among the rest, he was mortally weary. So it was that his gay talk and laughter were missing as the jokes passed round the table, and their challenges brought no answering banter from his lips.

"Rich is all in to-night," whispered one to another; "do you s'pose it's 'cause the old lady croaked?"

And the strange part of the remark was that, though the expression was most horribly irreverent and uncouth, it was said in sincerest sympathy and was received as it was meant.

"Sure!" said the other comrade heartily, with a sympathetic glance at Richard. "He'll be all right one o' these dry rains."

It was not till almost the last minute that he told them he was going away. It was characteristic of their code that they had not questioned him about his money and new clothes. They knew he would tell what he wanted them to know when he got ready, and not before. They would have done the same themselves. So now they listened as he told them briefly that he was going out to see his aunt, and might stay if he liked it; he didn't know.

Their faces were sober for a moment, but not with sorrow for his going. At that age they acknowledge no such thing as regret. They were each envious of his chance to see the world and wear those clothes and spend the money they heard jingling in his pocket.

They accepted his generosity, took chocolate and

chewing-gum galore at his expense, and attended him pridefully to the train at last, bearing his new sole-leather suitcase noisily aloft on their shabby shoulders. They marched in to the sleeper to the annoyance of the contemptuous porter, who lifted his discerning nose of contempt and lowered in vain his discerning eyes to their shabby shoes. They were utterly unabashed, and felt that they had as good a right as he—better, perhaps—to stand there. Had not their comrade a ticket and a sleeper berth? They intended to make the most of it until the train departed. And they were not even college boys! The porter was *sure* of that.

They hung on until after the train had started, and ran noisily along, flinging in paper wads, cakes of chocolate, anything, shouting at the top of their lungs; as tough and uncouth as possible, and highly calculated to make the entire carful look with disapproval on the young traveller taking his first long journey.

And yet, when they were gone, Richard sat back alone, and felt that he was deserted of all who knew him, alone in the wide, wide world!

Chapter V

THAT was a busy day in the Gracen home following the evening announcement of Miss Victoria that her nephew was expected. The old servants worked with a will, for was not "Mr. Dick's" child coming home to them at last after the long years of family alienation? Both Hiram and Rebecca, his sister, had been in the family when "Mr. Dick" was born; and Molly, Hiram's wife, had been his nurse. It had been a sad day for the servants when the young man left his home forever. They had mourned as if he were their own, albeit their loyalty to his mother and sister had been so great that they had kept it to themselves for the most part, and humored the irascible old father, to whom they had also given deep devotion, while thinking him altogether in the wrong concerning his son.

Molly and Rebecca were up early, giving the house a thorough overhauling, and especially making the room next to "Miss Vic's" sweet and inviting after its years of closed idleness.

Not a book that was not taken out and dusted carefully, not a fishing-pole or trinket of the elder Dick that was not tenderly handled and displayed to its best advantage. There were pictures of him everywhere about the room, taken with his school friends, his baseball-team, in his canoe on the creek; taken sliding down the great hill that started in the meadow back of the house; taken skating on the creek with his boy and girl friends. There was a large one with the dawn of seriousness in his handsome eyes taken just before he went away to accept that fine business offer in Chicago, and it hung surrounded by the pictures of his college life. Reverently the old servants touched the frames as they wiped off the dust, and more than one surreptitious tear was brushed away behind the closet door that day. They worked away with a will, and somehow contrived to give to the great room an air of expectancy, as if a boy might be coming home to it.

Old Hiram was doing duty with the carpets and rugs, and between times rubbing down the "colt," as the youngest one of the great black horses was still called, although it was several years since he had left coltdom. Hiram confided to the colt's ears that likely Mr. Dick would want to ride him, and he even went so far as to get down the elder Dick's saddle and rub it up, brightening the stirrups and buckles and bit, his face wearing a pleasant smile of reminiscence while he worked.

All this was well under way before they knew whether the boy was coming or not.

The Roslyn telegraph operator had gone to his lunch when Richard's telegram arrived; and so it was not until after one o'clock, while Miss Gracen was eating her belated lunch,—late on account of the extra cleaning that had been going on that morning,—that the telephone rang and the boy's message was repeated until every word was carefully copied down.

The three servants crowded near the library door, regardless for once of cooling tea and chops that ought to have been set in the oven until the lady returned, and boldly stood to listen.

"I think he's coming," said old Hiram, nodding his head happily; "I think Miss Vic's voice sounded that way."

Then, when she returned to the interrupted lunch, the copy of the telegram tucked inside the bosom of her morning dress and a smile of excitement and pleasure on her face, instead of rapidly dispersing to the kitchen they stood forth unabashed and eager.

"He'll be here to-morrow night at five-thirty," announced Miss Gracen. "Hiram, you may meet him at the station with the carriage and both horses. I think I will see him first at home. The boy may be embarrassed, and there might be people around watching. I don't want to have any talk. Molly, can you and Rebecca finish the cleaning this afternoon? Then you'll have plenty of time to do a little baking to-morrow."

So for the first time in their long service they forgot their relation of mistress and maid and grouped together around her, planning a welcome home for the boy to whom all their hearts went out with loving expectation.

Richard's first night in a sleeper proved to be anything but a restful one. The strange sounds and the stranger motion might have lulled his weary body to sleep sooner if the excitement of the day had not been keen upon him. He lay in the luxurious bed, wondering at everything that had happened to him, and tantalizing himself now with the thought that perhaps he had been disloyal to his mother by accepting this money and going to his aunt. But then came the thought of his father.

He knew that his father had anxiously desired a reconciliation, but would not accept it unless his wife were recognized equally with himself. But was not he the representative of them both, and had not his aunt invited him as such? If he found that she considered it otherwise, he could go away from her at once.

Having settled so much, he fell into a doze, but was soon awakened by the slowing of the train and the calls of the trainmen. He simply could not lie down and compose himself, for were they not continually passing strange new places, some of the names of which he could even read when they went more slowly through the sleeping towns? They were places of which he had often heard, and his interest was awakened. It was so wonderful to pass the lighted streets, and see now and again people here and there.

More than half the night he lay propped up on one elbow, staring out the window and watching the wonders of the way, but more and more this journey gave him a sense of deep loneliness.

It was nearly morning when at last he slept and awoke to the din of a great city station, having dreamed that the train had been going in a circle and was back in Chicago again, with his uncle and a long line of policemen waiting at the station to meet him.

He was greatly relieved to find the station a great, strange place, and that he was still on his independent way unhindered.

It was a new and embarrassing experience to get dressed in a sleeper berth, and he found that he was the last man in the car to rise. He made his way to the buffet-car, and enjoyed his breakfast in state alone, wondering what the fellows and his uncle's family would think of him if they could see him.

The window held new sights indeed now, for they were beginning to pass through the coal regions and over the mountains, and the boy was all eagerness to see everything. For a time this put his situation entirely out of his mind, and he forgot that ahead of him was a new and untried way, which he dreaded more than he had ever dreaded anything in his life.

However, as the afternoon waned, and he knew he was nearing his destination, his heart began to beat hard and his hands and feet grew cold with apprehension. Just what he feared he could not put into words or scarcely into lucid thoughts, but he knew that if he had the chance now he would never have come. He would have run away—west, north, south, anywhere—rather than face a new and unknown relative, who might expect all sorts of disagreeable things of him.

As the train came nearer and nearer to Roslyn, he sat stiffly in his seat, his fingers clinched, his feet braced, his jaw set. He must go through it now, of course, but he would not stay if he did not like it. Well, the running was still good, and he could run away here, of course, as well as he could in Chicago.

This was his last thought as the train slowed down and came to a full stop at Roslyn, and he knew that his time had come.

"Best hurry out, young man," the porter adjured him. "We only stop here for passengers or on flagging. You ain't got no time to waste."

The porter caught up the suitcase from his cold, trembling hands; and Richard, with his new raincoat over his arm, followed confusedly, and, descending the steps, immediately found himself standing alone in a dazed condition upon the platform of a pretty little station, with his train hurrying wildly down the track as if angry at the moment's delay he had caused.

The sweetness and quietness of the place, even with the vanishing screech of the train yet in his ears, fell about him like a mantle of peace. He had never been in so quiet a place before.

The station seemed to have nestled down between softly-rising hills; the tracks gleamed away and vanished in a cut; and everywhere there was autumn foliage, glorious and beautiful in the low sunlight of evening. Off at the right, rose a sloping green campus, with academic buildings showing their classic lines between the trees; and to the left were pleasant homes all set in late greens, browns, crimsons, and gold, with close-clipped hedges or open lawns and pleasant streets stretching in every direction, all giving the atmosphere of plenty—plenty of time and rest and comfort for all who belonged there.

Richard instantly had the feeling that he did not belong there, and cast one more hopeless look after his unfriendly train now vanishing in the cut.

But this was his first instant's impression. In the next second he became aware of a carriage and a pair of shining black horses standing close to the platform, and an old man in dark-green livery approaching him. His first thought was that this was a cabman asking him to ride, and he began to wonder what he should do next. He instantly decided he would not take a cab; that would get him there too soon. He would inquire the way, and walk, and try to get his mind composed.

Then old Hiram spoke.

"This must be Mr. Dick, I'm sure," he quavered, respect and glee mingled in his old throat. "I knowed you the minute you stepped out, you look so like your father. We're right glad to have you, sir, right glad to have you home at last. We've been a-wearyin' to see ye these many years. Me an' Rebecca an' Molly an' Miss Vic have. Just step right over this way to the carriage. My! But you do look like Mr. Dick when he was your age. I'd 'a' knowed you anywheres. Just climb right into the back seat; an' gimme your checks, an' I'll see they bring your baggage right up. Just one trunk? All right! Here, Jim," motioning to the station hand, "take this check an' see that Mr. Gracen's trunk is sent up immediate."

The old man hurried up the platform to give the check to the baggage-man, talking as he went; and Richard, amazed and somehow comforted, sat waiting for him in the back seat of the carriage,—his new suit-case beside him, marvelling over his reception.

Was this what it meant to get home? And who was this amiable old man? He had never heard of any living relative but an aunt before. But perhaps there were others. Whoever he was, the boy's heart warmed toward him.

He looked at the satiny backs of the fine horses, their long tails almost sweeping the ground, their noble heads curved proudly, their harness gleaming here and there with silver. He touched wonderingly the dark-green broadcloth of the cushions he sat upon, noted the shining immaculateness of everything, and realized with

awe the lack of poverty. It was so new, so wonderful,
to have aught to do with really fine, nice things, and
have a right among them. For the first time he recognized that it satisfied something in him which had always seemed starved, some native longing, perhaps,
that he had not understood. But he was only a boy, and
did not think these things out in words; he simply felt
them.

Hiram came back smiling, followed by a battery of
eyes from the men hanging around the station. It was
the first intimation that the town had had of a visitor
coming to "The Beeches," as Miss Gracen's home was
called. Hiram was enjoying the distinction of giving the
loungers something to wonder about.

Who, indeed, was Mr. Gracen? They didn't know of
any other Gracen relatives. Why had he never appeared
upon the scene before? He was exceedingly young, just
a boy. Whose boy was he?

The question started, speculation was rife. Hiram
went home serenely unconscious that he had untied the
bag and given the cat a good chance to jump out.

"Well, well, well, ain't this just great, havin' you
here at last?" exclaimed old Hiram, jumping in with
agile movements scarcely expected of his years.

He slowly turned the blacks with their heads toward
home, giving the bystanders a good chance to gaze at
the handsome young face of the boy in the back seat;
but he failed to hear the comment of an old resident as
they drove slowly down the street.

"By gum! Ef that don't look jest like Dick Gracen
did the year he went off to college!"

Richard was almost embarrassed by the attentions
of Hiram as they drove down the street, but he was
too confused to say much; and, indeed, Hiram did not
require it. He was only too glad to get a chance to in-
dulge in reminiscences about the boy's father.

Sunset again, and long, slanting, red rays lit up the
crimson of the foliage as the carriage turned into The
Beeches, and Richard saw lights appearing in the windows. The house stood far back from the street amid a

grove of wonderful beeches, approached by an avenue of tree-arched beauty. There were soft shades of the lights, green and crimson, and a glow of firelight that Richard did not recognize, because he had never known a fireplace in his home. Everything indicated warmth, comfort, welcome; and yet the boy felt again a great trembling through his frame and a distinct desire to turn and run away. Not that he would have done so for worlds; but he realized that the coward in him was to the front, and he had much ado to hold him down from looking through the windows of his eyes and showing himself to the world.

The carriage stopped and the house door was flung wide open, letting out a flood of light to mingle with the evening shadows and long, slant rays of the sun.

Hiram threw open the carriage door, and lifted down the suitcase. Dick climbed out, and for one absurd moment recalled the look of the culprits who climbed down from the patrol-wagons in front of the city hall, looked wildly about for a hope of escape, and seeing none, fairly bolted into the open door if their prison that was to be. He felt as if he looked that way himself now.

There were three women standing in the hallway, one on each side of the door, two with long, white aprons and caps; and just a little back of them, in the very middle of the hall, under a great globe of light, with a gracious air of welcome, stood another, a beautiful woman with white hair and young eyes.

She stood with both hands held out to him, a smile on her face; and to his bewildered vision she seemed the most beautiful woman he had ever looked upon.

He stumbled in, and took her hand awkwardly, letting her lead him into the library, past dim visions of great rooms on either side of the hall, and knew she was saying kind, welcoming things, and must be his aunt, but knew not what words she was speaking.

He felt the beauty of everything about him without really seeing it.

The air was pervaded with the odor of good things to eat, and Molly and Rebecca appeared smiling in the doorway, giving a reminder of the supper that was ready. The aunt turned smilingly toward them.

"This is Rebecca," she said to the dazed boy. "She and Hiram were here when your father was born; and this is Molly, who was his nurse. They have been very eager for your coming."

Richard shook hands with both the women. He did it awkwardly. He wasn't used to shaking hands, and it came hard.

"I made some spice-cookies for you this morning," said Rebecca, smiling. "Your father used to like 'em. Do you like 'em, too?"

"Sure!" said Richard, turning rosy red, and smiling in spite of his embarrassment. Then they hurried him up-stairs to get ready for supper.

There was stewed chicken, with plenty of gravy, on tiny, little, puffy biscuits. There were more of the biscuits to eat with red raspberry jam and clear currant jelly. There was succotash such as the boy never had tasted before, made of corn sweet as a baby's breath, and queer red and purple calico beans. There were delectable pickles, and mashed potatoes without any of the dull, heavy lumps he supposed always went with that sort of vegetable; and there was a great glass of creamy milk foaming beside his plate. For dessert there was floating-island white as snow in a custard of delectable gold, and maple cake.

But the tragedy of it all was that he couldn't eat, because something in his throat kept closing down and almost choking him.

He had just to sit and stare at the vision of his beautiful, young, white-haired aunt, and wonder how he was to answer her remarks.

Hovering over it all, like two old beaming angels, came and went Rebecca and Molly; with a glimpse now and then, through the door of the butler's pantry, of Hiram handing out more eatables. It was all a wonderful dream, and Richard wondered sometimes whether he were not really asleep and whether this was not the reason that he could not do justice to the good things. He never had had a meal like it in his life, and he could not realize that all his meals were to be pretty much on this order after to-day. He just could not realize anything at all.

After supper his aunt took him back into the library, and he sat on the edge of the Morris-chair, and tried to act polite while she talked to him; but presently he forgot all about having to be polite, because she was talking to him about his father. She told him how he used to study and play, about his taking music-lessons, and being captain of a baseball-team, and doing great feats in college; how he looked the last time she saw him; and a great many other wonderful and interesting things, just fragments of them, for she did not go into much detail with anything, only sketched bits of scenes that made Richard eager to hear more.

And the boy never knew that she was talking against tears, trying to keep them from her eyes and from her voice because he brought back so vividly the face and form of her dear lost brother.

Then presently the little clock on the mantel chimed nine in a silvery tone, and his aunt stopped, smiling, and said she knew he must be tired and that he ought to go to bed right away.

She went up-stairs with him herself, and showed him where to switch on the electric light, and pointed out to him the white-tiled bathroom just across the hall, with its silver trappings and its wealth of splendid towels; showed him the pictures of his father on the walls of his room, just to make him feel at home; and then, with a half-wistful hesitation, she paused at the door and after a second said a sweet, cheery good-night, with a wish that he would sleep well in his new room.

She was gone, and he looked about in wonder; the daze began to wear off a little. He realized that he was terribly tired, and his eyelids smarted with the light. The choking sensation was growing in his throat, too, and he craved more than anything a chance to lie down in the dark, to be alone, and think.

He did not linger to look around, more than for a glance at that great picture of his father on the wall.

He knew it looked like himself, though it seemed far handsomer than he could ever hope to be; but the look in those young, bright, kindly eyes was one that seemed to understand him; and, added to all that he had gone through, it was the one thing more that he could not bear. The choking in his throat was unbearable. Why had he missed having a splendid father like that?

Swiftly he undressed, and, turning off the light, crept into the great, lonely bed, burying his face in the pillow. He despised himself for it, but sobs shook his body and gasped in his throat; tears hot and fast blurred themselves into the pillow. He did not know what he was crying for; he only knew he was crying, shamelessly crying like a baby, and all because of a strange, unbearable something that yearned in his breast for a love he had never had. This, this home and kindliness that were offered him now, he did not seem to fit; it could never really belong to him. He had missed it all, and was alone, alone, alone!

He did not know how long or how short a time it was that this unforgivable emotion held him in its grasp before he heard soft steps coming down the hall to his door, and a gentle tap sounded through his muffling pillow. He only knew he held his breath to listen and wonder what he should do next.

Chapter VI

It was his aunt's voice that broke the painful stillness of his dark room. "Dick, dear," she called softly, "are you asleep yet? May I come in just a minute?"

He made a muffled sound in his pillow, not intending to answer her at all; but she waited for no more; she opened the door softly, and stepped inside, leaving the door ajar just a crack; and it sent a keen blade of light diagonally across the floor and wall, reflecting on her beautiful face and white hair.

He had raised his head partly from the pillow in consternation. To be caught crying by his aunt this first night of his arrival! This was too much! What would she think of him? A sissy-boy! That was the most awful reputation any boy could earn for himself. He would rather be thought *any*thing than a sissy-boy!

He held himself rigid, motionless in the darkness, and tried to get control of his voice and act as if he didn't mind that she had come in. Perhaps she only wanted to find something she had left in the closet, and wouldn't look toward him.

But she came swiftly, softly, over to the bed in the darkness, and knelt beside him, throwing one arm across his shoulders as he fell back dismayed on his pillow and faced her in the dark. She leaned her head over his, and whispered softly:

"I couldn't go to sleep without kissing you good-night, Dick. I always used to kiss my brother Dick good-night. It's been so many years now, and you are so like him! You won't mind if I do, dear boy, will you? I had to come and tell you how I love you. O Dickie, Dickie, dear, how I am going to love you!"

There was a sob in her voice, and as she bent down to kiss him the glint of light on the wall reflected on her sweet face, and showed it all shining and wet. Why, she was crying, too!

Then somehow Dick didn't mind any more. He put up his young, strong arms, flung them about her neck, and held her tightly in a fierce boy grip; and thus they mingled their tears together.

With her arms still about him, and her face close to his as she knelt, she whispered softly:

"O my heavenly Father, I thank Thee for sending me this dear boy. Bless him; and make him happy and good in this new home; and show me how to love and help him every day; and may we be a blessing to each other, for Jesus' sake. Amen."

Richard had never heard himself prayed for before. His mother had not prayed with him beyond teaching him "Now I lay me," which prayer he had long ago outgrown. But this prayer, coming as it did out of a

loving heart, filled him with awe, wonder, and a strange
new happiness.

When it was finished, she kissed him on the forehead
again; and as she said, "Good-night," he gripped her
hand, and blundered out:

"Thanks, awfully! I'm glad I came. I—guess we'll—
get on—all right."

It was a great deal for a boy like him to say. It was
equivalent to a hundred loyal speeches and kisses
thrown in, and it meant entire surrender. Perhaps her
intuition taught her by the thrill the tone gave her soul
as she slipped away and left him to sleep.

The boy lay back marvelling, and remembering. She
hadn't said a word about finding him weeping! Yet she
must have known. She was "game" all right. She hadn't
let him know how she knew. Yet he knew she knew.
She was the real stuff!

What was it that made him feel so different! Why,
she had said she loved him! She loved *him!* Nobody
had ever told him that before. Of course his mother
had loved him; that was understood, but she wasn't
the kind that talked of those things. But this aunt
didn't have to love him, didn't have any reason to
do anything but dislike him; and yet she had gone out
of her way to tell him she loved him! That was great!
And—*why, that made him belong! He belonged* there
in that house, *because she loved him!*

Then he fell asleep. He dreamed that he went to
heaven to tell his mother all about it; and she had
smiled and was pleased, and pointed out his young,
handsome father just like the picture on the wall.

When he awoke, it was morning, with the bright
autumn sun shining broad across his bed into the pictured eyes of his father, regarding him kindly from the
wall. He found himself filled with a kind of wondering
ecstasy, as though he had been changed into a new
being and all the old things were passed away. When
he stopped to think why he felt this way, he knew it was
because his aunt had kissed him and told him that she
loved him.

The breakfast-table was a revelation. Set in a glow of

autumn sunshine, the heavy linen, delicate china, sparkling silver, and cut glass made a deep impression upon
his beauty-loving nature. Never had he sat down to a
breakfast-table like this. People where he had come
from sometimes fixed up the table for a company dinner
or supper, but to take all that trouble just for breakfast
started an entirely new world for him.

In the centre of the table was a great bowl overflowing with late pears, peaches, plums, and grapes. The
oatmeal seemed to have no relation whatever to the
sticky mess that had gone by that name in his mother's
boarding-house, and the cream was rich and yellow. It
made a delectable combination. There were tender
beefsteak, fried potatoes, and golden-brown corncakes
with thick maple-syrup. His mental comment as he
surveyed the first plate of cakes that Molly brought in
was: "Gee! but the eats in this house are great! I wish
the fellows could have some!"

Richard had been almost afraid to come down-stairs,
lest the recollection of last night should be embarrassing, but his aunt met him with a smiling "Good-
morning," and no hint in her eyes even that there had
been anything like tears or prayers or kisses between
them. It put him entirely at his ease at once.

He looked with admiration at her in her pretty, pale-
blue morning-gown with deep lace frills about her white
wrists. The sunshine made her white hair into a lovely
frame for her face, and he found himself wishing his
mother could have seen her once. He was conscious of
a growing pride that she belonged to him. He had
never seen a woman of that age so beautiful before,
and he had never connected loveliness in any form
with growing old. His aunt fascinated him, and he
found himself watching her every movement. He
liked the fine lines about her eyes and the modelling of
her delicate features.

Every line that the years had graven in her beautiful
flesh was a pleasant line, as if she had always thought
the best of every one. It filled the boy with admiring
wonder. He had not known, he never even thought,
that any woman could be like that.

He went with Hiram to the stable while his aunt was busy about her morning household duties, and took his first lesson in harnessing the horse. The city-bred boy eyed the horses with delight, and his face lit with joy when Hiram showed him the saddle and spoke of his riding. He made the acquaintance of the "colt," and took a brief lesson in saddling him, mounting him, and riding around the stable-yard. He finally drove the carriage up to the door of the house, his eyes aglow with happiness. He felt as if he had suddenly been snatched from the hard, gloomy realities of the world and set down in heaven, a better heaven than any he had ever imagined for himself; and something of his own unworthiness of it all looked out of his eyes as he smiled half shyly at his aunt when she stepped into the carriage clad in a lovely long, soft, gray cloak and a gray felt hat with white wings. He was both proud and embarrassed to be riding out with such a queenly woman.

He rode behind with his aunt, and Hiram drove in the front seat. Richard watched him eagerly, and wondered whether he would ever be allowed to drive those two shining horses by himself. His heart swelled with the very thought of it, and Miss Gracen, watching his bright, eager face, with keen intuition seemed to read his thoughts; for almost at once she said:

"You'll like to drive the horses to the store and post-office sometimes when Hiram is busy, won't you? Hiram, you'll have to show Mr. Dick all about the horses. You know you taught his father to drive."

"Yes, indeedy, so I did, Miss Vic," said Hiram, his face lighting with the memory, "only he was a mighty leetle feller when he fust held the reins. I mind he used to sit atween my knees, an' holt the lines behind my hands, an' holler an' laugh, an' think he was drivin'; and his cheeks would be as pink as one of Rebecca's posies in the kitchen garden, an' his eyes as shiny as the stars.

"But I reckon this here Mr. Dick won't need much teachin'. He's almost growed up. Reckon he knows how to drive 'thout my teachin' him."

A wave of pleased consciousness rolled over the boy's

face in a faint flush, while he modestly disclaimed any
equestrian knowledge. Indeed, his knowledge of horses
was confined to driving a grocery-wagon occasionally
on a Saturday when there was a scarcity of hands; but
he did not like to tell that to the dignified Hiram, who
treated him as if he were a gentleman.

It was a new and pleasant experience to be treated
as if he were wanted, and to be actually planned for
as if he were a part of the things of consequence. He
smiled back at Hiram with a pleased surprise, but said
little. It was all too new and wonderful to last, he felt
sure; and his native caution, which had been his constant safeguard all his life against the hard brunt of
an unsympathetic world, warned him not to commit
himself.

When these people found him out as he really was,
saw what commonplace gifts were his, and knew about
his past inclinations to wildness, they would probably
not care to bother any further with him. It was the halo
of his father's likeness, very likely, that made them care
now; but they could not in the nature of things keep it
up. Nobody had ever paid much attention to him, unless it was his mother, and she scarcely ever had time.
Well, he would enjoy it while it lasted—and then?

But he had not opportunity to pursue his bitter
thoughts, for his aunt kept directing his attention to
things and people as they went along.

Up there on the hill was the college. That was the
dome of the observatory showing through the trees;
over there was the Carnegie Library, and next it the
gymnasium and dormitories. A number of great men
had been graduated from this college, and it ranked
well with others of its size. Over there were the athletic
grounds.

These last were a second thought. Miss Gracen had
never had much to do with college athletics. In her
brother's college days athletics had been in their in-
fancy, and regarded with doubt and suspicion by many
thoughtful people as being a menace to high scholarship. Her circle of friends had scarcely been one to

change this impression, though of course she had felt the general trend of thought of the day in regard to such matters, and was a broad-minded woman.

But now she saw like a flash the lighting of the boy's eyes as she spoke of athletics, and went on to tell of games that had been won from other large colleges, growing quite enthusiastic in her telling. So Hiram was told to drive up around the athletic grounds, and the boy feasted his eyes upon the wide stretches of velvety, green turf and the generous grand-stands.

Were there any games soon now? Football and basketball must be at their height, he said; and his aunt shook her head.

"I'm sure I don't know, Dick; we'll have to find out. I suppose, if that's the thing to be doing this time of year, our college is at it," she said; "but I know very little about such things. However, we'll take means to discover at once. Here comes our minister, and his son. Boys all know about the games, I suppose. We'll ask."

She leaned from the carriage, and greeted the pleasant-faced gentleman in a gray suit who was coming toward them; but Richard's eyes were on the boy who accompanied him. He was almost as tall as his father, well knit, with a homely, freckled face lit up by the handsomest pair of wine-brown eyes that Richard had ever seen. His hair, when he took off his rough tweed cap to speak to Miss Gracen, showed a deep, rich red; and there was a reckless grace in his movements and a mischievous twinkle in his brown eyes that made the other boy's heart warm toward him at once. The newcomer eyed the stranger curiously, as boys will, narrowly, sizing him up at a glance.

"Mr. Atterbury, this is my nephew, Dick Gracen," said Richard's aunt, leaning out to shake hands with the minister; "and this is Tom Atterbury, Dick," she said informally; and the two boys awkwardly and gravely acknowledged the introduction, each determined to be cautious in going a step further with the acquaintance until he was at least sure of its desirability.

"Dick was asking me about the games, and I couldn't tell him," said Miss Gracen with a pleasant laugh. "I wonder if you can enlighten us."

She looked straight at Tom Atterbury, and wondered why she had never noticed before what handsome eyes he had. She had always regarded him with a slight disfavor. He had a name for being in all the mischief in town, and she had always felt sorry for his father; but Tom's eyes softened her heart toward him greatly, and she had a passing wonder whether possessing a boy of her own would give her an interest in all boys.

"Sure!" said Tom Atterbury in a slow, drawling voice and with a smile that lit his freckles into a pleasant, merry face. "There's a game this afternoon, a big one. Our men play against Carnegie Tech. Would you like to go? I'll take you if you say so;" and Tom lifted a mischievous triumphant eye of inquiry toward his strong-faced, kindly father.

Now it happened that Tom carried under his arm a stack of school-books, and had just been undergoing a kind, but firm lecture on the subject of staying away from football-games and studying up some of the things in which his reports had been showing him to be sadly deficient during the past month.

Tom had no deep interest in taking Dick Gracen to the game; but he did have a consuming desire to go to it himself, and he knew that he was striking his father in a weak spot when he touched him on the side of parish work. His father would want him to be kind to Miss Gracen's guest of course, and he would be willing to have him go to the game under those circumstances, he was sure; and the kindly response in his father's eyes showed Tom that he had judged correctly.

In a moment more the arrangements were made, and Tom Atterbury went on his way to his belated school-day with a smiling countenance, to become the torment of his teachers and the despair of the principal for the day, in honor of the victory he had won over his father and the game he was so soon to see.

Miss Gracen, however, sat back in her seat as the

horses started on again through the college campus, and found her mind suddenly troubled. Here she had let that scamp of a Tom Atterbury make an arrangement to take her boy to a football-game! How had she so blundered? How had she been so blind?

She had planned in the watches of the night how she would introduce him to the boys who would be likely to be the greatest help to him in every way, and perhaps steer him clear of all the wickedness of the town, and keep him from knowing the wild ones at all.

She had completely forgotten the minister's son. Of course he had to be introduced, being the minister's son, but he was the wildest of the wild, if all the stories she heard of him were to be credited; and now she had put her Dick right into his clutches the first one.

If Dick began to go with Tom Atterbury, then none of the other nicer boys would have anything to do with him. There was George Barry, who lived with his mother and waited upon her so beautifully whenever they went anywhere; and there was James Clovis, who had won the scholarship in the preparatory school and had been chosen twice on the debating-team; and there were the Jarvis brothers, who worked every summer in the bank to save money for their winter's schooling so that their mother would not have to work so hard. They were all fine fellows. There was Brice Parker, the son of the burgess of the town, whose manners were perfect and whose character was both strong and charming. These were the companions she coveted for her boy. They all went to church and Sunday-school, and attended the Christian Endeavor Society regularly. They dressed well, and studied well, and behaved well everywhere, and never had a thing said against their reputations.

Tom Atterbury went to church and the Christian Endeavor Society, too; but he went because his father expected it of him, and he sat in the back seat if he could, and made mysterious noises that convulsed the little boys, who cheerfully bore the reprimands for the sake of watching his antics. There were notable pranks in the annals of the village years set down to the credit, or rather the discredit, of Tom Atterbury, the penalties of which had been borne by the younger fry, but which every one knew had been instigated and encouraged by the minister's son; and rumor said that he grew no better as he grew older.

Miss Gracen's soul was troubled more with every step her horses carried her away from the minister and his scapegrace son. How could she have been so thoughtless as to introduce Dick to him the very first one? She might have avoided it as well as not by telling Hiram to drive on quickly and by merely greeting the minister with a smile and a bow.

She had made a grievous mistake at the start. What should she do to rectify it? She tried to think as they drove to other places of interest; to the preparatory school, the high school, the church, the bank, the post-office, and the largest stores.

At last, after she had made some purchases and was back in the carriage again, she suggested that perhaps Dick would be too tired after his long journey to go to the game that afternoon, and that, if he would like to have her do so, she could telephone to Tom Atterbury and excuse him from the engagement; but Richard, beaming on her brightly, declared he was not in the least tired and would be delighted to go to the game. He added that Tom seemed like a good sort of fellow. He thought he should like him.

"He has a good father," said Miss Gracen cautiously, with a sigh of anxiety. "I'm not sure that Tom is always a comfort to him."

Richard said nothing. He did not know much about fathers or being a comfort to them. Her words made him wince over the fact that he had never been a comfort to his mother.

But he decided that Tom Atterbury was all right and that they would get on famously. There were hallmarks upon him that made him seem akin to the fellows he had left in Chicago, and it made him feel less alone here to find a boy he could understand. There had been the right kind of gleam in the eye of the minister's son when he spoke of the game. Other things didn't matter so much.

Miss Gracen, with many compunctions, watched her boy go off that afternoon, in company with the minister's son, and it seemed to her at the moment when they walked down the front path together that a great weight of responsibility settled down upon her.

The minister's son wore a rough brown Norfolk-jacket suit that just matched his hair and his wine-brown eyes, and there had been something altogether pleasing and engaging about him as he tipped his rough brown wool hat when he bade her good-bye and turned away smilingly to go with Dick.

Something in her—was it her misgivings?—had turned over in her heart as he looked at her, and suggested to her that perhaps Tom Atterbury was not quite so bad as people said; but still, when they disappeared behind the tall hedge and she knew that Dick was to be under his influence for two or three long hours, she turned away with the troubled feeling that a hen with one chicken wears on her brow, and sat down in deep thought to try to plan how to put Dick under good influences.

She decided that really no great harm could be done in one short afternoon, and she must expect to meet outside influences and cope with them; nevertheless, she was by no means at rest, and spent an hour in alternately seating herself in deep thought and walking to the window to look out, though she knew it was a long time before she could expect to see her boy coming back.

One thing was very sure; she must have a good talk with Dick that evening, and they must both know just where they stood. Then her mind would be more at rest, and she would know how to plan.

On her fifth trip to the window she saw a figure turn in at the gate and hurry up the walk with a quick, nervous gait. She recognized it at once as belonging to Miss Lydia Bypath, and turned with an impatient sigh. Ordinarily she was good nature itself to this most unwelcome of callers, for she knew and warmly loved the good side of Miss Bypath; but this afternoon, with anxiety on her mind, and her talk with her new nephew to plan for, she dreaded the bright, prying eyes, the cattish flings, and the curious questions that she knew she would have to meet.

Miss Bypath had of course heard of Dick's coming, and had come to inform herself concerning the stranger in her friend's home. There would not be a bit of tender heart history or family pride that would not be turned over and thoroughly aired before she was through with her subject. Miss Gracen dreaded the encounter.

Hitherto she had been able to keep on the right side of the village gossip and critic by never doing anything that Lydia Bypath disapproved and by being always ready to listen sympathetically to all the poor, little, narrow soul's grievances. But by all tokens she knew, as she turned away from the window and prepared to meet her guest with her most ceremonious smile, that her own turn had now come, and that she must meet it bravely.

Doubtless, too, the very thing that worried her most would be burned into her soul with scorching sentences, for in all probability Miss Bypath's sharp eyes had seen Dick go by to the football-field with the minister's scapegrace son. Miss Gracen girded up her strength, and went forth to meet her unwelcome guest.

Chapter VII

Miss Lydia Bypath had thin lips, eyes that bored like gimlets, though they were blue as the sea and had been pretty in their time, and a nose that was always ready to sniff at anything she doubted. She doubted almost everything that was told her, but told it as truth to the next person she met. She was slender and small, with an alert movement like a sharp blackbird, and she always wore dull black clothes with dazzling white lines near together. They seemed to reverse in color the fine lines of dissatisfaction in her thin, pursed lips, and up and down on her narrow forehead, vanishing under her gray, frizzy hair.

She came from a very fine old family, and had a patrician tilt to her chin, and most delicate little hands; but poverty and disappointment had so long been allowed to eat into her soul that nearly all the sweetness and beauty were gone. In their place had come only a most unworthy curiosity about her neighbors for the still more unworthy object of finding out whether they had been better treated by the world than she had been.

She had a poor opinion of all men in general, especially of husbands, a strong jealousy for all women, except perhaps Miss Gracen, whom she strongly admired, and a dislike for all young people and children. It was hard to find anybody that Miss Bypath quite approved, and harder to say anything with which she agreed.

So far no one but Miss Gracen, not even the minister, had been able to keep in her continual good graces; and now Miss Gracen was about to pass her first test by the sting of this most accomplished village gadfly. Her solitary condition, her pride and poverty, the fragments of her lost beauty, all appealed deeply to the sympathy of Miss Gracen, and had so far helped her to be patient with Miss Bypath's besetting sin.

The visitor perched herself on the edge of the Morris-chair, as if to lean back were to capitulate to a weakness of which she could not be guilty, and, having removed her cape, gloves and "fascinator," pursed her lips into a disagreeable smile, and began:

"Well, Victoria," fixing her sharp, gimlet blue eyes upon her victim, "I've come straight to you for information. I've always said, you know, that 'twas the only way to find out the real truth—to go straight to the fountain-head; and so I've come. I wasn't going to let anybody tell me things about my very best friend and not know how to deny them. I must say that I think you might have confided in me, an old friend, but, of

course, there may have been some excuse for your
not doing it. You know best about that. However,
I've come to find out before I said a blessed thing
about it to any one."

"Dear me, Lydia, is somebody saying something
about me now?" said her hostess with a forced smile.
"It was good of you to come straight to me, of course;
but, really, don't you think it's just as well not to pay
any attention to gossip? It dies down soon enough
when people find out there isn't any foundation for it."

She arose and placed a lovely bronze cushion behind her guest's back, rang for a cup of tea to be
brought, lowered the shades, then settled down to what
she now saw was inevitable.

"Yes, but Victoria, isn't there any foundation? *Isn't*
there?"

The blue eyes pierced her very soul as if they would
extract the information against the will of the other.
The two had gone to school together, had lived as
neighbors for many years, and Victoria Gracen knew
what she had to encounter.

"How am I to tell you, Lydia, when I don't know
what they're saying?" she laughed lightly, toying with
a carved paper-knife that lay on the table, and remembering with a curious pleasure that Dick had been
studying it just before lunch. She marvelled at the hold
the boy had upon her thoughts already.

"They say," said Lydia, and her voice took on a
terribly sepulchral whisper that held both imprecation
and implication, "they say that you have turned against
your dead father's wishes and have brought home the
child of your brother, the disinherited grandson. They
say, too, that if you keep him you will surely bring a
curse down upon your home and yourself."

Miss Gracen sat up very straight, a bright spot of
color in her cheeks and her dark eyes shining with
battle, an almost haughty smile on her sweet lips.

"Really!" she said, and then again, "Really!" Then
she laughed.

But little Miss Bypath sat still, held her thin hands
primly in her lap, and drew in her thin lips until they

almost vanished in a line of stern disapproval. She did not laugh. She conveyed the impression that she was most deeply hurt by Miss Gracen's laughter and that she considered it no subject for merriment.

Then Miss Gracen suddenly grew sober and dignified.

"Really, Lydia, I should scarcely think that was worth noticing," she said pleasantly. "It isn't any one's affair but my own, you know; and they can't bring any curses by their absurd remarks.

"If you really feel it incumbent upon you to say anything about the matter, you may just tell them the plain fact that my nephew, Dick, has, indeed, come to stay with me for a time, how long or how short a time will depend upon whether or not he likes to stay.

"I would have had him long ago if his mother could have spared him, but she could not see her way clear to do that. Since her death he has been lonely and accepted my invitation to come to me. I hope we are going to be very, very happy together."

There was something in the sweet dignity of the hostess that prevented the sharp queries the guest would have liked to make. Miss Gracen's tone said as plainly as words could have said that the subject was closed so far as she was concerned.

Lydia Bypath suddenly found an unaccountable lack of words wherewith to push her inquiries, though she was an adept in prying out and exhibiting to the world other people's private affairs. Now she could only shake her head ominously and murmur:

"Well, I'm sure I hope you will! I'm sure I hope you will! But the prospect looks anything but likely to *me*." What was there about Miss Gracen's direct and simple way of telling a few facts frankly that seemed to leave nothing further to ask, although the eager questioner would fain have known a thousand other details, but had not the effrontery to go further?

"Here is the tea," announced the hostess cheerily, as Rebecca entered with the tempting tray, on which were the delicious rolled sandwiches of brown and white bread for which Miss Gracen's receptions were

famous, and Lydia Bypath dearly loved, as well as the
delicate almond cakes and fragrant tea, with the choice
of lemon or cream. It pleased Miss Bypath that the
choice was always given her, although she invariably
answered severely: "Cream, of course. I'd as soon put
a pickle in my tea as lemon." Nevertheless, if the lemon
had not been on the tray, she would have felt that
Victoria Gracen thought her old-fashioned, and
hadn't considered it worth her while to observe all the
formality that she always gave to Mrs. Elihu Brown
and to Mrs. Norman Constable.

Miss Bypath waited in grim silence, save for the
usual lemon-and-cream dialogue, until she had had her
tea and sandwiches and Rebecca had withdrawn. Then
her voice took on its sepulchral whisper again.

"You've taken an awful contract on your hands,
Victoria; and you'll be sorry, or I'll surely miss my
guess," looking straight at her hostess. "Boys are terrible creatures to manage, and they will always disappoint you. I'm sorry to have to tell you right at the
start this way, but I consider it my duty to put you on
your guard before it is too late. Why, your young
scapegrace nephew is in bad company already. He
went by my house not half an hour ago arm in arm
with that good-for-nothing Tom Atterbury, and you
certainly know what he is! They were headed toward
the football-field, and I said to myself, 'Well that's the
end of him,'"—as if football were synonymous with
evil;—" 'Victoria Gracen had just better send him right
back to where he came from as fast as he can go, or
there'll be another disgraceful member of the family
to worry her into the grave.' I knew him by his close
resemblance to his father. He has that same reckless,
daredevil black eye——"

Miss Bypath here extinguished further speech in a
delectable bite of rolled brown bread and lettuce, but
it is doubtful whether she would have continued further in her remarks; for Miss Gracen had risen with
an air of finality, her deep eyes showing flashes of fire
that Lydia Bypath had presumed never to see directed

toward herself. She saw them now with dismay, and
shrank visibly before the look.

Miss Gracen stood thus looking at her guest scarcely
a second before she spoke; yet it seemed an aeon to
the presumptuous soul before her.

Then she merely said:

"Yes, I asked Tom to take Dick to the game. I want
him to feel at home as soon as possible, and there is
nothing like athletics to bring young people together.
But, if you please, Lydia, we will not discuss my family
any longer. Won't you let me give you a little more tea?
I'm afraid the cream has cooled it.

"By the way, did you know that we are to be favored with Professor Hammond's lecture on Shake-
speare at the next Club meeting? Won't it be great to
have him lecture for us? I hadn't dared even to hope
for anything of the sort, because they said he had come
here only to rest; but he told Mrs. Constable he should
be delighted to help us in any way we desired."

Miss Bypath, for once meek, readily caught on to
the thread of the new topic of conversation, yet she
realized none the less that she had indeed been on the
very verge of dismissal, not only from the house, but
from her friend's regard forever. She had dared many
things and she had outraged many people, but never
before had she been made so thoroughly to see and
realize the fulness of her offence; and yet no verbal re-
buke had been uttered. The remainder of her visit
—and she stayed until the shades of evening were beginning to fall—she spent eagerly trying to placate her
dignified hostess.

Perhaps it was as well that Miss Gracen had no
leisure to worry that afternoon, for surely she would
have worried about the very thing Miss Bypath had
suggested; but now her soul was roused in indignation
against the meanness of the village gossip, and she
began to find in her heart excuses for the son of the
minister. His wistful brown eyes haunted her, and
when, glancing out of the window as the dusky shadows of the early twilight drew on, she saw the two boys

coming down the street together, laughing and talking, a glad smile broke out upon her face. Her boy was coming back to her safe and sound. Nothing very bad could have happened to him in one short afternoon, although Lydia Bypath had said that he was going to a football-game in the same tone in which she might have told how fast he was going to destruction.

Miss Gracen felt a sudden unaccountable sympathy with the son of the minister, who had acquired a doubtful reputation, and wondered again within herself whether all that people said about him were really true, after all. Perhaps he was not so bad as he was thought to be, and anyhow his father was a good man.

When, a moment later, Richard, not knowing that his aunt was entertaining a guest in the library, entered with his new friend, Miss Gracen greeted him with an outstretched hand and a sweet smile of welcome. A sudden desire to show Miss Bypath how wrong had been her attitude toward Tom came over her.

"I'm glad you came back with Dick," she said. "I was wanting to ask whether you wouldn't stay to supper. I'm sure Dick would like it."

Dick's eyes lit happily.

"Sure," echoed the boy. He hadn't been in the habit of having friends home to supper. It was a new and delightful experience.

"Why, I just came in to see some photographs Dick was telling me he brought with him," drawled Tom in his soft, hesitant, appealing voice; "but I'd like awfully to stay; only dad said if I didn't come straight home and study I couldn't go to another game this semester. But it would be just jolly to stay. I'd like it awfully, Miss Vic."

Tom's brown eyes touched again the chord of sympathy in Miss Gracen's already awakened heart. She determined to have Tom stay, the more as she turned and saw Miss Bypath's cat-like eyes of disapproval fixed upon her, and suddenly realized her duties as a hostess.

"Excuse me, Miss Bypath," she said, turning toward her; "let me introduce my nephew, Richard Gracen of Chicago; and Tom Atterbury of course you know."

There was that in her tone that made Richard feel as though she had introduced the son of a millionaire, and his face flushed with pleasure. He liked his aunt for the deference she paid to him, a mere nobody of a boy.

He shook hands with Miss Bypath with an easy grace that astonished his aunt; and Miss Bypath was quite overwhelmed for the moment, though she could not forbear a jab of advice as she submitted her reluctant hand in greeting.

"I'm sure I hope you'll turn out to be a comfort to your aunt in her old age, and not bring trouble the way some boys do."

With the keen instinct of youth the two boys knew immediately that Miss Bypath had been talking about them to Miss Gracen, and Richard seemed to feel, for the first time since he had entered his aunt's house, the reproach of what his father had done, while Tom's face took on the sullen, dogged expression of the hunted one of whom no one ever thought any good.

An angry wave of color rolled over Richard's face, and he felt something throbbing and choking painfully in his throat. His fingers involuntarily clinched themselves, and he lifted his chin proudly in a way that his father used to have when he was hurt, which went straight to the heart of his aunt.

Instantly Miss Gracen stepped to Richard's side, and slipped her hand lovingly, confidingly within his arm, putting the other soft white hand gently over his fierce clinched fingers.

"Dick is a great comfort to me already," she said confidently; "and I am sure we are going to have delightful times together."

She felt his fingers relax at once under her touch, and saw with relief his wondering eyes turn to her with a pleased look. She smiled, and his face lit up with something beautiful to see, that the boy himself scarcely understood. It was a strange experience to have any one take his part, or show any outward sign of caring. His mother had been too meek and tired to answer back when his aunt and uncle blamed him for anything. He knew she cared, of course; but she never said so. He was surprised to find how sweet it was to have some one care.

Tom, meanwhile, was looking on surprised, his own expression changing back to wistfulness as he saw Miss Gracen's smile of understanding. He was glad for the other boy, glad that any one understood a boy as she seemed to do. Miss Gracen looked up, and caught his glance, and reached out her hand to him also.

"Now, Tom," she said with one of her bright, happy smiles, as if the other matter were entirely settled and forgotten, "would it do any good, I wonder, if I were to telephone your father and ask him to let you stay for supper? You could go straight home and study afterward, couldn't you? And you wouldn't be able to do much between now and supper-time, you know."

Tom's freckles melted into smiles. The sinking sun shot out a parting ray through the long west windows, and laid a touch of gold upon his deep-red hair, making the boy really attractive. Miss Gracen's heart went out to him in earnest now. If this boy was wrong in some ways, might he not be helped to be right? At least, she would get acquainted, and find out. If he was to be guarded against, she must know what she had to guard against.

Tom laid a rough red hand confidingly, wonderingly, on her white one, as he would have laid it on the head of his favorite collie, that loved him. It was his way of responding to Miss Gracen's kindness. He was pleased beyond measure at what she had done, and especially in the presence of this crabbed, sharp-eyed woman who had always seemed to have an especial spite against him.

"Oh, I'd like it just awfully, Miss Vic," he said gratefully, "and I'm most sure father wouldn't refuse you. That would be just fine—if he only would let me stay. Yes, sure, I could go right home afterwards and study. I'd study *hard,* too."

"Then I'll telephone at once," smiled the hostess.

But Miss Bypath made herself felt at that instant with her most effective sniff, as if to say that this was no company for a respectable woman like herself; and to the relief of all she made a stiff adieu, and took her way home, declining coldly the offer of company, though Miss Gracen suggested sending Hiram with her.

When she was gone, Miss Gracen went to the telephone and talked with Tom's father, who reluctantly consented to allow him to stay to supper; and the two boys went noisily and happily up to Richard's room to make ready for the evening meal.

"Gee! but that woman Bypath makes me tired," said Tom as he followed Richard up-stairs. "Father says she makes him more trouble in the church than any five other members put together. I'm glad your aunt didn't ask her to stay to supper. She never did like me, and she'd put one over on me whenever she could.

"Say, your aunt is all right, isn't she? I always did like her, though I never knew her very well. Father thinks she's just great."

Richard's face had darkened at mention of Miss Bypath, but it lighted with a tender smile when his friend spoke of Miss Gracen.

"Yes, she's pretty fine, all right," said Richard, half bashfully.

"She sure is! She's a peach!" proclaimed Tom, as they entered Richard's room and closed the door.

The echo of their voices had come down to Victoria Gracen as she stood still beside the telephone, wondering whether, after all, she had done the right thing; for she feared lest she had let herself be carried away by her indignation with Lydia Bypath, and had perhaps fostered an intimacy with this wild boy, who would do her boy no good. But, when she heard the unqualified approbation in the young voices, and realized that it was herself who was being discussed in these strange boy-terms, her heart beat with a wild thrill of happiness. She was not very familiar with modern slang, but she had discernment enough to know that when Tom Atterbury said in that tone that she was a "peach" he could give her no compliment higher, according to his way of thinking, and she resolved to hold and keep his admiration if possible. Like a flash her common sense showed her that, while she might have made a mistake in introducing her nephew to this boy in the first place, he would have had to meet him sometime, and it was better for them to meet in Richard's home and under her companionship than out and away from her knowledge.

It was not likely that the boy who had come to her had been brought up in pink cotton so far. He might indeed, for aught she knew, be even a more dangerous companion than the much-talked-of Tom. At all events, she would keep Tom's friendliness now that she had it, and see whether there was any way in which she could help him back to the confidence of the neighborhood.

It was with this in view that she sat down to her well-spread table and prepared to be as fascinating as she knew how for the sake of these two boys.

The supper table was very pretty in its usual whiteness of fine linen, its glitter of silver and its shimmer of cut glass, and the effect of it all was just as strange and just as wonderful to the boy from the parsonage as it was to the boy from a forlorn little Chicago boarding house. There was a great bowl of roses in the centre of the table, and touches of old rose showed here and there on the beautiful soft gray gown that Miss Gracen wore.

Tom suddenly became aware of the largeness and redness of his hands as they protruded from his last year's sleeves, that were too short. However, he was not much used to worrying about his appearance; and Miss Gracen and Richard were so hearty in their expressions of pleasure at his being there that he soon

forgot his hands, and made himself so agreeable that
Miss Gracen in her turn was surprised and pleased.

She decided that people had judged Tom without
knowing him. He certainly had charming ways, and a
wistful fashion of looking at one that appealed tre-
mendously to the heart.

The roast beef was of a quality that seldom came
the way of the parsonage, where the meagre salary
was always in the process of stretching itself to cover
the multitude of needs of a family of seven. There
was custard pie, plenty of it, with a crust like flakes of
snow, a golden luscious centre, and browned to a perfect cinnamon tinge on the top. Also, Miss Gracen not
only offered, but urged, two pieces on the hungry boys;
and Tom, whose methods of obtaining the second piece
at home were not always the best, was overwhelmed
at such open bounty.

The conversation finally fell on football; and the
hostess, who had never been to a football game in all
her life, and had indeed shared the feeling of more
than half the village that it was a terribly useless and
dangerous waste of time, began to see an entirely different side to the question. She saw the eagerness with
which both boys entered into the merits of the game
they had witnessed that afternoon, describing the different plays, denouncing or praising this or that
player, rejoicing that the home college team had
won. She asked questions, and the boys proceeded eagerly to instruct her, using the salt and pepper bottles
to illustrate the different plays and an olive for a ball.

Even Rebecca lingered in her waiting, watching the
little green ball move from one pepper bottle to another as Tom gave a demonstration of the game that
afternoon; and Hiram was seen to apply one eye to the
crack of the door of the butler's pantry, both servants
beaming over the good cheer that had so suddenly
come to the home after the long years of silence.

Miss Gracen's eyes were bright and her lips smiling
with interest as she began to understand the game,
and she laughingly agreed to go with the two boys to

watch the next big game that was played in town, wondering furtively what Lydia Bypath would think of her now, to be contaminated with football at her age.

But then probably the boys would forget all about it before time for the game to be played; and it pleased her that they had asked her.

"I haven't had so pleasant a tea-party as this since my dear brother went away," she said happily, as they rose from the table. "Indeed, you must come and see Dick again, Tom." And with a sudden loving thought she reached over, selected two of the most beautiful buds from among the roses, and pinned them to the boys' coats before they left the dining-room.

As he made his adieu, Tom Atterbury came impulsively over to his charming hostess; and, putting both big, rough hands confidingly on her sleeve, he said in his most winning drawl:

"Miss Vic, I want to thank you for that dinner. It certainly was simply great. I'm awfully obliged to you for inviting me to stay."

With that look in his brown eyes Miss Gracen's heart was entirely won over to champion the cause of the minister's wild young son.

"I'm glad," she said brightly. "Then you'll come often again. And now you must study hard all the evening, as you promised, so your father will be willing for you to come the next time."

"All right, I will, I surely will. You'll see, Miss Vic. I'll bring my report-card down to prove it to you next week, when we go to that game."

He bade them a laughing good-night, and Miss Gracen turned away from the door with a qualm of conscience. What had she done? Committed herself to a standing friendship between her nephew and this youth who had hitherto been considered dangerous? Nay, she had done more. She had even encouraged it.

But a glance at the look of deep admiration in the eyes of Richard as she closed the door made her forget all in a rush of joy that she had this boy. Her home was no more lonely; she had some one to love; and something in his eyes told her that he was not averse to loving her. She slipped her hand within his arm, and so they walked back to the cheerful light of the library fire.

Chapter VIII

"Nice fellow he is," said Dick with a shade of embarrassment in his voice. He didn't know how to talk to a lady very well. His aunt was so delicate in her make-up and so dainty and refined in her dress that she filled him with a sort of awe.

"He does seem nice, doesn't he?" said Miss Gracen, watching him thoughtfully. "He has the name of being rather wild, but I couldn't help liking him to-night. Perhaps he has been misjudged."

"Hardly anybody's as bad as folks think they are," vouchsafed the youthful Richard with a frown, remembering his own case and how he had been, as he felt, misjudged. "I'm not any angel myself," he added belligerently. "I don't s'pose you'd have asked me here and done all you have for me if you'd known all about me."

He turned and looked at her half defiantly, as if he would give her opportunity even now to withdraw her kindness and send him back to his own place.

It had come—the opportunity she had been longing for and dreading,—the opening to have a personal talk with the boy for whom she had become responsible. She knew she must not let it slip, and that it must be talked out to the finish, faithfully, patiently, and with infinite wisdom. She put up a breath of prayer for help, while her heart began to beat wildly. Never in all her quiet, well-ordered life had she met with a task more difficult and more unequal to her experience.

Pressing her fingers gently on the boy's arm, she said, after a moment's searching, tender look into his eyes:

"That wouldn't have made any difference, Dick.

And it doesn't make any now. You are my dear brother's child, and as such I wanted you. Now that you are here I love you. Whatever you are, I shall have to bear with. If you choose to do wrong, I shall have to suffer."

The boy's eyes grew cloudy with moisture. He had never heard anything like that speech in his life. It touched him, comforted him, and made a baby of him all in one.

"I don't want to make you suffer," he growled in a choked voice, lowering his eyes and half turning away.

A sudden great joy sprang into Victoria Gracen's eyes.

"O Dick, dear, thank you! I don't believe you're going to. Sit down and tell me all about it, won't you? I think we have made a good beginning."

They had come into the library, and were standing in front of the fire; but Richard drew away from her, and brushed his hand hastily and angrily across his eyes as though the lights hurt them; then he leaned his elbow on the mantel, and rested his forehead on his hand so that his face was shaded from her view. He made no move to sit down, and his very back was eloquent of deep disturbance.

"I'd better go away," he growled out at last. "I don't belong here. I'm not fit to be in a home like this. Don't you suppose I know it? I knew it when I came, I guess. I could tell from your telegram you were different. Mother was a good woman, and did the best she could; but she wasn't like you. And I've knocked around a lot and done a lot as I pleased. You wouldn't like what I've been, I know, and I ought to go away right off. I'd better go at once before it's any harder."

A choke in his voice ended the speech; the boy dropped his head on the mantel, and his shoulders drooped piteously. The heart of the woman went out in great motherliness, and she felt the tears filling her own eyes. She got up from the chair in which she had been sitting, and came and stood beside him, putting her hand shyly, unaccustomedly on his thick brown hair.

"Dick, dear, didn't I tell you that I love you? Didn't I tell you that doesn't make any difference? I'm going to keep right on loving you in spite of everything you may say you have been. Can't you understand that? This is just as good a time as any for us to understand each other. Come, sit down, dear."

With ready tact she drew a chair opposite her own low one in front of the fire, and turned out the lights in the room; for the fire was burning brightly, and soft, flickering leaps of light and shadow played about the walls and floor and on their faces. She had seen that the boy was stirred to the depths of his nature, and readily guessed that the talk would be less embarrassing for him if his own face were not subjected to the glare of the bright electric lights.

He dropped into the chair she had drawn, and watched her furtively, his brows attentive, his eyes full of a growing admiration. She made a charming picture there in the firelight, the play of shadow over her soft, gray dress, and the light glowing in the touch of rose color and illuminating her white hair and sweet face. Richard, as he looked, thought he had never seen any one so lovely, not even a young girl. And this beautiful, motherly, understanding woman loved him, and wanted him!

His soul was filled with a deep comfort such as he had never known before, and he found himself wishing his mother knew about it.

Miss Gracen began by telling a little story of her brother Dick and some escapade of his which had put him into disgrace. She pictured herself and her brother sitting in this very room talking it over, and told the younger Dick how she had loved her brother in his trouble, and wanted to protect him, because she felt that he was truly sorry, though his elders did not seem to be thoroughly convinced of it.

Perhaps what she said might not have been considered wise by trained educators and psychological experts; but she followed the promptings of her heart, and was perfectly frank with the boy. She felt that what they needed first was perfect confidence in each other, and then they could go ahead.

"Now, Dick, dear," she said as she turned from the incident of his father, "I'm getting to be an old woman; at least, I'm on the way there; and I don't suppose I'm very wise. I'll not be able to do all for you that your father would have done in helping you to be a splendid man; but I thought if we could just begin by being good friends, and always perfectly frank and true with each other, it might make things easier. I'd like it very much if you could feel you would never hide things from me, even if they were things you knew I didn't like. I'd promise always to be ready to talk them over fairly and try to see your point of view as well as my own. Do you think you would be willing to do that?"

Richard's eyes were upon her earnestly, and they took on a glint of appreciation. His look spoke volumes, but his lips only said in a low, reserved growl:

"Sure!"

It wasn't much of an answer, and yet his aunt felt that he had given her full assurance. Something in his eyes and in the loyalty of his tone filled her with joy inexpressible. She had not thought it would be like this to have a boy of her own. She had hoped she would like him enough so that his presence would not be a burden, but that her life should suddenly be filled with a great glory and beauty because of his coming she had not dreamed.

"Dick, tell me," she said, looking at him earnestly, and speaking low and tenderly, "are you—do you think you are going to like to stay here? Do you think you can learn to love me a little?"

The boy tried to take his eyes away from her face, but before he succeeded he gave her a look of so deep reverence and affection in answer that she felt she never would forget it; and then his voice, hoarse and gruff, and sounding strange to his own ears, growled out again:

"Sure. I like it better than anything that ever happened to me before, and—I like you already." He couldn't make his lips say "love"; but he thought it in his heart, and the aunt felt that was what he meant.

They were silent for a moment, looking into each other's eyes in the firelight; then the boy looked down embarrassedly, and said quickly, sharply:

"But I know I'm not fit to be here in this beautiful home, and with you. I know well enough I don't belong here, and I ought to go back and work in the slaughter-house where my uncle wanted to put me. I hate it; but that's all I'm fit for in this world, and I've got sense enough to see it. You'd better send me right back."

He drew his hand across his eyes hastily, and his throat moved convulsively. Miss Gracen was on her knees beside his chair in a second, with her arm about the strong, young shoulders, and her white hair close to his dark head.

"Dick, my dear, dear boy," she said tenderly, "don't ever say that again. You do belong right here in your dear father's house, and you are fit for it, I know; or, if there is any way in which you are not fit, we will make you fit. You shall never go away unless you do not like to stay. Do you understand?"

For answer Richard's fingers closed tightly about his aunt's hand that had crept into his.

"Thank you; you're awfully good to me," he managed to murmur hoarsely after a minute. "I'll try hard to deserve it all."

"I hope you will, dear," said his aunt gently; "but remember that, after all, it isn't a matter of deserving. It's your inheritance. It is your right as your father's son. You must try to live up to what your father would expect of you. Will you try to do that?"

"Sure," said Richard tersely, though evidently deeply affected.

"And now, Dick," said his aunt after a minute, feeling that the strain must be relieved, "suppose you tell me all about yourself. Remember I don't know anything about your past, nor what you've been used

to; and I think perhaps we'd get along a little better if
we understood each other's ways. I'll tell you in turn
anything you want to know. Shall we do that?"

Richard assented almost inaudibly, and his aunt
arose, and stood beside him for a moment, passing her
hand lovingly over the dark bowed head; then, drawing her chair quite near to his, she sat down.

"Now, will you begin?" she asked pleasantly.

"What do you want to know?" asked the boy.
"How bad I've been?"

The woman smiled tenderly.

"Why, yes, if you care to tell me," she said, "and
how good you've been, too. I'd like to understand all
about you; then perhaps I wouldn't make so many
mistakes at the beginning."

"There hasn't been much good to tell, I guess," muttered the boy, "at least, not what you would call good,
I suppose. I haven't been so awfully bad, either, though
I guess some things you wouldn't like. But a boy has
to have a good time somehow, you know, and there
weren't many good times coming my way unless I went
out and made them for myself."

Miss Gracen's hand stole out sympathetically, and
touched the hand that lay on the arm of his chair. The
boy seemed to gather courage from the gentle touch
for what he had to say.

He talked slowly, in broken sentences that seemed
somehow to have little relation to one another, and
there were long pauses between them; but, when he
was through and turned with an apologetic laugh to
say, "That's all, I guess," there were tears in his listener's eyes, and she found she had a very clear picture
of the life her brother's boy must have led. It made her
heart ache. She wanted to say so much to him, and
felt herself so unequal to the task she had before her.
How was she to get wisdom to guide this fervid, pas-
sionate, lonely young soul into the right way? It seemed
as if he had so far been struggling through life prac-
tically alone. She prayed for just the right word to say
first.

Before she had spoken, however, Richard broke the silence again.

"You think I'm only fit to go back and work in the slaughter-house, now don't you?" There was a curiously hard, fierce tone in his voice that almost broke his aunt's heart.

"Oh, Dick!" she cried out, hardly able to keep the tears back, "don't say such a thing——"

But the boy, mistaking her meaning, brushed her hand away roughly, and sprang to his feet with an unpleasant laugh.

"I know that's what you think; only you don't want to say so; and I'll go the first thing in the morning. I won't stay around here and disgrace you——"

Cut to the heart at the desperate look in the boy's face, his aunt went to him, and drew him down on the couch beside her.

"Dick," she said, "dear Dick, my own dear boy, how can you say such things? It is awful to me to think of your going back to work in the slaughter-house, and nothing you have said has made me feel you do not belong here. What more can I say to make you feel at home than just to tell you once more that I love and always shall love you? You belong right here, and here you are going to stay as long as you are willing to stay. Do you believe me?"

There was a long pause during which the boy's head was turned entirely away from her, and she could see only the strong, attractive outline of fine head and well-knit shoulders. The boy was thinking hard, and trying to gain command of his voice.

"Do you believe me, dear?" she said softly again; and at last the boy replied hoarsely:

"Yes, if you really mean it."

"I do."

"Then I want to stay," he said, fiercely gripping her hand in his eagerness. "And I'll try every way I can to do what you want me to do. I'll try to live up to your standard as much as I know how."

"Dear boy, that's all I could possibly ask," said his

aunt, deeply moved; "and I'll try to help you and to make it as easy as possible for you. There are certain things which this community will expect of your father's son. I am sure you will want to come up to their expectations and bring no dishonor on your father's name. Am I right?"

"Sure," came the muffled voice, with nevertheless a deep, true ring.

"They'll expect you to be law-abiding and courteous, honest and true, not to drink intoxicating liquor, nor smoke, nor swear, nor loaf around in idle ways, but to take your place in the community in a pleasant, useful way; to go to church on the Sabbath, and to stand well in your classes at school. That is also what your father would have expected of you, and what I want. Does that sound too hard?"

The boy looked up startled.

"School?" he asked.

"Why, yes, didn't you expect to go to school? You didn't think you had finished your education yet, did you, Dick?"

"I don't see how I could go to school. I'm way behind, and it's a long time since I stopped."

"Why did you stop?"

"I had trouble with the teachers. I guess it was my fault," he added shamefacedly.

"Never mind, Dick. Perhaps they didn't understand. And anyhow you are older now. You will know better how to conquer those things. I should be greatly disappointed if you didn't go on with your education."

"I'll go if you want me to," said the boy, as if that settled it; "but I don't see how I'll ever catch up."

"You won't have much trouble if you're anything like your father. Besides, I can help you some. I used to help him. I enjoy that, and you'll soon be up to the boys of your age, ahead of them, perhaps. You'll like to go to college, sha'n't you?"

"Mother always talked about it. She wanted me to. She'd have liked it."

"And so would your father," added his aunt softly. "What grade were you in when you left school?"

They turned up the lights, and sat down to a thorough canvass of the school question. Miss Gracen sent up-stairs for some of the elder Dick's school-books, and telephoned to the principal of the high school for information; and before Dick knew it he was poring over books, and remembering things that he had in some way imbibed from the atmosphere of the school-room during the days when he fooled away his time and opportunities in nonsense.

For the first time in his life he realized just how serious a matter it had been, and more than once he threw down the books and told his aunt that there was no use at all in his trying, he was too far behind; but always she opened the books again, and went on encouraging him, asking him quiet questions, until his desire to conquer began to grow.

When ten o'clock finally came, Richard was surprised, and laid aside the books and plans almost reluctantly.

"We'll go over to the high school Monday morning," said his aunt, smiling. "I've made an appointment with Professor Holloway to meet you, and he will tell us just what we ought to know. Then you and I will get to work next week and brush up a few things before you go, so that you will not feel uncomfortable.

"Now, to-morrow is Saturday. How should you like to take a long walk down the meadow and out through the ravine where your father used to go? There is a beautiful creek there, and a swimming-hole, and I know all the spots where your father used to fish and go canoeing and camping. I haven't been on a tramp in a good many years; but if you think I'd do for a companion, we'll go."

Richard was delighted. He had never been in the country in his life, save on Sunday-school picnics. For him, born and bred in the city, nature held a certain charm that was entirely new.

He came over to his aunt, great embarrassment in his face, but determination in his manner.

"You're awfully good to me," he said shyly. "Good-night."

Chapter IX

REBECCA and Molly were making sandwiches the next morning, and Miss Gracen was arraying herself in a short walking-dress and stout walking-boots, her eyes as excited and happy as a girl's in view of the pic-nic she and Richard had planned, when, happening to glance out of the window, she saw to her dismay two boys entering the front gate. One of them she felt sure by his walk was Tom Atterbury, and who was the other boy? Instinctively she knew that they had come after Richard, and both alarm and disappointment arose within her.

In the still watches of the night, thinking over her boy's prospects, in spite of her anxiety, she had been very, very happy; and she had decided that even a friendship with Tom Atterbury might not be so bad if it were tempered judiciously with other friendships.

She had resolved to see whether she couldn't do something for Tom, invite him to the house often, and try to make it pleasant for him. If Richard saw him at home, perhaps there wouldn't be so much danger of his wanting to go off with him.

But now here he was the first thing in the morning, coming just when they were going off together; and Richard would, of course, prefer going with the boys. What should she do? And who was the other boy?

She came closer to the window, and her heart was suddenly filled with trouble when she saw that it was Harold Constable.

Now, Harold Constable was as much worse than Tom Atterbury in the estimation of the entire village as Tom Atterbury was worse than some of the more exemplary boys. Mrs. Constable was a society woman, spending much of her time in the near-by city, always entertaining and being entertained. She was also an ac-

tive club-woman in a very superficial sort of way, and
these two vocations gave her little time to look after the
welfare of her family. Harold was always well dressed,
had plenty of spending money, and an automobile
of his own, although he was still slightly under the law-
ful age to run it. This fact, however, did not in the least
hinder him from running it to exceed the speed limit
whenever he thought he could do so without being
caught. He loafed and smoked continually, had been a
pupil in nearly every school in the locality and in several at a distance, and he was now enjoying a season of
idling at home.

His reputation had grown more and more unsavory
during the increasing years of his life, though nothing
more definite had ever been said than could be expressed in a phrase "wild," conveyed in more or less
eloquent terms, according as the speaker could use a
shrug of the shoulders and a meaning glance of the
eyes.

Harold was handsome, daring and reckless. He had
gained the ill-will of almost everybody in town, but
went on his way as serene as a summer morning, doing
whatever he pleased and only daring the more because
people looked coldly at him.

And Harold Constable was coming to see her Richard! She felt appalled. For a moment she had the attitude of a mother hen who sees a hawk about to swoop
down upon her chicken. Then her eyes flashed. How
dared he come there? How dared Tom Atterbury bring
him? She would have to hurry down and make Tom
understand that this was the end of all relations if he
was going to bring boys like this to her house.

In feverish haste she put on her hat and coat, and
went down; but Richard was already talking to the two
visitors. She caught his voice with a wistful tone, saying:

"I'm awful sorry, but I guess it can't be helped.
Aunt Vic planned something else for this morning,
and I mustn't disappoint her."

Her heart warmed in sudden gratitude to her own
dear boy. He wasn't going to ask to run away and leave

her, after all. He was loyally going to stick by their
plan, although she could plainly see that, whatever the
invitation was, he was longing to accept it.

Then she turned to look at the other boys, and saw
both their faces fall in blank disappointment. They had
really wanted Richard to go with them, and it was going to spoil all their fun; yet she could not, *could* not
trust her boy in such company as that. How thankful
she was that he had refused of his own accord!

Tom Atterbury spied her coming down the stairs,
and raised his red-brown eyes to greet her.

"Oh, Miss Vic, good morning," he said in his pleasant drawl. "Say, Miss Vic, couldn't you just change
your plans a little, and spare Richard? We want to take
a hike, and we want him to go with us. You know
Harold; don't you, Miss Vic?"

Now it happened that Miss Gracen, although she had
known the boy by sight for several years, had never
spoken to Harold Constable, nor he to her; and, as she
turned, half vexed, to acknowledge the introduction,
he flashed his fine white teeth at her in a confiding
smile, and opened at her his big, gray, handsome eyes,
shaded by long golden lashes; and a remarkable thing
happened to Miss Gracen.

Had she suddenly become daft, she wondered, because she had one boy all of her own, that she should
now find a most unprecedented interest in her heart for
all boys? What was the matter with her that she could
not look at Harold Constable in cold disapproval, as
she had fully intended to do, thereby conveying both
to him and to Tom Atterbury, who had presumed to
bring him there, the knowledge that he was not at all
welcome? But indeed she could not. She could only
smile and give him her hand in friendly greeting.

Harold took it with a grace and ease that showed
the one thing his elegant mother had taught him, and
in his winning way he proceeded to speak.

"I don't believe we know each other, but I wish we
did," he said gracefully. "I've always admired you, and
Tom here tells me you are great. He says you're as
good as one of the fellows, and that you're going to a

football-game with him next week. I wish you'd let me
go along."

"Why, of course," said Miss Gracen in utter rout
and confusion; for who could resist the disarming look
of innocence in those gray eyes, the fine possibilities
expressed in the half-formed lines of the face, the sunny
smile, the daring waves of light-brown hair tossed carelessly back from a fine forehead, the whole spoiled only
by the look of recklessness half graven over it?

She looked the boy over, smiled back at him pleasantly, and felt that she liked him, yet was still fearful
of herself, because she *knew* this boy was not all that
he ought to be, and she had her own boy to think of
now. Yet she was conscious of a passing wish to do
something also for this child of luxury, this boy who
was so evidently being neglected by his own mother.

She smiled at Tom Atterbury, and began to say how
sorry she was that she must be in the way of any pleasure, but, as she and Richard had planned to do something special this morning——

At least, that was what she intended to say; but, as
she looked from the red-brown eyes of one boy to the
wide gray ones of the other, and then into the great,
dark ones of her own boy, she suddenly did the unexpected, *most* unexpected even to herself.

Instead of sending those boys on their way disappointed she said:

"Why, Tom, why shouldn't you and Harold come
with us? You'd like that, wouldn't you, Richard? We're
going on a hike ourselves. At least, I guess you'd call
it that, and we'd be pleased to have your company.
Maybe you won't care to have an old woman along,
though. I suppose I can't walk so fast nor as far as you
can."

"Oh, Miss Vic! That will be great!" shouted Tom
joyfully. "Of course we want you along. We'd have a
great deal nicer time, and we don't care how far or how
fast we go. We just want to get out and have a jolly
good time together."

Richard's face was all alight with joy, and he looked
adoringly at his aunt as though she were some angel

who could divine and always give him just what he
most wanted. Well pleased, his aunt turned to the
third boy, half hoping the affair would be too slow
for him, and he would courteously decline to go, and
withdraw from the scene; but, when she saw his expression, her heart went out to him with a sudden sympathy; for the gray eyes were alight with a real pleasure,
and the whole face had softened with a look she could
not quite understand.

"I'd love to go, Miss Gracen," he said earnestly.
"Are you sure I wouldn't be intruding? I don't want
to butt in where I don't belong."

His gray eyes searched her face longingly, and she
suddenly realized, to her surprise, that she no longer
hoped that he would not go.

"You're not intruding one bit," she said graciously;
"we want you very much. It will make the day a great
deal pleasanter for Dick. Come in and sit down while I
tell Rebecca to put a few more cookies and sandwiches
into the lunch-basket."

"Cookies! Ohh! Ummmm!" drawled Tom, drawing
his breath in a suggestive sound. "Say, Harold, we've
dropped right into a good, soft place to-day. Some hike!
Real cookies!"

Miss Gracen flashed a look of pleased sympathy at
them, and vanished into the dining-room, where she
gave directions for more sandwiches to be made in a
hurry, and then herself slipped up to her bookcase to
find a book that might perhaps interest the boys in
case they sat down to rest for a few minutes.

She didn't want to give any chance to those other
boys to harm her boy, but she meant in her heart to
make them all have the best time she could.

She felt almost guilty going off this way with two of
the worst boys in the town, and her own dear boy un-
warned and unguarded; but somehow she could not
help feeling very happy about it. If indeed she was doing wrong, at least she would be on the alert; she
would discover it at once, and perhaps never do it
again; but she meant to find out just exactly for herself
whether these were bad boys or not. Her boy was to be

of their world now; she could not hope to keep him utterly apart from them, even should she wish it. It would be well for her to know exactly what they were. One day together ought to tell her something.

Of course, she supposed, they all would far rather have gone without her, but she must do so much for Dick to guard him; and so, whether they liked it or not, this once she would go along.

The lunch was packed in two boxes, so that it could be easily carried and the boxes thrown away when empty. Tom and Richard took possession of the boxes, slinging them knapsack-fashion on heavy cords from their shoulders. Miss Gracen was deeply touched and greatly relieved when, as they started out the door, Harold Constable walked beside her and lightly helped her down the steps, saying:

"Miss Gracen, may I walk with you?"

It suited her plans exactly to walk with Harold, for then she could find out about him, and then also she might prevent her own boy from being in doubtful company.

Down through the brown meadow, wind-swept and dry; out under tall oaks, whose rustling leaves were falling in great golden heaps; down the steep, winding way to the little creek they treaded their steps; and Harold Constable, as carefully and thoughtfully as a man would have done it, helped Miss Gracen over every root, rock and rough place in the way; and, as they walked, he talked.

"I'm awfully glad you came along with us to-day, Miss Gracen," he said earnestly, when they had reached the bank of the creek and were walking slowly along the mossy path among the rocks. "I'm lonesome, I guess. You see, my mother sailed from New York yesterday for a three months' stay in Italy; and somehow home seems kind of empty, just dad and myself, and dad off on trips most of the time. I didn't realize it till mother went; but they have shrouded everything in our house in denim and netting, and it looks like ghosts everywhere. Dad and I could hear our voices echo back to us last night when we were eating dinner, and I guess dad'll stay at his club in town after this for dinner mostly. I could have gone to boarding-school, but I didn't want to. I'll just bum around, I suppose; but you can't think how I appreciate your inviting me this morning. It looks like a regular peach of a time to me. Look out for that branch, Miss Gracen; it's too low for safety. Here, I'll cut it off. It might have got in your eyes. Watch that rock there; it's slippery, and inclines right over the swimming-hole. Ever go swimming, Miss Gracen?"

As if she had been a girl again, an intuition seemed to come to her now to talk to this attractive, lonely boy; and her whole heart went out to shelter him from all the dangers that she knew must surround a boy left as he was, without his mother or his home or much of a father. Her indignation boiled inwardly that a mother should so neglect a splendid fellow like this one, and allow him to get the reputation that he had gained in the community.

Then with a glance at her own boy in front she breathed a quick prayer that she might not make such mistakes; that she might not be blind to the dangers that Richard must pass through, or neglect any opportunity for strengthening him on every hand.

She discussed swimming with Harold Constable, and talked of canoeing. He said that his canoe was still down by the water-side, just about a mile up the creek, and suggested joyfully that they walk to it and then paddle up to the head of the stream.

Now, Miss Gracen had always been informed that canoeing was the most dangerous form of navigation, and she was secretly very much afraid of the water; but with three eager pairs of eyes upon her, and three eager voices telling her that a canoe was the safest thing in the world, she could not spoil the sport.

She would be "game," as they called it, and even get into a canoe if they so desired. For one day, at least, she would do as they asked her; and then perhaps she would be in a position to ask favors of them sometime.

Into the canoe she submitted to being put, with plenty of cushions pulled from the locker under a tree, and stuffed around her, and a great streamer-rug from the same receptacle tucked about her. She sat for a few seconds in some trepidation, expecting every instant to be tipped into the water; but there was, after all, a serene consciousness that the day was not cold; and, if she did fall in, there were three strong swimmers to rescue her.

The boys clambered in, and the little craft was shoved silently into the stream. Then there came to Miss Gracen a sense of surprised delight and delicious restfulness such as she had not known before. She perceived suddenly what a joy all its own there was in canoeing, and rested back among her cushions as cosily as she would have done in her own rocking-chair at home, and watched the ripples as they glided up the stream.

Wonderful and beautiful colors came into view, and were pointed out familiarly by the amazing Harold, who developed a poetry of thought and a keen appreciation of nature that was most unexpected in the boy the whole town had always supposed him to be.

"Look up there, Miss Gracen," he called from his seat behind her. "Now watch as we round this bend. You'll see some mighty pretty coloring. There! See that crimson maple against the background of the other golden leaves. And did you ever see anything slicker than that red vine climbing up that gray old stone, and the dark spruce-trees leaning over to watch? It always makes me think of a real old man smiling at a lot of gay little kids playing in the sunshine. I come up here early every fall just to look for that vine to turn red, and it keeps pretty till all the others have dropped off. Do you see that bit of squawberry-vine netted among the roots of the spruce? It has a lot of red berries already. Say, would you like it to take home? Wait, we'll go over that way and get it."

In a moment more the canoe was steered close to the bank, and the red-berried squawberry vine was reposing at Miss Gracen's feet.

They went on up the stream as far as it was navigable; then, fastening their bark to a tree on the bank,

they climbed the hill over crackling brown and yellow
chestnut leaves, and went hunting chestnuts, the boys
filling their blouses and sleeves in lieu of any other receptacle, and keeping a great handkerchief-full of
choice ones for Miss Gracen.

They found a flat rock, and spread out the lunch-
boxes. They were all famously hungry, and Rebecca's
chicken sandwiches, stuffed eggs, potato salad, baked
beans, peach turnovers, and sugar cookies disappeared like dew before the morning sun, to say nothing
of the cup-custards in tiny blue jars. The jars were taken
to the spring and washed and brought back full of sparkling cold water. There was gingerbread, too, and
sponge-cake, and olives tucked in between things here
and there, some delicious cheese and crispy crackers;
and one end of the box was filled with black and white
grapes.

The boy from the parsonage, where eating was plain
and scarce, the boy from the handsome house on the
hill in the distance, where eating was abundant and
appetites pampered by skilled servants, and the boy
who had spent his life in a poor little Chicago boarding-house, alike ate with keen appetites; and every one
voted it the greatest lunch a picnic ever had.

"Big eats! Big eats!" said Tom Atterbury solemnly,
as he emptied the last custard-cup into the stream, and
prepared to fill it at the spring.

"Yes, big eats, son," said Harold soberly. "Hand
me over that last cooky. If nobody wants it, I can't
see it left alone. We never have cookies like that at our
house. Miss Gracen, I wish you'd invite me along
again when you're going on a hike."

There was a wistfulness in his tone that went straight
to that good lady's heart, and she straightway did what
earlier in the day she would have been filled with horror
at the very suggestion of doing; she invited Harold Constable to come to her house as early and as often as he
chose.

Perhaps in sober thought alone at home she might
regret what she had done; might wish that she had
kept some reservations until further revelation made

her way clearer; but at present she had decided that this boy, too, was well worth helping, and that the whole town must be mistaken in their estimate of him, for certainly no boy could have been pleasanter, kinder, and more courteous than he had been all through the day.

He had made her his especial care, and the others had vied with him in trying to give her a good time. They went ahead and cut down branches; they gathered sprays of scarlet leaves because she admired them. They pointed out the easiest foot-paths, and praised her endurance every step of the way, so that, had she been worn out, she would never have been willing to confess it. But she was not weary. The air and the unwonted brightness of the young company about her filled her with a new exhilaration. She almost felt like a girl again, and her cheery laugh rang out clear in the fine autumn air.

Coming back to the canoe, they established her among her cushions, and started slowly down the stream. There were little drifted huddles of curled brown beach leaves lying here and there upon the water, like tiny boats moored together for protection. When the canoe slid through them, they gave forth a soft, rustling music like the gentle touching of violin strings by a master hand.

It was Miss Gracen who noticed it first and cried out with pleasure, telling the boys that it was the music of the stream and of the day. They all looked at her wonderingly, and then, gravely listening, they turned their attention to the little singing leaves. When they came to another patch of the fallen leaves, Harold gave one mighty, silent sweep with his paddle, and then held it up from the water; and so with bated breath they drifted through, playing the mimic harp as they went.

A little way down the stream Harold steered the small craft between two great bowed branches of a spruce-tree that had broken away from the parent tree, and were now dipping into the water like two mammoth plumes; and there, with a beautiful arch of green over them, feathering down about their shoulders

in delicious fragrance, they held the little boat. Miss
Gracen exclaimed rapturously over the loveliness of
the spot.

"It only needs one thing to make it perfect," declared Tom; "and that's a book and somebody to read
to us. Miss Vic, why didn't you bring a book along?"

"Why, I did," said that good lady with a sudden
remembrance of how much she had enjoyed the afternoon. "I did bring a book, but I'm afraid it won't be
just what you would like."

It suddenly seemed the most uninteresting book she
could have found, and she wished heartily she had
made a better selection.

"Spill it out, and give us a try," said Tom, and then
sat up quickly in his place with his cheeks as red as his
hair and a most contrite look in his red-brown eyes.

"Indeed, indeed, Miss Vic, truly I didn't mean to say
that," he drawled anxiously. "I do surely hope you'll
forgive me. I never thought for a minute who it was I
was talking to. You see, Miss Vic, you don't seem the
least bit like a—a—lady——"

But his speech was drowned in shouts of laughter
that echoed back and forth from rock to hillside.

"Better button up your lips, At," called Harold between the shouts of laughter; "you're just making things
worse all the time. What do you mean by telling Miss
Gracen she isn't ladylike?"

"Why—I—I didn't say that," cried the distressed
Tom, his face growing redder and redder. "I meant
just that she seemed like one of us," he finished desperately.

"That's the very worst thing you could tell her, old
man," laughed Harold. "Now you better subside, or I'll
give you a ducking, talking to our guest like that."

"Now, Miss Vic, don't you understand?" said the
horrified Tom. "You'll forgive me, won't you?"

"Of course I will," said Miss Gracen, laughing heartily with the rest. "Don't you suppose I know you've
given me the finest compliment you know how to give?
I don't suppose a lady would have been much fun to
have along to-day; but, if I've managed to make you

think for a little while that I'm one of you, why, then I can hope that I haven't been a bore nor completely spoiled your little expedition. Thank you very much, Tom."

"Great woman!" cried Harold; "she knows how to be a boy with us. She shall be our queen, and be crowned. Here's for our white queen;" and he reached out and secured a delicate crimson trailer of woodbine from a dead tree-trunk at the water's edge, placing it carefully like a fillet about the white coil of her hair, for she had long ago discarded her hat and laid it in the bottom of the boat.

Miss Gracen lifted her merry eyes to see her own nephew looking at her with a face filled with deep admiration and love. She knew by his expression that he was proud of her, and it gave her a thrill of joy.

At that instant as if by contrast she seemed to see what Lydia Bypath's expression would be if she could stand up above them on the bank, and hear and see all that was going on. Lydia Bypath would be thinking that not only the nephew, but the aunt as well, was on the rapid road to destruction. Miss Gracen could only hope she would never know, and continued to rejoice in the good time she was having and giving.

Chapter X

"AND now, if you have got quite done making fun of your only old guest, I will read a little," said Miss Gracen merrily, pulling a tiny volume out of her pocket and opening it slowly.

"I think it must have been in some such spot as this that this beautiful story opens. At any rate, there were water and trees and rocks, and a steep bank like that over there; I am sure there must have been. Listen, boys." And she began to read:

> The stag at eve had drunk his fill,
> Where danced the moon on Monan's rill,
> And deep his midnight lair had made

In lone Glenartney's hazel shade;
But when the sun his beacon red
Had kindled on Benvoirlich's head,
The deep-mouthed bloodhound's heavy bay
Resounded up the rocky way,
And faint, from farther distance borne,
Were heard the clanging hoof and horn——

Tom Atterbury started upright in his place with a smothered exclamation; and Miss Gracen looked up, already sure that the book would not attract her audience; but the light of interest in Tom's eyes surprised her.

"Say, Miss Vic, that's 'The Lady of the Lake,' isn't it? Say, do read that, please. I'm mighty glad you brought it along; for I have an exam on it the first thing Monday morning, and I promised dad I wouldn't flunk this time. It's been worrying me all this day, because I knew I ought to be home studying it, for I just can't get that poetry stuff into my head."

"Why, surely, we'll read it; won't we, boys?" she said, looking around on the rest of her audience for approval. "I was afraid you wouldn't care for this at all; but, if Tom needs it——"

"Sure! Go ahead!" assented Harold with interest. "Guess we can take a little dose of poetry if it's going to help you on your exam any. We don't want to make you flunk, At."

A light suddenly came into Miss Gracen's eyes, the fire of a great resolve. What if she could really conquer the interest of these boys? If she could make them actually *like* that reading? Her own boy needed it, too. True, she saw no enthusiasm in his face, and she felt he would probably care as little as the others if he were made to tell what he really was thinking. But he, too, would probably have to take an examination on the book some day if he went to school. Why could she not make the story so fully his this afternoon that he never would forget it?

With one swift look across toward the shore she made her plans.

"Then suppose we get to work and teach this lesson to Tom," she said; "and then I'll invite you all home to dinner, and we'll see whether we can make up for the hard work by a little extra fun."

Her proposition was greeted with a shout and cheer, and Richard's eyes shone. Life seemed to be going to be one continued fête hereafter, with an aunt like that, who understood.

"Very well; then suppose you paddle over to that green mossy bank, and let's have a map of the place. We'll understand it better that way, you know. There's a map in this book, and we'll copy it in moss and stones and earth. Harold, you take the map and locate all the places; and Dick, you and Tom cut this card into small sign-boards while I read. First, we will locate Glenartney, where the stag was taking his evening drink, and then Benvoirlich and Uam-Var. You know these places are all real, and Walter Scott must have known them well."

Then, while she hastily removed the map from the book, giving it to Harold, and hunted out some calling-cards from her jacket-pocket, she told briefly of the great man who wrote the poem, until with her few words he had become a living being to the boys, and she saw their attention was held. While Glenartney was being modelled from moss and ferns and its name eloquently printed with Tom's fountain pen, she plunged into the poem again, and found no wandering audience this time. They were all attention in the hunt and in laying out the land and getting it just like the map. Child's play, perhaps; but Tom's examination was its excuse, and they all three were but little out of childhood, though they never would have owned it.

It was in the dipping shade of a great spruce-tree that they tied the canoe; and the moss rose green on the bank beside them, peopled presently with the characters of the story. Miss Gracen read on rapidly, stopping only when there was a decided difference of opinion about the size or exact location of some mountain, glen, or lake.

Then the sun dipped low, and the story went on until the dusk gave sudden warning. Reluctantly they left their mimic Scotland, and the paddles silently bore them back to the landing-place.

"That certainly was great, Miss Gracen," drawled Tom. "I never'll forget it now. I can see every one of those places, and I'm afraid I'll scare the 'prof.' He'll think I had the book open. I'm sure I can pass now. Won't dad be surprised when he sees my mark? Say, couldn't you finish it for us after supper? Is there so very much more, or are you too tired?"

"Not a bit tired," said the triumphant lady, her eyes gleaming with pleasure in the darkness; "but maybe the other boys have had enough."

"No, it's interesting," said Richard, who had not spoken about it before. "I'd like to see how it came out myself. We started reading it in school; but I left before we finished it, and anyhow I didn't care much for the teacher. I didn't get on to the story at all then."

"Here too," called Harold, as he skilfully brought the canoe to the landing.

They climbed the little hill through the dusk. Miss Gracen, with her pretty hair all tumbled and fluffy and the red garland wreathed gracefully about its white masses, her hat swinging in her hand, and Harold helping her up the steep places, was laughing like a girl at the funny things the boys were saying.

"Don't hurry, Miss Gracen; you'll be all out of breath at the top," declared Harold.

"Yes, Miss Vic, I'm afraid you're expeeding the seed limit," drawled Tom comically. "There's plenty of time, I'm sure, though I left my watch up-stairs when I came away this morning."

"Let it run down," quickly finished Dick; and then they burst into a torrent of puns, plays upon words, and comical phrases such as their cultured, quiet companion had never heard before.

What delightfully merry, bright boys these were! The things they said were really witty, though they were couched in the vernacular of modern slang; and she perceived, too, with a great pride, that her own boy could hold his own with the rest.

By this time Miss Gracen had actually so far forgot-

ten herself as not to be shocked at the excessive amount
of slang to which she had been listening all the afternoon. She was laughing in happy abandonment as
Harold let down the meadow bars and helped her into
her own yard; and Hiram heard the echo of it, and
called Molly and Rebecca to the window of the butler's
pantry to see and listen. With awe they looked at one
another, a great light spreading over their faithful faces.

"Now hear the pretty voice of her!" exclaimed Rebecca. "Ain't it fer all the world like she was a little
girl again, and coming home from school afore her
brother went off and made all the trouble? Oh, I wish
her poor mother could hear her!"

"It's all that young Mister Dick," averred Hiram.
"He's goin' to make the house that cheerful again,
with plenty of young folks. I can feel it in my bones.
Got plenty to eat to-night, Rebecca? She might want
'em all in to stay for supper."

"Ain't there always plenty to eat?" tossed back Rebecca, holding her gray head high and hurrying back
to give the mashed potatoes another good beating before they were to be taken up.

The three boys went noisily up to Richard's room,
and Miss Gracen could hear his proud young voice
pointing out the pictures on the wall. "That's my father when he was captain of the baseball nine."

Her heart swelled with pride and joy, and the tears
started unbidden to her eyes, as she went to smooth
her hair in her own room.

Harold Constable's clear voice rang out:

"Say, your father's all right. Gee! but you must be
proud of him, Gracey."

They had nicknamed him Gracey that afternoon,
and she had perceived that it was their way of christening him as one of their own.

"He's got an awfully fine face. Say, Gracey, turn
around to the light. Say, I believe you look like your
father. Sure you do. Can you play ball? At, you must
get him on our team right away."

Something in the tone and the tribute to her dead
brother made Miss Gracen pause in the act of removing

the gaudy garland from her hair and smile at herself in
the glass. No, she would not take it off; she would leave
it just as the boy had placed it for the evening. It
would please him, and wouldn't hurt her. The servants might think it silly; but the boys would be
pleased, and, after all, what harm could it do? She
smoothed the hair about it as best she could, and
slipped on a soft pearl-tinted gown that seemed a fitting
background for the crimson wreath in her hair; so
she went down to meet her noisy, eager guests.

There was roasted veal with stuffing and plenty of
gravy for dinner. The dessert was a beautiful brown
baked Indian pudding heavy with raisins and currants
and smothered in whipped cream.

"We never have anything like this at our home,"
said Harold wistfully, handing back, with a polite show
of reluctance, his dish for a second helping of pudding. "Gee, but it's good! I wish mother knew about
it."

Some one called Miss Gracen to the telephone just
as they rose from dinner, something about the next
topic for the missionary meeting and who was to look
after the mite-boxes. While she was talking, the boys
drifted into the big parlor. It was perhaps Harold who
led the way.

Harold was used to great, stately rooms and was
accustomed to ceremony. It was perfectly natural for
him to drift into the wide doorway, and the formality
of the place held no restrictions for him, as it did for
both Tom and Richard. In fact, that big, formal, serious room had not as yet been appropriated by Richard
as a part of his new home. It seemed to him to be a
place only for strangers, written with a large "S" and
represented by Lydia Bypath.

But Harold walked in quite naturally, as though that
was what would be expected of him; and quite as naturally seated himself at the piano, touching soft chords
at first, and then striking the piano with a perfect crash
of jolly, happy-go-lucky sounds chasing one another
up and down and rippling hilariously over the keys

with all the wild abandonment of the pianos in the "movies."

Richard drew near in open-eyed amazement, wondering that a boy of his own age could bring forth such effects. They seemed marvellous to him. Of real music he knew almost nothing.

Harold, never embarrassed by his surroundings, broke forth into the raggiest sort of a rag-time song. He had a clear, high tenor, a trifle strained and rasping from continuous rag-time and "rooting" at football games, but entirely capable of better things; and he had a way of bringing out the words with distinctness and dramatic effect which made them extremely funny.

> Will that young man go home to-night,
>   Or eat his breakfast here.
>   Out on the old front porch?

he chanted, and Richard and Tom were convulsed with delight. In the chorus of the second verse they chimed in with various growls, for they were both quite familiar with the monotonous melody, though neither of them could have carried it alone.

When Miss Gracen came back from the telephone and paused in the doorway, wondering, to listen, Harold had just struck into the choice selection of "The Noodle Soup Rag" and the other two voices dropped obediently into the really pretty harmonies of the opening lines:

> O, the old folks seem to like it;
>   They would sit all night and listen.

Suddenly Harold spied Miss Gracen standing against the soft gray-green of the portières, smiling; and he sprang from the piano-stool in mock dismay, breaking off at the very instant of the entrance of the soup upon the scene.

"Oh, Miss Gracen, I didn't know you were there. Maybe you don't like rag-time played on your piano."

Now Miss Gracen had never even heard of "The Noodle Soup Rag,"—though in theory of course she deplored the presence of rag-time music in the world, being somewhat of a delightful musician herself,—and she had no idea what the words of this new song might be, that sounded like the beginning of "Old Kentucky Home" or some sweet old ballad; so she stood smiling happy approval.

"Is that rag-time?" she asked innocently. "It really sounds quite pretty to me. Won't you sing the rest of it for me? You all have wonderfully good voices. I like to hear you sing. Do go on."

Thus encouraged, Harold turned to the piano, and rattled into the "Noodle" again, while his hostess settled herself to enjoy. It must be confessed, however, that, as the song progressed and it became plain what the old folks enjoyed sitting around to listen to, she drew in a quick breath of surprise, much as if a sudden dash of cold water had met her face.

The boys, however, were intent upon the rhythm of the jig and the fun of the words. It was just funny to them, that ending of the sweet, pathetic strain with "When father eats his soup."

Watching them with a half-shudder as they rollicked out the careless disrespectfulness, she suddenly realized that they were not quite to blame for liking such things. It was just a part of the recklessness and the daring of the age in which they lived. It held a certain rough challenge to their fun-loving natures and gave them a license to say under the protection of the song things that were forbidden otherwise. Then there was an irresistible "swing" and a rollicking "go" to the music that caught and held them fascinated. They did not mean any coarseness or any disrespect either to age or station. It was simply unmitigatedly funny to them; and fun was the one thing they liked best of all in life, no matter what it was about.

As she meditated, the rag-time clattered on. It struck her as being the most noisy, monotonous music she had ever heard; perhaps that was why they liked it. Would it perhaps be possible to interest them in anoth-

er kind, and make them dislike this because they grew
to like the other better? Perhaps they enjoyed this because it was easy and they could do it themselves.
Better music was beyond their powers, and they didn't
understand it.

> I should worry like a tree
> And have somebody trimming me,

shouted the clear young tenor, and "Who put the rove
in Rover?" he asked in a minute more; and then the
sharp chorus of confused whistles blended with the
song, and she watched the faces of the trio, happy,
care-free, having a good time with all their might.

It came to her to wonder what Lydia Bypath would
think now if she could suddenly enter the room, and
see her, the heretofore respectable Victoria Gracen, sitting by and smiling while the two most condemned
boys of the neighborhood sang rag-time with her
nephew.

She wondered whether the minister, even, would
approve of her course; and a swift vision of the horror
in the faces of the women of the music section of her
club caused her to draw a quick breath.

But at that moment from her position near the
open doorway she caught a glimpse of the smiling face
of Hiram peering interestedly from the half-open pantry door, and Molly and Rebecca smiling and stretching their necks behind him; and she smiled a quick
sympathy with them. They were glad to hear the silent
old house ring with laughter and song, rag-time or no
rag-time; and in her own heart she knew she was glad,
too.

Suddenly Harold wheeled toward her on his stool,
and demanded:

"Have we driven you half wild, Miss Gracen? We're
going to stop now, for I know you don't really like this
rag-time."

"Why," hesitated that truthful lady, "why—I really
never heard it much before. Some of it sounds rather
—lively and pretty. Don't you think the songs are a

good deal alike? There isn't much real melody to many of them, is there? But they are all right for a change, I dare say." Her smile was even more of an admission than her words; and she thought again of her mentor, and was glad she had not asked Lydia Bypath to run over this evening, as she sometimes had done on Saturday nights, to make it less lonely for her.

"Harold, I'd like to hear your voice in something else. Won't you sing for me?"

"Oh, I don't know anything else, Miss Gracen; really, I can't sing. I've got a voice like a fishman," protested Harold, rising in dismay from the piano.

"Try this," she suggested, coming forward to a pile of music, and selecting some songs. "Here is 'Love's Old Sweet Song'; I'm sure you've heard that," and she sat down at the piano and touched soft chords.

Harold was interested at once, and bent over the piano to study the words. Yes, he had heard it before; he didn't know whether he could sing it or not; and he began to hum the notes as she played the accompaniment.

The other two boys stood with their arms across his shoulders, and so for almost an hour they sang, going over the old ballads and the well-known songs, sometimes singing solos and sometimes in chorus, until they were all hoarse and had to stop.

"Play us something, Miss Gracen," pleaded Harold, dropping into a chair as the last note of "The Rosary" faded softly into silence. And without comment she played a part of "Elsa's Dream."

They knew nothing about Wagner, any of them, nor had they heard much real music; but they listened intently, respectfully, with a new kind of absorption in their eyes, though she could not tell whether the real message of the music had reached their souls.

"That's surely got tune enough," commented Tom. "I like it immensely. It seems sort of like going to sleep. It's mighty pretty."

"Yes," said Harold, "I'd like to hear it again sometime soon. It's the kind of a thing that gets into your mind, and goes over and over. If I come to see you soon again, will you play it for me, Miss Gracen? I like music. Mother hardly ever plays."

Miss Gracen turned a radiant smile upon the boy, and, searching his face, saw that he really wanted it; so she readily promised.

But Tom turned their attention back to literature at this juncture.

"Say, Miss Vic, you're too tired to read us the rest of 'The Lady of the Lake' to-night, aren't you? Maybe you'd let us come a little while to-morrow afternoon, and finish it. I never know what to do with Sunday afternoons. It would be awfully nice if you'd read to us awhile."

There was a wistfulness in his slow speech that quite touched her.

She looked at him, startled, and suddenly saw into the emptiness of a Sunday afternoon for a boy who had no religious interests.

"Why, Tom," she smiled indulgently. "I'd be glad to read to you awhile on Sunday afternoon if you would enjoy it; but we don't want to read lessons on Sunday, do we? That would be a good deal like work, and I think we might find something that would be more in keeping with the day, don't you? But we want to finish that poem to-night, for you need it Monday, don't you? Dick, get the book, will you, please? I left it on the library table—or wait! Suppose we go in there. There are more easy-chairs, and it's cosier. Dick, light the fire in the grate. I think we can finish by ten o'clock. Your fathers won't expect you home before ten, will they, boys?"

"Father won't expect me at all. I come and go as I please," said Harold, with a shrug of his handsome shoulders. "Like as not father won't be home till the midnight train himself, if he comes then."

Miss Gracen's eyes lingered sorrowfully, pitifully on the hard, handsome young face; and her smile warmed his heart as he looked up surprised.

"Ten o'clock's all right for me," drawled Tom, settling down in front of the fire lazily. "If you're sure you're not too tired to read, Miss Vic."

It was five minutes to ten when she finished, and the boys got up from their comfortable positions reluctantly, and prepared to leave.

"It's been awfully nice, Miss Vic, all day," said Tom in his confiding tone of gratitude. "We just can't thank you enough——"

"It certainly has," said Harold gracefully; and then, with a wistful glance into her face, "It seems presuming to ask you, after the peach of a day you've given us, but would you really mind if we came a little while to-morrow afternoon? Sundays are awful. You didn't want to study lessons on Sunday, but I guess you'd think what I did was worse. I go fishing or canoeing, or play tennis, or go out in my car; but the day is miles long. Father often stays in town over Sunday. It's all right when I can get some fellows to go off and have a good time, but sometimes it rains. It would be just awfully good to come and see you. Maybe you'd play for us again, too."

And thus she promised, wondering meanwhile what her respectable and horrified neighbors would think of her allowing boys—and *such* boys—to come to her house on Sundays. And would even the minister understand it? Still, how could she refuse such a request from a boy who was, for the time being at least, worse than orphaned?

"I'll tell you, boys," she said with sudden inspiration, "I'll read to you to-morrow if you'll promise to go to church with me to-morrow evening."

Tom made a wry face, but Harold responded quickly and willingly.

"Sure! Miss Gracen, we'll go anywhere you want us to; won't we, Tom?" and Tom bowed a willing assent.

"Then come at four o'clock," she said, and bade them good-night.

As they turned from shutting the front door, Richard threw on his aunt a look of adoration.

"I say, Aunt Vic," he said, "you're just great! The fellows think so, and I'm mighty glad you sent for me." He reached out, gave her hand a squeeze, then bolted up the stairs, and left her standing in a tumult of wonder and joy in the hall.

This, then, was what it meant to have with her in her home a boy of her own!

Chapter XI

MISS GRACEN, in her soft gray robes and gray hat wreathed in gray plumes, that looked like the clouds at sunset when a touch of pink is shining through, walked down the church aisle the next morning, attended by her handsome young nephew in his new dark-blue suit, the observed of the whole congregation.

Lydia Bypath watched them jealously as they passed her seat, and sniffed. It had been made known to her by some occult method all her own that Miss Gracen had wasted a whole day going off on a tramp with this boy and two others of the village's worst. To a late hour the evening before sounds had proceeded from the hitherto respectable mansion of Gracen which had not gone to the furthering of the honorable name of Gracen. Miss Bypath classed these sounds with the rioting of the college students on the street at night, and, knowing little of rag-time, called them "revelry," thinking possibly of Belgium's capital and the disaster that her school reader had portrayed so touchingly.

She watched her old friend go softly to her seat in the church, and sniffed again as Miss Gracen sat down with bowed and reverent head. Victoria Gracen needn't think she could carry on like that on Saturday, and then cover it all up by a reverent attitude in church. She, Lydia Bypath, could see through it all. Victoria had taken a white elephant on her hands, and was trying to make it appear that she approved of what she could not control. Any one could see at a glance that the black eyes of that nephew by her side had deviltry in them, and of course it would come out. His father's had. Very likely Victoria hadn't been able to keep the boy away from those other two, and so had gone with them to give the expedition countenance. Well, Victoria Gracen would find herself in a kettle of hot water if she tried to keep up that sort of thing.

The jealous eyes of the woman fastened themselves like claws of a vampire on the backs of the two innocent worshippers, and seemed to seek to draw from the smooth, thick black hair of the boy and the soft pinky-grayness of the feathers of the aunt some idea of the sinful thoughts hidden beneath their quiet attitudes. She fancied before the sermon was over that she could see the worry in the puckers around Miss Gracen's eyes, and in the set of the boy's handsome shoulders and stolid determination to have his own way. But she was quite mistaken.

Miss Gracen was sitting happily by her boy's side, conscious of the joy of again having some one who belonged, to sit at the head of her pew and be her protector. It had been a great joy to have her boy help her over the curbstones and open the doors for her this morning with all the ease and grace of Harold Constable. Had he learned it from Harold yesterday, or was it just innate, the heritage of his blood? She glanced sideways at him, and was filled with pride over his handsome bearing. He was a boy to be proud of; and, to add to her thrill of joy, as if he understood, the boy turned at that moment and glanced at her, with a look of deep admiration and perfect content. It was just a mere flicker of a smile that passed between them, but a flash of perfect understanding and love had been in it that made them both feel the hour and place sacred. Miss Bypath saw it pass, and said sourly to herself:

"Victoria Gracen is going to make a perfect idiot of herself over that wild boy, and she'll rue it; she certainly will." She said it as though she would be glad of such a result.

Dick could not remember ever to have enjoyed church so much in his life as he did that morning. He used to go with his mother sometimes when he was a little fellow; but the seats were hard, the air was bad, and he could not understand anything. After he began to grow up he never went if he could help it, unless some of the fellows took a notion on a rainy night to sit in the back seat and make each other laugh. He had gone once or twice to please some interested Sunday-school teacher, but he had not been regular at Sunday-school; so that had not occurred often.

But now he sat proudly beside his beautiful aunt, found the place in the hymn-book for her, joining his voice in the hymns, and even mumbling a little in the responsive readings. It was dear and pleasant to be near her, to belong and to know that she cared.

He didn't analyze his feeling; he only knew he was happy and liked to be there. He "liked" his aunt; that was the way he put it to himself, this strange new delight in belonging to a lovely, loving woman who wanted him and tried to make him happy. He couldn't get over the joy it gave him to have her look at him in that understanding way, almost as if she herself were another boy, and knew just how he felt about everything.

Tom, sitting in the pastor's pew, turned furtive glances in his direction, and Dick smiled back as if they had been old chums.

Dick wondered what the fellows in Chicago would think of Tom. He wondered what they would think of him. He wished they could be there, some of them, and have some of the good times. They never had had such good times as yesterday—none of them. There was Jim, who had never had half a chance. Would Aunt Vic perhaps sometime allow him to have one of them on for a visit, just so he could tell the rest? But no; of course that wouldn't do; they weren't her kind—and yet—there was no telling but sometime she might let him do it.

He smiled another recognition of Tom's greeting, and this time Miss Bypath sniffed so she could be heard half-way up the aisle. Such actions in church! The minister's son, too! And there sat Victoria Gracen under her gray plumes, quite unaware. It was plain she was going to be entirely blind to her protegé's faults. Next thing the boys would be snapping rubber bands back and forth over the heads of the congregation.

Tom Atterbury was quite capable of it. She had seen him do it once when his father was conversing with an elder, and on Communion Sunday, too. It showed how utterly brazen he was that he would smile right during the sermon, when his own father was preaching. The curse of the Lord was on children who did not honor their parents, and Miss Bypath felt it would fall with full justice upon luckless Tom. She had disliked him heartily all through the years, and now she fairly hated him. It seemed that he had had something to do with her first quarrel with her only friend and she could not forgive him.

She shut her thin lips tight; and, while she sat and hated the ruddy glow of Tom's hair under the sunshine that fell through the yellow glass of the Constable memorial window, and inspected the many finely-matching freckles on his kindly, wistful face, she planned what she would say to Mrs. Cora Craig, who sat in the next pew, about Miss Gracen's indiscretion in adopting a nephew of so uncertain character and lineage at this late date in her career, and its probable disastrous outcome. She could see by the set of Cora Craig's shoulders, and the turn of her head as she looked at her husband when Victoria came up the aisle, that Cora Craig would fully understand her and agree with her. Mrs. Craig had once been overheard to remark that she didn't see why Victoria Gracen should be chairman of all the committees and vice-president of all the societies merely because she had more money than some other people who were just as good. Mrs. Craig had a boy of her own, a sly creature with white eyebrows and a skulking look, whom she never could make go to church. Mrs. Craig had not been a success in bringing him up; but that would not matter; she would understand all the better why boys were degenerate and that unmarried women without experience should never try to bring them up.

As they passed down the aisle after service, the minister laid a detaining hand on Miss Gracen's arm, while Tom took possession of Dick and walked on to the door.

"Tom tells me that you have asked him to come over for a time this afternoon," said the minister in troubled hesitation. "Miss Gracen, you have been most kind to my boy, but I don't wish him to trouble you—and Sunday, of all days——"

"Why, I've promised to read to the boys a little while this afternoon," said Miss Gracen, suddenly wondering whether the minister would approve. "They said they didn't know what to do Sunday afternoon, and I want to make the day a happy one for my own boy. If you are willing, I shall be glad to have Tom join us."

"Thank you," said the minister, his brow still troubled. "I have never quite believed in Sunday visits; but you are most kind, and I can see how the right kind of reading might be most profitable. To tell you the truth, I have never been able to get Tom interested in keeping the Sabbath in the way we have brought him up. We have provided religious literature, but he does not seem to take to it. In fact, I do not think he cares much for reading to himself, at least, not as I did when I was his age. I am very much troubled about him sometimes. I don't seem to understand him."

His tired brown eyes reminded her of Tom's, and she longed to comfort him. People had criticised him for having been so indulgent a father; and many of them had said he was blind, or didn't care; but the eyes told their story of anxiety, and she could see that it had been merely that he hadn't understood the boy.

"Well," she said brightly, "I guess I've got a lot to learn about bringing up boys; but I'll have to learn it for my boy's sake; and, if there is anything I can do for yours at the same time, I'll gladly do it. He is a dear boy. I fell quite in love with him yesterday. We are very good friends already. I'm sorry I haven't known him all these years. You see, I've got to know boys now because I have one."

The minister's face relaxed. It was the first time since Tom was a baby in a perambulator that any one had said anything loving and kind about him. People had always found fault with him since the day of his christening, when he had dipped his fist into the christening-bowl and splashed the water full in the face of the senior elder who held it, and then with his tiny kid shoe had kicked the bowl out of the outraged elder's hand and splashed water down the front of his mother's new gown. The gown had been a silk one, the kind that spotted, a present from the Ladies' Aid, and worn for the first time that day. There had not been enough to make over the front breadth, and it couldn't be matched; so his mother had shamefully worn the spotted silk, a symbol of her son's lawless nature, and tried her best to cover it with her hands in her lap or some furtive arrangement of girdle-ends or mantle-ties; but the spot had been patent to the whole church for years as a sign of the blight on her boy's character, and nothing would ever make them forget it.

"You are very good, Miss Gracen," he said. "I thank you. No one seems to like my boy very much. I'm afraid it's his father's fault. I wasn't sure when he told me about this afternoon. I have tried to restrain him from going out on the Sabbath; but if you say you wish him to come——"

"I have a good religious story to read aloud that I think the boys will enjoy," said Miss Gracen eagerly, for she had begun to look forward with some interest to her afternoon, "and I thought perhaps they would also like to sing hymns for a little while afterward. I hope it will be a good, quiet way to keep the Sabbath afternoon, and yet make it pleasant for them."

She spoke shyly, half doubtfully. She had been brought up most strictly as regards the Sabbath, and yet she had felt the need in the wistful tones of the boys as they complained of the usual dulness of the day.

"I am sure it will be all right, Miss Gracen," said the minister with relieved brow. "To tell you the truth, I was half afraid Tom might be deceiving me and that he was inventing some way to get out away from the home restraint for a little while. I shall be very glad to have him come over this afternoon, but you must promise me not to let the boy intrude upon you too much. He is very much in love with you already, and would live at your house continually if allowed. You must be frank and send him home when he is not wanted."

Miss Gracen promised, and went on down the aisle to find her boy, her heart aglow at the thought that Tom was fond of her. Perhaps, after all, she might be able to help the dear boy a little. She would try. A fleeting memory of the time some years before when she had been asked to take a class of boys in Sunday-school, and, being appalled at the very idea, had refused, assailed her now. Might it be possible that she would have enjoyed it, and been able to do some good? Had she perhaps missed a great opportunity? She had not known that one could get joy from association with rough, unformed boys; for, theorize as she would, the astonishing fact remained that she looked forward to her afternoon with her companions of the day before with not a little feeling of pleased anticipation.

She had spent a couple of hours the night before in carefully selecting the book that she would read; and Rebecca, unbeknown to her mistress, had worried not a little and got up three times after retiring, to look from her window in the servants' wing of the house and wonder why Miss Vic kept her light burning so late.

Miss Gracen had carefully gone over several books of thrilling interest to herself, but laid them aside as not fitted for the immediate purpose, and had finally decided upon a story of Western life with all its wild adventure and thrilling situations, with one man single-handed struggling in the name of Christ against the vice and evil influences that had dwelt in the place since its beginning. She knew the boys would like the setting of the story, and she felt sure the climax in which death and hell struggled for the souls of some of the characters would stir their hearts and make them thoughtful. She hoped the ending would give them a vision of the Christ that would at least make the Sabbath a profitable one, if it did no more.

The story was a religious one, not in any milk-and-water sense of the word, but treating religion as one of the great facts of life. It was a tale to make a reckless, care-free, adventure-loving boy think, without making him feel that he was being preached to. Miss Gracen had found herself all during church service that morning praying quietly that God would use her reading that afternoon to help the three boys who were coming to her that she might brighten what seemed to them a dull day without meaning.

Perhaps it was her intense desire for the success of her afternoon that made her eyes so bright and her cheeks flush so prettily pink as she walked down the church steps by the side of her boy. Passing Lydia Bypath she smiled happily into her spiteful eyes.

"She'll smile on the other side of her mouth when that pretty nephew of hers brings her into disgrace," snapped that soured soul to Mrs. Craig.

But Victoria Gracen passed happily on with her boy, and was saved from a knowledge of the poor lady's ill-will. She was rejoicing in the ease with which her boy lifted his hat as she bowed to her friends, and she took pride and pleasure in stopping to introduce him to her intimate acquaintances. Somehow she had never realized before how lonely it had been always to go and come everywhere alone.

They walked down the wind-swept autumn street, and Miss Gracen was unspeakably happy. She thanked God that he had sent this boy to her, and she prayed in her heart that she might be shown how to lead him in the best and wisest way.

Chapter XII

IT was in the cosy library that she awaited them, a big easy chair apiece in readiness, and plenty of cushions piled luxuriously on the couch. The fire on the hearth was blazing cheerfully, and a great platter of molasses candy in delicious golden squares that Molly had made the night before stood alluringly in the broad window-seat. Miss Gracen's own little reading-chair was placed at just the right angle where the light from the bay window would come over her left shoulder, and she could see the occupants of the three big chairs. The book lay innocently under a pile of religious papers, and even Dick did not suspect its presence as yet.

Dick's pleasant whistle could be heard up-stairs in his room. He was beginning to feel quite at home in that big new home of his. He had been out among the horses with Hiram after dinner, and wandered about the place a little; and now he was up-stairs exploring some of his father's books and pictures.

His aunt fancied that already his face seemed to have lost some of its hard, defensive look, and his eyes were glad when he looked at her and smiled.

On the piano in the parlor Miss Gracen had collected all the hymn-books in the house. She would get the boys to sing a little while, she thought, as she hovered about the rooms, putting a touch here and there as though she were expecting grand company. Somehow she was as eager as a child over a party. She wanted the place to look pleasant and attractive to them all, not only for her boy's sake, but for the sakes of them all; and how strange it was that a few days ago she had no interest whatever in any of them! Was it because they had each given her a bit of a glimpse into their hearts, and she had seen the restlessness and longing, and really wistful looking out to life for something more than it had as yet given them?

It wasn't in nature that they should notice the big bronze bowls of red and gold chrysanthemums that stood on mantel and table; yet she touched their bright masses happily, and looked about on the pleasant rooms with a hope that it might seem good to the boys. What would Lydia Bypath think now, if she could see how interested she really was in those terrible boys?

She walked the length of the great parlor, and drew aside the costly curtains of frostlike lace to look out. The sun was shining, and the world held that autumn-gold look in the atmosphere. It was almost too pleasant to expect the boys to care to come indoors. Perhaps, after all, they would not come. She wondered a little at

the twinge of disappointment this thought presented to
her mind. Yet even as it passed, and while she yet stood
looking out the window, she saw them coming down the
street; and there were *three of them!*

At that moment the silver chime of the library clock
tolled half-past three, and she had not told them to
come until four; yet they were even now turning in at
the gate, and who was that with them? She did not
know him. Perhaps they had company, and did not
care to come, but were stopping at the house to excuse
themselves. Very likely they were going to take a walk,
and wanted her Dick to go with them. That would be
another problem for her to face; Sunday walks and all
sorts of companions.

A feeling of blankness and disappointment grew upon her, after all her pleasant preparations. She shrank
within the screening lace to think what she should do.
Of course it had been foolish to think that she, an elderly woman, could hope to hold a lot of big boys against
the attractions of the great, free world. How silly she
had been!

Then a sudden panic, lest they leave a message and
depart without her seeing them or having a chance to
find out what was the matter, seized her; and before
they could ring the bell she had hurried through the hall
and opened the door herself, not waiting for the servant.

There they stood waiting, eager, their hats off, with
not a thought of going walking, all ready and anxious to
come in. She saw it in their manner at once, and she
was glad. But her eyes were held by the face of the
third boy, who stood slightly back of the others, respectful, waiting, keenly observant, almost hesitating,
she thought. She smiled at the rest with a warm greeting, putting out her hand to each; but at the stranger
she gazed earnestly, meeting his eyes and his questioning look with one as questioning and intent; and his
face interested her at once, even though she did not
know him. He had a dark, unhappy look, and deep
lines about his mouth and eyes for one so young. His
brows were dark and distinctly pencilled. He drew
them down over his deep-set, almost lowering, eyes in

a strange way for a boy. He looked as if he had suffered much and doubted nearly everybody and everything; yet had left, hidden deep somewhere, wonderful, beautiful possibilities in his nature, and an unsuspected sweetness of temperament if only the cloud could be lifted from him. His face was finely cut, and showed strong character, yet all was masked by that haughty withdrawing and the defiance in his manner.

"We've brought Wayne Forrest with us, Miss Gracen," said Harold Constable lightly. "He hadn't any plans for this afternoon, and we thought you wouldn't mind. He's my friend."

Harold cast an arm about his friend's shoulders as he spoke, and drew the other tall fellow forward. Miss Gracen noticed the loyalty and deep admiration of his tone as he said, "He's my *friend*," that meant something more than just a schoolboy attachment. They made a marked contrast, too, as they stood thus together, the one boy handsome, airy, care-free, sure of himself, light in his manner, smilingly at ease, and dressed in the costly attire of a rich man's son; the other, fine and strong, but almost severe in his manner, frowningly defiant, holding back from all advances, and dressed in much-worn garments that would have been shabby if they had not been worn with the air of a conqueror who needed no accessories to give him pre-eminence among men. He stood, resisting his friend's drawing, refusing to say a word or break the darkness of his countenance by even a smile, awaiting her word.

She felt that he was searching her face for any sign of disapproval of him, and that, if she should hesitate by so much as an instant to second his coming to her house, he would break away from his friend's arm and flee from the place forever. There were not only keenness and defiance in his glance; there was a heart-breaking hunger in it that went straight to the depths of her soul; and with a clear, sweet look of welcome from her kind and understanding eyes she held out her hand, and a smile broke over her face.

"I'm so glad you brought him!" she said in that rich, musical voice of hers. "I like him right at first sight, and

I know he's going to be a great addition to our little company. Besides, if he's your friend, of course we want him."

The boy's face, which had been almost like a thunder-cloud in its intensity, broke suddenly into astonished light. The hard lines relaxed; the forehead cleared; the dark brows went up from lowering into startled, amused attention; the fine eyes showed their beauty, and almost danced with a merry appreciation of her greeting; and the strong yet sensitive mouth curved into a reluctant smile. He held back for just an instant more to study her and make sure it was really true that she wanted him; and then he put a shy hand forward to take the white one she held out. Standing so with that warm hand-clasp, and her eyes looking steadily into his for a full, long gaze, she began to know the spirit of the boy, who more than all the others, perhaps, needed her, and by association in her home was uplifted and helped to be what God meant him to be.

Wayne Forrest accepted the challenge in her eyes, and showed her in that long, clear look the answering challenge in his own. She knew from that time forth that, whatever the meaning of the hard, reckless lines she had seen at first, he had not wholly gone away from the right, and that he still had a decent, loving, hungering soul behind his hard exterior. Then suddenly his face broke into a smile, and she knew that he felt she was a friend.

"I'm sure I thank you very much," he said as they turned finally to go in; and the maturity and dignity of his voice startled her. It sounded like a voice that had suffered and grown old while it still should have been young in experience.

"Forrest, Forrest, where have I heard that name?" she questioned herself as she led her little company into the library and seated them. And why did she not know the boy? His face was not familiar. Perhaps he was some one from the city down to visit Harold over Sunday. But, Forrest—ah! Was that the name of the man who had been imprisoned for forgery five years ago? The wife was an invalid, and they were in poor circumstances. They lived at the other end of the village, quite out of the section where Miss Gracen's carriage was seen.

It was said that Mrs. Forrest would not go out to see visitors since her husband's disgrace. Miss Gracen herself had called twice, but received no response to her knock. They had come to the town shortly before their trouble, and had remained utter strangers by their own choice. Could this boy be the son? A sudden wave of pity swept her face as she turned and looked into the boy's eyes again, reading in the hard lines written there his story of bitter shame and disgrace. Her heart went out to him suddenly. If this were really his story, how he needed someone, something, to help him!

Then suddenly she remembered Lydia Bypath, who represented what the town would say; and she thought of her own boy. What was she doing? Gathering from the offscouring of the town to form a coterie for her boy's companionship? Was she doing right? Probably everybody would tell her she was not, and yet—it seemed as though she had not sought this herself; it had come to her. Could, *ought,* she to have turned these boys away who seemed to want her—even to need her —and seek only those who were perfectly refined and entirely good and reputable for her boy to know?

Well, it was a question for her to think of at leisure, and prayerfully. The boys were here now; and, having invited them, she could not turn them away. It remained for her to do what she could for them in this present, and it certainly would take all her thought and energies.

Her troubled eyes met the merry ones of Tom as he turned from a friendly scuffle with Harold for the corner of the couch that had the most cushions, and at once her anxiety and dismay fled.

A week ago she might have stood cold and disapproving if these boys had entered her house and made free in this way. She might even have called them rude, bad boys and have turned them severely away; but a wonderful change had come over her way of looking at things. Yesterday's experience in the canoe had given her a new viewpoint, and she was conscious of a distinct feeling of pleasure that they felt enough at home with her to act just their natural selves. What did a pillow and a couch matter, even if they were roughly handled? It was not the act that was rude; it was the boy that felt at home and happy, and was expressing his good will by acting as if she were another boy. The true values of couches and cushions and other people's houses had nothing whatever to do with the matter. They were having a good time, and she was a part of it. They were not afraid of her.

She found herself still hampered by that thought of Lydia Bypath, and was glad she was not present to see, for she would never understand. Blessed little Miss Gracen, that she did understand!

Wayne Forrest stood by, smiling half uncertainly at the pleasant contention, and watching her furtively to see how she would take their being so free in her house. It did not occur to her that the two might be showing off a little before this third one, to let him know how much at home they already were with her. But she saw the question in his eyes, the half-deprecating smile of apology as he turned toward her, and she met his look with a bright smile.

"While they are having it out with the couch, suppose you and I look after ourselves. You take this big chair by the fire. It really is more comfortable than the couch, I think," she said.

She was surprised at the ready grace with which he drew it forward and urged her to take it herself. His manner was as easy as Harold Constable's, although his ways were quieter and graver. Where had he got his ease and refinement, living in the shabby little house on the out-of-the-way road? Surely she must be mistaken. His ways were those of one accustomed to culture and refinement, although she saw there was an outer crust of hardness about him, perhaps something that would almost be called in common slang "toughness." Yet every time she looked at him she liked his face better. It was as if the hardness had been forced upon him, but was not native to his soul.

She decided that he must have come from the city to visit Harold as she had at first surmised. But before she could put any questions Dick came down, and it appeared at once that Dick had met him before. They had been together at the football game the day after Dick's arrival, and there was something about the new boy's face as he stood greeting her boy toward which her heart warmed. She could see at once that they had taken to each other; and somehow, though her heart misgave her with secret fears, she couldn't help being glad.

"Shall we go into the parlor and have a little singing before we read?" she asked as the noisy greetings of Dick subsided. Now that they were here, she began suddenly to doubt whether she had selected the right book to read to them, and to wish to put off the reading for a little till she could think more about it.

"Sure!" chorused Harold and Tom, rushing headlong from the seat for which they had contended, and then rushing back to escort her to the piano. Perhaps they were hoping for more rag-time; there seemed no Sabbath hush upon their eager spirits; but the hymn-book was open at a hymn Miss Gracen thought they would like. She handed the pile of books to Dick to pass around, and began at once to play, Tom catching up the melody and following it in a clear whistle.

The new boy accepted his book with a curious manner, as though he did not quite belong to the group, and was uncertain about partaking in the exercises; but he turned to the place, and followed the music. Miss Gracen watched him furtively as she played.

He did not sing at first, yet watched the book interestedly; but at the second verse he began, softly at first, then louder, in a clear, high baritone as mature as a man's. It rose and swelled above the other voices, and sent a thrill of delight through the music-loving heart of the hostess. What a voice was this, all in the rough! Did he know how wonderful, how marvellous it was for a boy of his age to have a voice like that? She studied him as he sang; but he seemed not to know that he was bringing forth unusual sounds, and he sang on, gaining confidence, and wholly absorbed in the pleasure of the music.

"You have a beautiful voice," she said to him in a low tone, bending toward his chair and laying her hand on his arm to attract his attention. They had stopped for a moment to search the index for a special hymn Tom wanted, and the others were not noticing. The boy looked up quickly, keen suspicion in his eyes; but when he saw the sincerity in Miss Gracen's face, his look quickly changed to one of pleased surprise.

"It's not much," he said embarrassedly. "I don't know anything about singing, but I like it."

"You must take good care of your voice," she went on. "It has a remarkably sympathetic quality. It should be worth a good deal to you some day after you have had it cultivated."

He laughed.

"Not much chance of my ever getting my voice cultivated," he said in a bitter tone.

"Oh, but you *must,* you know. Such voices are gifts that must be counted precious. There will be a way some day. You must make it."

He stared at her with eyes that seemed to say she knew very little about it, and his whole face took on the hard, resentful look; but he did not answer. Just then Tom announced the number of the hymn; and she noticed that Wayne joined in with zest.

When they had sung one verse, she paused.

"Suppose we ask Wayne to sing the next verse," she suggested, looking at him pleasantly; "and we'll come in on the chorus."

It was a venture following a sudden impulse; and, when the words were spoken, she was sorry, because if he should refuse she would have lost a point in her acquaintance with him; but, to her surprise, after an embarrassed hesitation of a second or two he stood up and began to sing, and his voice sounded even better than it had promised.

He did not seem to be shy about it, and was evidently doing his best. There was a clear resonance about it that held the other boys silent, wondering, somewhat awed. She could see his singing pleased them, and they were proud, not jealous, of him; nor was he by his expression in any wise set up about what she had said of his voice. He was simply, earnestly trying to do his best. Her heart thrilled at the sweet sounds that her words had evoked.

"That was beautiful, beautiful," she said when the song was over. "It is great for a boy to have a voice like that." The boy sat down, suddenly abashed, and looked at her piercingly from under his dark brows, as though he would be quite sure she was sincere; and there was something in his face which seemed to say: "Yes, but you don't know who I am, do you? When you do, you won't say such things to me."

He seemed to have withdrawn from them all in spirit, and Miss Gracen perceived that some subtle change had come over him. By this token she knew that the singing was over for the present.

She led them into the other room, seated them comfortably, told Dick to pass the platter of candy; and, sitting down, opened her book and began to read.

Miss Gracen was a good reader, with a sweet voice and a natural way of making her story live before her hearers. At the club meetings she was often asked to read some poem that was being studied, or some rare bit of prose sketch, because she could read so well; but she had never read to so inspiring an audience before.

Harold, from his corner of the sofa, sat bolt upright, his eyes upon her face every instant, attention held from the first words, his speaking face changing with the story; ready to laugh and bring out a bright comment now and then; his eyes clouding with sympathy during the more pathetic parts, or lighting with triumph or delight as the story progressed.

Tom, lolling luxuriously in a nest of pillows at the other end of the couch, was inclined to fool and laugh a little at first; but his interest was soon caught and held, his brown eyes lost their mischief, and were filled with earnestness. It seemed as though he had dropped his mask of impishness for the time and let the true soul of the boy look out from them with all its longings, failings, disappointing repressions, and occasional attempts at goodness.

Dick sat in one great leather chair on the right side of the fire, and Wayne in its mate on the left side. Dick's eyes were watching the flames as they flickered and leaped, and his face wore a look of content and pleasure that was good to see. He was enjoying life as he had never enjoyed it before, and there were whole vistas of such enjoyments in the possibilities of the future. What would his uncle and aunt say if they could see and know? How glad he was they were not here to try to spoil it, for spoil it they would, he was sure, if they got anywhere near him.

Then the story got its hold upon him, too, and the firelight took on the form of the scenes through which its characters were passing. He, too, became absorbed in listening, and forgot everything else. No one had ever tried to interest him or make him happy before, or to cultivate the latent forces of his mind and soul; and this first experience was a wonderful one to him.

From the big chair on the left of the fire the boy Wayne, his head slightly bowed upon his hand, raised a pair of intense eyes under his defense of dark brows, and watched her unflinchingly. Whenever she raised her eyes, she felt his eyes upon her, questioning, analyzing, weighing every word that dropped from her lips. She had a strange feeling that a man's mature mind dwelt behind those eyes, and that the story meant more to him than to any of the others. Perhaps it was with an intuitive divining of some hidden need of his that she put her own soul into what she was reading, and brought out the fine shades of helpfulness in the well-balanced story, making a truth live before her hearers that was scarcely even expressed in words on the printed page. She knew how to read such things into the words, just with the varying of her tones, and it was thus that she always swayed her listeners.

The autumn twilight deepened; and Dick, with a little proud thrill of being at home and having duties as host to perform, slipped silently up, and switched on the electric light in the reading-lamp on the table, leaving the other lights off, so that the corners of the room were still in shadow. The boys' earnest faces glowed out of the dusky places in the room; and Miss Gracen, her voice quiet and sweet, read on, knowing that she held her audience as she had never held an audience before.

They had reached the spot in the story where death and the devil contended with the man of God for a soul, and where simple purity and sincere faith made good under terrible stress. Harold Constable's alert, watching eyes suddenly closed, and he rubbed them as if there was something in them. Wayne Forrest's gaze was down now, with the kind of look that often accompanies anguish-wrung tears, though one could see that the boy would suffer anything rather than let a tear appear in his fierce young eyes. The reader was aware of all this, and prayed in her heart, as she read, that the story might touch some hidden spring of longing that should lead to better things for these young souls.

Softly Dick reached for more wood from the big wicker hamper near the fireplace, and put it on the fire. The flames leaped up lighting the young faces, and Miss Gracen knew that for the time being each one of her hearers was alone in the room with the story and with God.

Chapter XIII

THE candy-platter, which had gone its silent rounds during the afternoon, was now standing empty on the floor by Dick's chair, and the story had reached its first climax when Hiram opened the door and brought in a tray.

The boys suddenly drew up alertly, and realized for the first time that they had been listening. The consciousness that they had been off their guard was embarrassing to them; and they sought at once, boy-like, to cover this with a degree of hilarity out of all proportion to what they felt. Only the boy Wayne did not join in. He sat silent, thoughtful, with a softened, yet deeply sad, look on his face, gazing into the fire. Miss Gracen, as she looked at him, longed to ask him to tell her what was the matter. There must be something terribly wrong when a young face could wear a look of anguish such as that.

On the tray were delicate sandwiches of brown and white bread with delectable filling, and a pot of hot chocolate with a bowl of whipped cream; Rebecca stepped softly behind Hiram, bearing a plate of little frosted sponge-cakes.

Wayne Forrest looked at the tray startled, and arose as though he had inadvertently committed a terrible breach of etiquette.

"It's time we beat it," he said in an undertone to Harold, whose end of the couch was near his chair. "I didn't know it was supper-time, did you?"

But Tom Atterbury sprang up to help pass the plates, and cried out:

"Gee! Isn't this great? I say, Miss Gracen, you're the right stuff!"

It required Miss Gracen's gentle, persuasive hand on Wayne's arm, and her earnest insistence, to make him sit down again and partake of the good things. He seemed all too conscious of his shabby suit, his sleeves, which were too short, and his hands, which reached too far out from them; but his hostess noticed that he ate what was given him like a gentleman.

She took her own plate, and drew her chair over beside that of the boy.

"I'm very glad you came," she said in a low tone that the others could not hear. "I hope you'll come again and let us get real well acquainted. It will give me great pleasure to hear that beautiful voice often."

"I should think you'd had enough of us staying all this afternoon," he said pleasantly; and she noticed that his speaking voice was deep and musical.

"Indeed, I've enjoyed it," she insisted. "Will you come again?"

His eyes went keenly to search her face again with that wordless questioning, "Do you mean it? Do you know who I am?" in them; but she met his look with a steady smile, and after a moment he answered:

"If you really want me, I'll come all right."

"Thank you," she said, smiling; "I really want you." And the boy's eyes showed her he was pleased and almost happy.

When the tray was nearly empty and the brief clamor of serving had subsided, Miss Gracen spoke.

"Boys, there's one thing I should like to do before you break up and go into the parlor to sing a little more—if you don't mind."

She hesitated and looked around.

"Anything you say goes, Miss Vic," declared Tom joyously. "What is it?"

"Well, boys, I'd like to read just a short story to you from the Bible; that would give a true touch of the Sabbath to our gathering."

She looked about on them appealingly with her sweet eyes, and a dead hush filled the room. Dick felt a queer, cold chill creeping down his back, and a hot anger rising at any possible opposition to his aunt's proposition. He didn't care much about the Bible himself, but he didn't want these fellows to be rude to his aunt.

For once Tom's vivacity was hushed, and his mischievous eyes dropped. Wayne's eyes swept the face of every one in the room, and waited with his tense expression to see what would come.

It was Harold who rose to the occasion.

"Sure, Miss Gracen, we'll be glad to hear *anything you* care to read to us."

"We'd *rather* hear some more of the book," drawled Tom wistfully, the mischief appearing in his eyes.

"We'll have the book again next Sunday," said Miss Gracen, and wondered if she had given herself another uncomfortable time to regret the promise, yet knew in her heart that she was glad she had said it; for at once a subdued cheer arose.

"Oh, that's good! Fellows, say!" called Tom. "No more stupid Sundays. Miss Vic, you're a peach!"

"Cut it out, Tom," said Harold, placing a sofa-pillow firmly over the mouth of the minister's son. "Miss Gracen only said 'next Sunday.' Don't go to taking it for granted that means forever."

"Say, Miss Vic, you won't stop at next Sunday, will you?" pleaded Tom.

"We'll see," said Miss Gracen, smiling. "That depends. You know your side of the contract is that you are to go to church———"

"Sure," said Tom, "I have to do that anyway; so it doesn't faze me."

"Of course we'll go," said Harold quickly, "that's a dead cinch."

But Wayne started, and looked around darkly. Had he been caught in a trap? His eyes sought the open doorway for a second, like some wild creature seeking to flee. But he sat quite still, and listened intently while Miss Gracen read the story of the arrest of Jesus in the garden and of His trial and crucifixion, from the eighteenth and nineteenth chapters of John.

She made no comments upon it; but, when the reading was finished, the whole story was pictured vividly for them; the dark garden, the questioning, troubled disciples, the rough, cruel soldiers, the smug, deceitful Judas, impulsive Peter, the firelight, the condemning maiden—all stood out like a living drama upon the stage before them. "Peter's 'turned yellow,'" muttered Tom, as she read of the denial; and the reader understood, and went on with an appreciative nod. Their faces grew grave with awe as the story of the cross unfolded itself before them, and she noticed that Wayne especially looked deeply thoughtful and startled as if the story were almost new to him.

They were all quite still as she closed the Bible and arose, laying a hand on Wayne's shoulder.

"Come, I want to hear you sing again," she said, and smiled down at him. He looked up sharply.

"Oh, I couldn't," he refused. "I really must go. I oughtn't to have stayed so long."

"But you are to go to church with me to-night. You

knew that was the agreement. I was to read if they would all go to church."

"I didn't know," he said, flinging his head back almost defiantly, as if he would even then escape from the room. "I really couldn't go. I'm not fit;" and he looked down at his shabby clothes, and then held his head proudly like a young king.

"You're perfectly all right," said Miss Gracen, "just as you are. We don't wear full dress to church; and, besides, I want you." She smiled a winning plea into his frowning eyes, and a strange thing happened. He looked down at her with refusal in his eyes, but after a second his brow cleared and a tender look broke over his face.

"Well, it's up to you," he said, "if you're sure you're not ashamed of me."

"Not in the least, my dear," said his hostess lightly. "Thank you. Now, come on and sing. There's a song in the other room that I'm sure will fit your voice. Suppose you try it."

And Wayne, surprised into happiness, went smiling by her side, and was soon singing his best for her.

They started early to church, but Lydia Bypath was there ahead of them, whispering in sepulchral tones to her neighbor in the next seat; and when Miss Gracen, attended by her four stalwart escorts, came down the aisle, she settled back and fixed each one with her piercing glance as they passed by, her thin, sharp face growing more and more filled with disapproval as the identity of each boy became known to her—the son of a forger, the son of a disinherited brother, the prodigal son of an indulgent minister, and the handsome, daredevil son of an unmitigated society woman, than whom, Miss Bypath felt, there could be no worse on the face of the earth. Poor, little, narrow, old Pharisee! What a lot she'll have to learn in heaven! If Miss Gracen was chilly in church, it surely must have been due to those cold eyes piercing her back all during the service.

By some strange happening Wayne had followed Miss Gracen next in order; and, when they reached the pew door, she motioned him in first and sat next to him, the minister's son coming after, with Harold and Dick at the end. The minister, as he took his seat in the pulpit a few minutes later looked down upon his congregation, and saw with relief his oldest son sitting next to one of the best women in his church; the son who went to church always on protest, and who often was missing at the hour of evening service, in spite of his father's most urgent efforts and commands. It is true the other boys in the company were no guarantee of virtue, but to see his son sitting beside Miss Gracen and hunting for the place in the hymn-book for her made his weary heart warm and kindle.

How wonderful to have those boys there, anyway! Oh for a touch on his lips from the altar of God, that his words might have power to reach those young hearts!

Does anything just happen in this God's world of ours? Was it happening that made the minister select that nineteenth chapter of John for his sermon that evening? And his text was "Behold, the man!" As he began to read, there was a flash of wonder and interest in the faces of the four boys, and especially in Wayne Forrest's face. He bent his head as though to look down, but fixed his eyes on the minister's face from start to finish, with that odd upward look under his dark brows that made him so noticeable a listener; and the minister, whose apathetic congregation often filled him with heart-sickness and discouragement, saw him, and took courage. If just one soul wanted to listen, he had a message worth the telling; and in his heart he prayed for the blessing of the Spirit.

Watch as she might, even during prayer-time, Lydia Bypath could not find anything in the conduct of the son of the forger to criticise; for a more quiet, earnest, thoughtful face was never set upon young shoulders; and he sang the hymns with his beautiful voice, looking over the same book with Miss Gracen, whose gray feathers came only to his tall shoulder, and looked down upon her almost reverently when she glanced up at him.

Dick grinned once when Tom snapped a rubber band and slyly hit the toe of an elder across the aisle, who crossed his feet twice and uncrossed them, and never knew why he did it. Several times Tom and Harold exchanged rattling confidences in the form of small articles from their respective pockets. Miss Bypath saw it all with her eagle eye, and set it all down against them, adding to the curse of sorrow that she saw with her mind's eye rapidly approaching the house of Gracen; but she was uncomfortably conscious of the fact that she could not see anything wrong in the conduct of "that disreputable young Forrest fellow with the hardened countenance." She supposed it was because Miss Gracen had him cornered off by himself in the seat that way. She didn't know his father well enough to trace a resemblance, but she spent much holy time tracing out signs of an evil inheritance in the strong, fine, young face, and she joined with fervor in the closing hymn,

> When, free from envy, scorn, and pride,
>   Our wishes all above,
> Each can his brother's failings hide,
>   And show a brother's love,

and knew not what a travesty it was upon her soul.

It was the first time that Wayne Forrest had been inside any church in Roslyn, and the first time that any minister in the town had taken him by the hand; so Mr. Atterbury's warm clasp, and hearty "Glad to see you, Forrest. Wish you'd come every Sunday," did a good deal toward helping him to bear the curious scorn of some other people who stared at him and whispered openly about him. He walked home in the starlight, listening to Miss Gracen's pleasant talk, and bade her good-night at her door with real gratitude in his voice as he said:

"I want to thank you for the nicest Sunday afternoon I can remember."

And Miss Gracen wholly committed herself to the future as she replied:

"I hope you will let me give you many more of

them. I shall look for you next Sunday, early. Remember!"

Home through the starlight he walked after parting from the boys, out past the village, into the lonely road of the country, and opened the door of the unattractive little house he called home fully two hours earlier than usual. His sister looked up sharply from the book she was reading, and called out half anxious, wholly pleased:

"What's eating you, Wayne, to come home so early?" She was a pretty girl with a fine mind and rather old manners upon her young shoulders. "Where've you been?" she persisted.

"Been to church," said Wayne gravely, as if that were his habit every Sunday of his life.

"Church!" his sister exclaimed. "Church! What do you mean Wayne?"

"Mean what I say. I've been to church." He sat down without smiling, greatly enjoying her bewilderment.

"Yes, a lot you've been to church. Mother," raising her voice to reach the invalid in the next room, "listen to Wayne. He says he's been to church."

"I only wish he had," sighed the feeble voice of the mother. "I always went to church twice on Sunday. I never meant my children to come up this way."

But the sister, with a keen look into her brother's face, slipped from her seat, and came and stood beside his chair, touching his hair lightly with her fingers, and brushing it back from his forehead.

"What's the matter, Wayne dear?" she said, and her sweet voice had grown gentler. "Has somebody been being mean to you?"

"No," growled the boy, half laughing. "I tell you I've been to church. I'm not kidding you. I've really been to church."

His sister sat down suddenly as though she were too much astonished to stand.

"What made you do it?" she asked, watching him intently.

THE OBSESSION OF VICTORIA GRACEN

"Oh, some of the fellows were going; so I just thought I'd go too."

"Where did you go? Which church?"

"Presbyterian."

It happened that the Presbyterian was the church of the wealthy and scholarly in Roslyn, and this made the surprise all the greater.

"You went to the Presbyterian church, and in those clothes, Wayne!"

"Hadn't any others with me, had I?"

"But suppose you had happened to sit with some of those rich swells. How would you have felt?"

"I did," said Wayne. "The fact is, I went with one of them, Sis."

"Who?"

"Miss Victoria Gracen."

"Wayne, I wish you'd stop joking and talk sensibly. Where have you been to-night, anyway? You don't suppose I'm going to believe all that nonsense. Wait! I'll get you some supper. There's some hot johnny-cake put away in the oven for you, and I saved a little of mother's cream. You'll like that with it, won't you?"

"No, sit down, Rhoda; I'm not hungry to-night. Eat the cream yourself. I know you went without your supper to save it for me. Now go and get it, and let me see you eat it. No, you're not going to save it for my breakfast, either. I want to see you eat it. I tell you honestly I'm not hungry. I had a grand supper."

"Where?"

She faced him curiously.

"Why, I took supper with Miss Gracen."

He sat watching her with keen enjoyment as she dropped into her chair again and stared at him.

"You took supper with Miss Gracen?"

"I did."

"I don't believe you. It's one of your miserable jokes; and by and by you'll tell me what you mean, I suppose. Well, if you had supper at Miss Gracen's, what did you have? Come, you can't tell."

"Sure I can. I had sandwiches, little, thin, rolled ones, lots and heaps of them, with chicken and nuts and

all sorts of nice stuffings in them. Had so many I put
one in my pocket to show you. Thought you'd like to
use it for a pattern the next time you gave a pink tea to
your college friends——"

Rhoda gave a quick glance about the bare room, and
tears came into her eyes. It was an old joke between
them, this about her college friends and her round of
society duties. It was their way of making light of the
long days of hard toil, the lack of books and opportunities to study, and the absolute lack of any friends whatever. But to-night her nerves seemed to have stood
more strain than usual for some reason, and the thread-
bare joke fell keenly on her tired heart. The little mother had seemed frailer than usual, and there had been
less in the house to eat than last Sunday. It was still two
weeks till Wayne's next pay-day, and how were they
to make things go much longer?

"Oh, Wayne, I wish you wouldn't tease to-night,"
she whispered. "You're just making a miserable joke,
and I know there is some trouble or other behind it
all."

"Nothing of the sort," said the boy in gruff tenderness; "everything I said is true. Put your hand in my
pocket, and get that sandwich. There's some cake
there, too. She kept passing the plate, and passing it; and
I ate all I could swallow, and thought it wouldn't be any
harm just to let you see a sample. Chuck your hand in."

He held out his sagging pocket, and Rhoda put in a
disbelieving hand, and pulled out the piece of cake,
somewhat crushed as to frosting, but still intact, and
the delicate rolled sandwich, all thoughtfully wrapped
in a crumpled railroad time-table. She gazed at them a
minute, took one small testing bite of the sandwich, and
then put her head down on the table, and cried.

Her brother looked on in amazed perplexity.

"Well, what's eating *you*? I'm sure, if I'd known it
was going to affect you that way, I would have eaten
them myself, if it choked me."

Rhoda lifted a sparkling face.

"Don't mind me, Wayne; I just lost my nerve for a
minute. I thought perhaps you'd been to that saloon

down at the corners where they give away fried oysters with every drink. I saw the sign in the window the day I walked to Mrs. Cranford's with her mending. You never tell us where you are at night, and I got to worrying lest you boys went there sometimes, perhaps——"

Wayne turned away with reproach and disgust in his face.

"What do you take me for?" he asked roughly. "Did you think I was that kind of a guy?"

"Well, no; only everything was so horrid, and it wouldn't be strange if you did as the others do; you never have any good times like other boys."

"Well, Rhoda, I had one to-day all right," he said emphatically; "and I rather guess I'm in for another one next Sunday, too."

"Did she ask you to come again?" Rhoda was now almost breathless.

"Yes, she did," said Wayne, his tone only half concealing his own feeling that it was nothing short of a miracle that she had. Then he gave her a detailed account of the afternoon, her eyes sparkling with astonishment and pleasure as he went on telling the nice things Miss Gracen had said to him. But, when he had finished, they were both silent for a few minutes; then Rhoda leaned forward, a trouble evidently rankling in her mind.

"Wayne," she said in a low tone that could not reach the invalid in the next room, "Wayne, are you *sure* she knows who you are?"

The boy's face clouded; and a dark, forbidding look enveloped and transformed him into another being. He did not answer at once; and, when he did, the wretchedness and despair in his voice made it like an old man's.

"I don't know," he said hopelessly, then added after a minute: "I don't suppose she did, but I guess she'll find out before another Sunday. She don't look as if she went around with her eyes shut. Oh, I don't suppose she'll want me again. I guess I sha'n't go unless she sends me word somehow, and I don't suppose she'll do that. I don't suppose I'll ever have another afternoon like that again; it was great! Simply great! And, if she turns me down," he added blackly, "if she turns me down when she finds out, I *have got that!*"

His sister reached out her rough, little, toil-worn hand, slipping it into his big strong one, and together they sat for an unusual moment of silent understanding. Then Wayne arose, and prepared to go to his room for the night. It was the way with most of the good things that flashed across his way; they never came again; and those he had turned bitter with his own thoughts afterward. It was hard, hard to be turned down everywhere, and for no fault of his own. And what was even harder was to have Rhoda, his beautiful, gifted sister, hidden away with the responsibility of a woman upon her young shoulders, and not even so much chance as he himself had to get out and away from it.

He seldom voiced these bitter feelings even to himself, but they swelled and rankled in the anguish of his young soul till sometimes he lost all faith in everything and wished that his life were over.

Chapter XIV

WAYNE was right; Miss Gracen was not one to go about with her eyes shut; and the thing she had upon her heart the next morning was to find out about the strange, silent boy whose face had attracted her at the first glance. Yet she already had too much loyalty to the boy himself to go about her discovery in any public way. She meant to keep her eyes open and discover for herself. She felt in a sense allied to him, and did not wish to break the unspoken contract of friendship between them by trying behind his back to find out about him. Neither did she care to have any one know that she had invited a guest to her home of whom she knew nothing.

However, her opportunity presented itself at the breakfast-table the next morning, and it was Dick who began the conversation.

"I'm awful glad you were so prime to that Forrest

fellow, Aunt Vic," he said as he ate his luscious grapes and reflected on the comforts of a home like this. "He's up against it hard, the boys say. I guess you know more about him than I do, but it must be tough to have your father do a thing like that. It must be worse than having him dead. You can be proud of him if he's dead, but not when he's committed a crime. The boys say he's awfully proud, and won't go anywhere. At asked me if I thought you'd mind about his bringing him here. He asked me after church yesterday morning. I meant to tell you on the way home; but those folks walked with us, and I forgot it. You ought to see Forrest play football. He has more nerve than any two others put together, and he's always everywhere that he's most needed. He played at that game up at the college. Some fellow got hurt and they got him to take his place. It was great to see him. If he ever plays again here, I hope you can go. But it was dandy of you to make him feel at home that way. At says he thinks you're great. He says he had all kinds of a time getting him to come. He thought you'd think he was butting in; and, if he'd seen the least little sign that you didn't like it, he would never come again. The fellows were awfully pleased that you were so prime to him."

His aunt smiled. She had her information and without the asking.

"I liked him," she said warmly, "and I'm glad if he enjoyed himself. We must try to give him some happy times. He has a wonderful voice. I wish I knew his mother. I called there twice, but never got in. I must try again sometime when I know him better," and she fell to planning how, without hurting his pride, she might find out more about the boy's home and his needs.

Later in the day, after the momentous visit with Dick to the high school, she sat down at her desk, and wrote this little note:

"Dear Wayne:—
     I've found a song that I have a fancy to hear you sing. I would like you to sing it for us next

Sunday afternoon; so, if you can find time to run over to my home on Thursday evening for a few minutes, we can try it over together. Hoping you will be able to come,

Sincerely your friend,
"VICTORIA GRACEN."

Wayne, coming home from his poorly paid office-work, dropped into the post-office more from habit than from any hope of finding mail. He took the letter, and read the address in great surprise. The envelope was of a soft pearl color, exhaling a delightful fragrance of violets; and somehow his own familiar name, written in that clear, strong, fine hand, took on a kind of dignity and beauty of which he had never suspected it before. He carried the note home in triumph to his sister; and together they took it to the poor little invalid mother, who listened, smiled feebly, and when they were gone out turned her sad countenance to the pillow, weeping for the boy whose birthright had been taken from him, and who was forced to depend upon the paltry whim of a stranger for all the pleasant things of life. She was glad that this joy had come to him, but wept that she had never been able to give him any good times.

Meantime Dick had found that he knew more than he had given himself credit for. In spite of the careless, studyless habits of his school-days he had managed to imbibe from the school atmosphere a large amount of knowledge concerning a number of studies. He had remembered many things from hearing others recite, though he had never studied them himself; and he possessed a native talent for mathematics which made him quick at figures. The school principal, being a man of discernment, decided that Dick could easily enter the second year of the high school, and might possibly be able in two or three months, if he studied, to skip into Tom Atterbury's grade. Whereupon Dick made up his mind to study. He had a feeling that he could do better than Tom if he had Tom's chances, and he meant to prove it. It was due to his father's memory that he should.

So Dick did not return to the house with his aunt that first Monday to be coached by her until he was able to enter school, but he delved straight into school-life with all his might. If anybody had told him three days before that he would have done this, he would have stolen a ride back to Chicago on the freight-cars, and would gladly have worked in the slaughter-house rather than go to that school for the first time; but somehow that talk with the principal and his newly-formed acquaintance with Tom had made a wonderful difference, and he went bravely through the eventful first morning, and came home at lunch-time with eager, shining eyes. His talk was all of the football team. They wanted him for left guard if he could make it; but you had to stand just so in your marks in class, or you couldn't play. He would have to make his first week's marks come up to the required measure, or there wouldn't be any chance at all for him.

It was all so breathless and happy, and for his aunt so like having a real boy of her own, to have him look to her to be interested in these things. It was so nice to feel that he was going to hold his own, and pleasant to urge him to take more soup and take time for another helping of rice pudding, and to promise to look up all the subjects that he had to study for the next day, so that she would be able to help him at night.

That first evening together around the light, puzzling over the next day's problems and hunting out Latin verbs and finding their derivations, was a delight far beyond any study she had ever done to write essays for the Woman's Club. She felt as if she were a young girl again, going to school herself on the morrow; and her heart kept growing lighter all the time.

Tom dropped in for a half-hour about nine o'clock. He said his father had given him permission to come over to see whether there was anything Dick wanted to know about his work for the next day; and he sat on a low hassock at Miss Gracen's feet, and played with the ribbons of her gown while she showed him how to read a paragraph in his English which he confessed didn't make any sense to him. When he had gone home, it sud-

denly came to her that Tom had in these short three
days become to her a being entirely different from the
disagreeable, red-haired, bad boy she had heretofore
thought him. She had begun to see the real boy in him,
and to love it. He, too, had been grateful for her treat-
ment of Wayne Forrest.

"Miss Vic, you were just prime to Forrie," he said,
twirling the rose and gray tassels on her ribbon-ends.
"He enjoyed it here immensely. He said he'd go to
church seven days in the week for you."

And Miss Gracen found her hitherto well-conducted
heart dancing gayly with delight.

From that time forth life to Miss Gracen began to
take on an entirely new aspect. The boy, and after him
the boys, became the centre of her existence.

The regular Club meeting, usually a brilliant social
affair with some speaker from town, and charming refreshments, where every one wore her prettiest frock,
and the finest musical talent of Roslyn did its best to
make the occasion a notable event, happened that week
to fall upon the very day of the game to which she had
promised to accompany the boys. It had not occurred
to her when she had promised; and on the morning in
question Dick reminded her of the game with bright,
shining eyes, telling her that the boys were "way-up
pleased" that she was going with them. They were planning to keep the very best seats to be had on the stand
for their party, and to take cushions and rugs and a hot
brick for her feet if it seemed to be cold.

Like any girl her eyes sparkled with anticipation,
and she promised to be ready for them the minute
school was out. No thought of the sacred Club meeting
entered her head—she had never been absent from the
regular meeting since the Club was formed, unless
she was out of town—until a neighbor called her up
and asked whether she could take her place on the
serving committee, as the neighbor had a dressmaker
and couldn't get away.

"Oh, I'm so sorry," exclaimed Miss Gracen into the

receiver in dismay; "but it's going to be absolutely impossible for me to get there this afternoon. I—have—another engagement," and she laughed, half ashamed to think what the engagement was. "I really had forgotten it was the Club day when I made it."

"For pity's sake, Victoria Gracen, what possible engagement can you have in this town on a Friday afternoon? Nobody has anything then. You surely can't be going to run away to town to attend the symphony concert, are you?"

"Why, no," said Miss Gracen, feeling more young and foolish than ever before in her life, and half vexed with her friend for being so inquisitive, "I'm only going with my boy and his friends to a game at the athletic grounds. I didn't know it was Club day when they asked me, but they will be disappointed if I back out. I'm sorry not to oblige you, but you surely won't have trouble in finding plenty of people to serve in your place. Clementine Holmes will be delighted, I know."

"A game! You go to a game this cold day! Victoria, you'll get pneumonia as sure as you live. Tell those boys you can't possibly go. Don't be a silly at your time of life. Take my place, and pour tea, do. Besides, I want somebody who will be responsible for the whole committee. Clementine would forget to pass the sugar and cream. I can't trust it with anybody but you. Do take my place, Victoria."

But Miss Gracen, with dismay in her face, gathered her forces, and answered decidedly:

"Indeed, Caroline, I couldn't think of breaking my promise to the boys!" And Caroline with a vexed "Well, of all things!" hung up the receiver with a click that told her state of mind.

Miss Gracen, flushing like a guilty schoolgirl, sat in her chair happily, and reflected that she had brought the gossip of the town upon her head now, hot and heavy, and must be prepared to meet it. Well, what of it? She had a right to stay away from the Club and go to a ball-game if she chose, and she did choose, most decidedly. She wouldn't disappoint those boys, and her

boy most of all, with his shining, trustful eyes, and his
brow so like his dear father's, not for all the clubs in
Christendom.

She went to the game in Harold's automobile, attended by the three boys and smothered in fur rugs and
foot-stoves. She could not have been more comfortable
in her own parlor. They explained each point of the
game to her carefully, and she entered into their enthusiasm as if she had played all her life.

Then, when it was over, they whizzed by the Club
house just as the meeting was out, and the ladies in
their best attire were pouring out into the street. It
wasn't exactly the way to Miss Gracen's home, but
Harold was bent on meeting Wayne's train and giving
him a glimpse of the good time they had had. The
ladies, as they walked leisurely down the street in the
gathering twilight, or stood in groups about the steps
and on the sidewalk, looked up in surprise, stared and
bowed, and stared again.

"Why, isn't that Victoria Gracen in the Constable
car? Why, she wasn't at the Club meeting, was she?
How very strange!"

Caroline came down the walk in time to hear the
remark. She had puckered herself together and left
her dressmaker to her own confusion, while she herself
did her stern duty by the Club.

"No, she wasn't," she snapped. "She went to a ball-
game instead. What do you think of that? Victoria
Gracen at a ball-game! I tell you that woman is just
obsessed by boys!"

"Obsessed" was one of the new words that the Club
had taught Caroline. She enjoyed an appropriate
occasion on which to use it.

"H'm!" said Mrs. Hiram Rushmore meaningly, as
she gazed after the flying car. "Well, that's the way
with some unmarried women when they get hold of a
man creature; they just go crazy. But I thought Victoria Gracen had too much sense."

But Victoria Gracen, happily unconscious of the
gathering storm of disapproval, rode away to the station.

"Now I'll tell you what we'll do," she said, as Wayne, his eyes shining with the attention shown him, leaped in and took the vacant seat beside her. "You'll all go home with us to supper. I told Rebecca to cook plenty of chicken and make pies enough for a regiment. I think there's pumpkin pie, if I'm not much mistaken."

A shout of joy from Tom and Harold hailed this announcement, but Wayne looked down at himself in dismay. The grime of the office was upon him, and he felt an unspeakable shrinking from going out to dinner, much as he would like it.

"Oh, thank you, but I'll have to get home," he declared with one of his dark looks. "They expect me. I really couldn't go, you know."

"Of course they expect you," said Miss Gracen. "It wouldn't do at all to let them worry. Couldn't we telephone them?"

The moment she had said it she knew what a mistake she had made, and Wayne's face darkened; but she caught up her own words with:

"But maybe you aren't bothered with a 'phone. Harold, suppose we drive out there; it wouldn't take long, would it? You see, I'm determined to have you, and you can't possibly get out of it."

Wayne looked down with tender awe at the small gray glove on his rough coat-sleeve, and actually smiled, although his whole being was in a tremor of expectation.

The door of the shabby little shingled cottage burst open suddenly as the car stopped noisily before the gate; and a young girl with her sleeves rolled above her elbows and her brown hair tumbled back from her face came distractedly out, exclaiming in a frightened tone:

"Oh, Wayne, what is it? Has anything happened? You haven't had an accident have you?"

And Wayne sprang out deftly over the car door without opening it, and shouted hilariously: "Not on your life. I'm going out to dinner. Step out of the way till I get a clean collar."

The last words were spoken just as he dashed into

the door, but they were distinctly audible to the four people in the car.

Miss Gracen leaned forward, and raised her voice.

"My dear, we're carrying Wayne home with us to dinner. I hope his mother can spare him for the evening. We really couldn't get along without him."

Rhoda, her fears relieved, gave a gasping "Oh!" pulled down her sleeves, and fluffed her pretty, rumpled hair all in one movement, and came slowly, shyly a few steps down the path.

"You're awfully kind, I'm sure," said the girl with a touch of her brother's haughty dignity, yet a hidden pleasure showing in her gray eyes. "He appreciates so much being at your house, I know. He just can't talk of anything else any more."

"I hope I may soon have the pleasure of knowing his sister," said Miss Gracen with her pleasantest voice and sweetest smile; and the girl grew rosy with pleasure in the rapidly growing dusk.

"Oh, thank you," she said, withdrawing at once into her shell again, "but I couldn't leave mother."

"Well, then, may I come to see you—and mother, too, I hope, if it won't tire her too much—some day soon?"

Rhoda was spared further conversation by the reappearance of her brother, his face shining from a rapid toilet. He sprang into the car, and called boyishly to Harold:

"Let her go-oo!" And Harold waited not on ceremony; but, as the car swept away from the door, Miss Gracen waved her hand in good-bye, and called out, "Don't forget! I'm coming soon."

Miss Gracen went giddily up the stone walk of her own house, and entered into her hall attended by four of the noisiest boys that ever entered a respectable home; but she never even noticed that they were noisy until she threw open the door of her own library for them to enter, and saw, sitting stiffly in the straightest chair, with retribution in her eye and relentlessness in her thin face, little, sharp, vindictive Lydia Bypath!

Chapter XV

DISMAY fell upon the joyous group as they stood in the bright room and stared blankly at the formidable occupant.

"Gee!" said Tom under his breath.

"Gee!" echoed Dick in the same instant, and:

"Gee!" whistled Harold softly.

But Wayne only stood like a wild thing at bay, and frowned darkly.

It must be admitted that Miss Gracen herself felt slightly as though she had met with a dash of cold water in her face as she went graciously forward to welcome her most unwelcome visitor.

"Well! You're come at last, have you?" was the severe greeting, like a teacher to a naughty child. "I've been waiting here since the Club meeting let out——"

"Oh, I'm sorry you were detained so long," said the hostess sweetly. "Won't you sit down and lay aside your wraps? The room is warm."

"No, I wish to speak with you in private. I'll just wait here until you are done with these——"

She waved her hand, and looked severely at the group of boys, as if they were a set of criminals who had obtruded themselves into her friend's house and must be attended to first. She did not need to add a noun to give a full and finished idea of what she thought they were. One felt that she would have liked some expression like "generation of vipers" to express her sentiments entirely.

Wayne's brow grew darker, and he half turned toward the door. Harold's chin went up in the air haughtily; Dick's eyes flashed fire from their dark depths; but Tom's kindled with mischief. He had been the butt of this mistaken woman's wrath for many a year, and had found it harmless. He rather enjoyed her remarks; they added zest to the occasion, especially when they were attended by the unusual circumstance of his not being in the wrong or to blame in any way.

But Miss Gracen was equal to the situation, and with her gentle face raised just the least bit in dignity she smiled toward the boys reassuringly, and answered:

"Oh, these are my friends, and they are going to stay to supper with me to-night. Won't you stay also? Then after supper we can take a little time together——"

Three of the boys were appalled at the prospect of a spoiled frolic, but Tom's sense of fun was uppermost.

"Yes, do stay, Miss Bypath," he drawled in his most dulcet tones. "Miss Vic said there was to be chicken, and we'll give you the wish-bone."

There was a joke of some kind, old in the village, connected with a number of wish-bones that had once been tacked to Miss Bypath's front door. Tom had not been the boy who put them there; but he knew all about it, and could not resist the temptation to remind her of it. He felt that she deserved it for the way she talked to his hostess.

Miss Bypath withered him with her glance, and, turning to Miss Gracen, angrily said:

"Oh, if you have company, I won't intrude. I see my errand is quite useless after all my trouble. I'll go at once," and she swept indignantly from the room, with a furious glance toward the defiant boys, who, if she had been a man, would gladly have thrashed her.

Miss Gracen followed her into the hall, but purposely left the door of the library open. She had no mind to be browbeaten by Lydia Bypath, and kept her sweet dignity as she said gently:

"I am sorry you have taken trouble. Was it anything I could do for you?"

"No, it was something I could have done for you, if you are not too far gone. 'Obsessed' was the word they used about you at the Club, a word that may be new and fashionable, but it never seemed quite respectable to me. They said you were obsessed by boys, and I came to warn you of it; but I see it is true."

Her eloquent speech was interrupted most unexpectedly by a ringing laugh from Miss Gracen.

"Is that all?" she asked merrily. "I thought you must

be ill or in trouble. So that is what they are saying
about me! Well, it cannot hurt them or me. Just tell
them I said it was perfectly true." And she broke into
another silvery laugh.

Two steel points were Miss Bypath's pale blue
eyes; flat and straight was her indignant back. She stood
and looked at Miss Gracen in speechless wrath for the
space of a full second, and then turned and marched
from the house without another word; and the boys, the
naughty, triumphant boys, joined in an ill-suppressed
cheer as the door closed upon her.

"Miss Vic," called the irrepressible Tom, "your name
is not Miss Gracen any more, for now you are Dis-
Gracen."

Miss Gracen was really more annoyed at the passage
at arms than she cared to show. It was the most unwise
thing that could have happened in the hearing of the
boys; but it had happened, and she could not help it.
It had been in no wise their fault, and she must not let
them feel any discomfort from it.

"You see, boys, what kind of a scrape you have got
me into by inveigling me off to a wicked football game
when I should have been serving tea and pink cakes at
the Club; so now you will have to make up for it by
having the very best time you know how this evening.
Run up-stairs, and wash your hands if any of you want
to, while I see that there are plates enough on the table."

She hurried into the dining-room, but the echo of
their voices came distinctly to her.

"Say, she's the real stuff!" came Wayne's clear baritone, and her heart told her that she had a new friend
among the boys.

"Isn't she, though?" answered Harold. "She's surely
a peach."

"You bet your life she is," said Tom, noisily, "a regular pippin!"

And then Dick's endearing growl: "Who is that old
tartar, anyway? What business has she got coming
round here trying to tend to *my aunt?*" There was own-
ership in his voice, and "my aunt" could scarcely re-

strain herself from rushing up-stairs and embracing him. She felt rich in his love.

Nothing was said at the supper-table about the unpleasant occurrence; for Miss Gracen kept the conversation humming on all sorts of interesting topics appealing to boys. They knew her well enough by this time to talk freely in her presence and to express their hearty approval of the bountiful supper which the wise Rebecca had prepared.

It was Wayne, the thoughtful, who later in the evening broached the question in a roundabout way.

"Miss Gracen, aren't we taking too much of your time from other things? It's awfully kind of you, but we mustn't presume."

Miss Gracen laid her small, white hand on the boy's arm, and smiled up at him.

"I've not had anything in years so interesting as you boys to take up my time, and I want you to take just as much of it as is pleasant to you. My boy is going to be the main object of my life from now on, I hope,"—she smiled lovingly across at Dick, who answered with a soft light of understanding and gratitude in his eyes,— "and I guess I shall have to take in and love all his friends as well. If you don't get tired of me, I shall not get tired of you."

"Not much danger of our getting tired," said Wayne huskily; and she could see that he was deeply affected by her kindness.

She was quick to seize her opportunity.

"I want to know your beautiful sister. She is your sister, isn't she? The one who came to the door to meet you? And your mother. Will she let me call?"

The boy looked down embarrassed, half pleased, half troubled.

"Mother isn't well," he said in a low tone; "she doesn't see people."

"I know," said Miss Gracen, her own tone so low now that the other boys who were talking could not hear, "she has suffered. I am so sorry. But I do wish she would make an exception of me and let me get to know her, because I love her boy."

The slow color stole into the boy's face and up into his soft, dark hair, and the hard lines softened into gentleness. He lifted his intense eyes, and looked into the gentle, true ones that were lifted to his; his own kindled into trust and answering affection. Then she knew who he was—and she still cared to have him come! It was wonderful, but it was true!

He put out his strong, young hand, taking her fine, small elderly one in an earnest grasp that sealed a compact of love and trust between them; but all he said was:

"Thank you! I'll tell her what you said."

That night, when she was alone and thought the evening over, Miss Gracen found little space in her mind for the incident of Lydia Bypath. If Lydia wished to be foolish, and interfere in her affairs as she had done in other people's, it was time to make her understand that it could not be done. She dismissed her disagreeable incident, and went singing back over the signs of progress in her boys, the little indications that they thought and cared for higher, better things than merely having a good time. She had begun to see great possibilities in every one of them, and she knew that her readiness to take in the other boys had only endeared her the more to her own nephew.

But the next morning there came an indignant letter from Lydia Bypath, insisting that she had been insulted within her former friend's door by the minister's son, and demanding retribution upon him for his impudence. She also made it quite plain to her correspondent that unless Victoria Gracen should immediately change her way of doing she would be the town talk. She gave valuable and untrue information concerning the ill deeds of every one of the boys, and declared that she felt it her duty in the face of all insults to make it plain to Miss Gracen that she was doing wrong to bring her young and innocent nephew into dangerous companionship with boys who were marked for the prison cell and the electric chair. She finished with a scathing picture of the elderly female who made a fool of herself with boys just out of leading-strings, broadly

hinting that because Miss Gracen had never been married she had lost her head and was infatuated with
these boys, a thing which she, Lydia Bypath, could
never be guilty of, for she knew too much about the
wickedness of the male creation. They never came
near a woman but to bring her trouble, as Victoria Gracen would soon find to her sorrow.

She had scarcely read this letter, and laughed over
it, before the telephone rang, and another friend called
her up with fifteen minutes of good advice to the effect
that she had chosen the wrong kind of companions for
her nephew, and she ought to have asked her about
boys. She was the mother of two sons who were models
(only in their mother's eyes), she could have told her
what boys to invite to her home, and she named a few
eligibles, her own among the number; but she informed
Miss Gracen that she must get rid of the others at once.
Harold Constable, of course, was respectable, though he
didn't seem to amount to much; still, he had manners
at least; but the others were an actual disgrace to the
community. Everybody knew how worthless Tom Atterbury was, of course, and that Wayne Forrest! Why,
his father was serving a term in the State prison for
forgery. Of course Victoria hadn't known that, or she
wouldn't have had him about——

Miss Gracen here interrupted to say in most decided
tones that she knew all about Wayne Forrest and liked
him very much; that he had been at her home a
number of times, and she felt the boy had been sadly
misunderstood. She went into a few details of facts
which caused a cessation in the volubility at the other
end of the line, as the informer dissolved into "Ohs!"
and "Ahs!" and, "Why, you don't mean it! Has a voice?
How interesting! I suppose we ought to be kind, of
course, but——" and, when Miss Gracen finally hung
up her receiver, she was boiling with wrath.

This, then, had been the matter with these boys; they
had been tagged bad boys because of mischievous
things they had done, and the village was determined to
keep them bad boys. No one was to be allowed to help
lift them up to anything better. Well, she would see

whether she was to be prevented. God had sent her these boys unexpectedly, without effort on her part; and she would do her best for them. If the town disapproved, let it disapprove. When had ever a Gracen bowed to public opinion enough to give up a righteous deed when the need was for it?

So the days went by, and the three boys became regular, almost daily, visitors at the house. Sometimes they only ran in for a minute to see Dick, sometimes to borrow a book or try over a song, sometimes to bring a great branch of red leaves still found clinging to some sheltered tree; and once Harold came breathlessly to the door, on his way to meet his father at the train, to leave a clump of squawberry-vine dotted with bright red berries, which he had found and carefully dug up for her.

It grew to be a regular thing that they took long tramps on Saturdays when Wayne had an afternoon off; and sometimes they inveigled Miss Gracen into a moonlight walk, just to see how the light shone on the little falls below the creek, with the branches of the tall, bare trees stencilled clear against the night-blue sky.

But the Sunday-afternoon meetings were not long confined to the four, for every now and then a new boy would be brought along, and would somehow steal a place in the heart of the hostess and be asked again.

Willing hands prepared on Saturday night the delicate sandwiches and cakes, the little tarts or crisp cookies; or set away dainty dishes of salad and bowls of delicious broths that needed only a few minutes over the gas-stove to make them ready for serving with the accompanying toasted wafers. Rebecca and Molly and Hiram rejoiced over this opportunity of helping on "Miss Vic's good work," as they called it; for in their good old souls they felt that a wrong had been done the father Dick, and it must be righted for his son, and that through him these other boys were being uplifted and helped as all boys had a right to be.

Expensive? Yes, the good things to eat cost a little; but it was a mere trifle to Miss Gracen, who might have spent it otherwise on going to the city to the opera, or giving bridge-parties, or taking trips to Europe; and she enjoyed it as no society woman ever enjoys her follies.

Just how the story of her doings got out is uncertain. The boys did not tell it; that is, they never intended to do so. They may have let it out sometimes more by what they did not say than by what they did; but it got out somehow, in distorted form, all about Miss Victoria's ridiculous and disgraceful goings-on. It may have been the time when Miss Earwig from the next door ran in late Saturday afternoon to borrow some soda for her gingerbread, and found Molly making rolled brown-bread sandwiches with minced chicken filling. Or it may have been Mrs. Harold Constable's letter from southern France to her most intimate friend, Mrs. Cornelius Cornell, secretary of the Club, wherein she made some jocose remark about Harold's having written that he took supper with Miss Gracen every Sunday night, and she wondered whether Miss Gracen was losing her Puritan ideas about keeping Sunday so strictly, and getting like other people at last. However the story came, it was out, with all the embellishing that much telling can give.

"Feeding them! Actually pampering their stomachs, and making them think they're just the greatest things on earth! Those *bad boys!*" almost screamed Mrs. Dr. Toosun when the story was told to her at a Club meeting. "Why, it's the worst thing she could do for them. They'll all end in jail, and she'll be to blame for it!"

"Yes, feeding them, and on Sunday, too! I think it's wicked," said fat Mrs. Thorndike, gulping her last drop of strong coffee. And all those who sat in condemnation, as they finished their delicate ices and cakes, sat back and agreed that it was a dreadful thing to do on the Sabbath, and never remembered how they resembled the Pharisees who found some such fault with Jesus on the Sabbath day.

But Victoria Gracen, independent of nature, and happy in the new work that God had given her, went serenely on her way, hearing little of the scandal about herself, because now Lydia Bypath, whose letter of vituperation had been answered by a brief, calm note of dignity, came no more to tell, and to warn, and to cast the eye of scorn.

The Sunday meetings had become quite an established fact, and were no longer confined to four boys, but had a regular attendance of from ten to twelve; and among these were numbered both high and low; for somehow a few of the really "respectable" boys, whose parents disapproved of the whole performance, crept stealthily in now and then until their presence became a regular thing; and, on the other hand, four or five fellows of the lowly walks of life were brought by the original boys, who felt that these needed it. A word of low explanation from one of them to Miss Gracen was enough to bring out her smile of welcome, and thus her house became the resort of some of the outcasts among the boys of Roslyn.

These were not all of them so intimate as the original four, nor did all go on the pleasant little tramps and expeditions, and occasional evening trips to the city to hear some fine singer or great orchestra; but they all were welcome to share the reading and the luncheons on Sunday afternoon, and all of them afterwards tramped their unabashed way into church with Miss Gracen Sunday night to pay for it. The minister eyed the growing company with interest and hopefulness. His own boy was becoming more thoughtful, more obedient, more attentive to his lessons and duties. Surely, this strange experiment Miss Gracen was trying in the goodness of her heart was not wholly a bad thing, even if she did give them things to eat on Sunday.

Also, they all shared in a good time about once a month, which Miss Gracen got up for them at her home, in which games, music, readings, mirth, and food were judiciously mingled. At such times the noises that arose from the staid and dignified Gracen mansion were such as to cause the elderly and respectable passers-by to look in horror and in wonder to see who was being murdered, and rag-time frequently vied with shrieks of laughter so loud that it reached clear down the street to Lydia Bypath's windows, which, in spite of the bitter cold that winter, she kept open a trifle on the evenings when Victoria Gracen's "wild mob," as she called them, were to meet for "another hullabaloo."

Lydia Bypath was biding her time, but she had not given up her one-time friend utterly to the error of her way. She meant to rescue her yet when the right time came, and until then she meant to keep well informed. Oh, if old Mr. and Mrs. Gracen could only look down from above and see the disgraceful actions that were going on in their dear old home, and how their daughter had become utterly foolish and reckless in her "obsession,"—yes, Lydia Bypath acknowledged in the secret of her soul that it was an obsession,—they surely could not be happy in heaven. It was not in Lydia Bypath's nature to enjoy having anybody happy even in heaven, when she was so wretched on earth.

But the climax came one day late in December when a beautiful blanket of snow had covered field, hill, and valley, and the boys, Tom, Dick, Harold, and Wayne, —for it was Saturday afternoon,—had coaxed their comrade, "Miss Vic," to go coasting with them.

They brought up their double-decker just at lunch-time; and about two o'clock they all started off to the hill at the back of the house; the long, gracious hill that lent itself to the snow in curves and bends and downward glides such as were not to be found anywhere else in that part of the country.

And Victoria Gracen enjoyed it as she had not enjoyed an afternoon since she was a girl. She wore an old gray serge dress, a white sweater, and a knitted woollen cap; her eyes were like stars and her cheeks like roses. She was having the time of her life. Her hair was all in a lovely tumble of misty white about her face; the little cap was set jauntily back on her head; and her face seemed to have grown ten years younger with the laughing and exercise.

At three o'clock sharp, Miss Bypath, having taken long counsel of herself in the night-watches and for many days, locked the door of her modest and respectable dwelling, and walked down the snowy path in her large, neat arctics, shuddering as the frosty air caught her thin nose and nipped it spitefully, for all the world in the same fashion as her words sometimes nipped other people.

Chapter XVI

It was not far to Victoria Gracen's house, and Lydia Bypath stalked up the steps—if so little a creature can be said to stalk—like a Nemesis come at last.

She was rather balked when Hiram told her that Miss Gracen was out and might not be back for some time. Hiram did not like Miss Bypath. It dated back to a time when his Molly was a little girl, and Miss Bypath had looked down upon her as a servant. He was secretly glad that his mistress was not in.

But Lydia Bypath was not easily balked. She demanded to know where her victim might be, and Hiram discreetly told her that she had gone out with her nephew, and hadn't intended coming back till suppertime.

Now, Miss Bypath was sharp; Miss Bypath was keen; moreover, from her little back-kitchen window she could easily see the small, black, bobbing specks of boys as they coasted down the Gracen hill. She knew the town and its habits. She knew that coasting was the order of the day among boys, and that the hill had been covered all the morning with many shouting, gesticulating, ridiculous, little black figures, "fooling their time away like apes," as she put it.

Moreover, her unusually sharp eyes had discerned the marks of a double-decker in the snow tramped about with many footsteps, going around the side of the house toward the pasture fence that led to the top of the coasting-hill; and at Hiram's second attempt to mislead her she looked down at those same footprints in the snow. Then she turned to the startled, easily abashed servant, and fixed him with her eyes, saying:

"Hiram, you don't mean to tell me that Miss Victoria Gracen has—*gone—coasting!*"

Hiram's sheepish face left no doubt in the matter, though he did not open his lips.

"Gone coasting with the boys at her time of life!" she fairly screamed.

Hiram stood mute.

"Hiram, conduct me to the spot. I have important immediate business with her. I say, conduct me to the spot at once."

But Hiram was rheumatic, and the thought of all the overshoes and mufflers he would be obliged to put on if Rebecca found out what he was going to do, as well as the impossibility of the idea of presenting himself to Miss Gracen with the disgrace upon him of having given away her secret to the enemy, was more than he could bear.

"Indeed, miss, you'll have to excuse me, miss; I've something very important to do in the house just now, miss. I can't say just which way Miss Gracen has gone, miss; but, if you follow the tracks through the meadow, I've no doubt you'll find her if she's there, miss."

And so with his most studied manner he managed to close the door upon her and not actually seem to have insulted her.

"Well, upon my word!" ejaculated the worthy woman. "I never thought it would come to this in the house of my friend!"

She studied the landscape for a little season, and then with an appealing glance at her trusty arctics she plunged into the snowy footprints, and wallowed bravely forth to the battle.

It was a long, hard struggle for the weak little respectable legs. The arctics were heavy, and her breath came painfully; but she managed it at last with only two or three actual falls, in which her inadequate cotton gloves dived helplessly into billows of cold feathers, and arose struggling with the snow that had gone up her sleeves. Each time she gathered herself from a fall she gathered more fury to her wrath; and her face was distorted with ugliness when she appeared at the top of the hill down which Miss Gracen, in all the glory of her wild dishevelment, in the seat of honor on the double-decker, with four tall gallants to guide and protect her, had sailed joyously away. Victoria Gracen should pay for this; O, *she should!*

And so in lonesome wrath she stood and awaited the return of her victim as she came, laughingly assisted by first one boy and then another, joyfully climbing back for another coast down the long hill.

They were almost two-thirds up the hill before Dick, looking up, discovered her, and gave a dismayed whistle of warning.

"Good-night!" he exclaimed, and then they all looked up quickly.

"Say, fellows," whispered Tom, nothing daunted, "let's put her on the sled, and give her a ride down the hill. That'll take the pep out of her all right. Come on, what do you say, boys?"

The three, Tom, Dick, and Harold, were off up the hill in a trice. Wayne happened to be conducting Miss Gracen, and until the boys rushed ahead with that peculiar air of having sudden urgent business neither of the two had seen the new arrival.

But, as Harold tore by Wayne, he murmured roughly under his breath:

"Get on to the skeleton at the feast?" and Wayne, looking up, saw Miss Bypath. His face overspread with the dark look that Miss Gracen had come to watch for that she might discover the cause; and she knew instantly that something was the matter, even before he exclaimed:

"Say, isn't she the limit?"

Looking up, she saw with dismay the small, gaunt figure in black, and realized her own tumbled hair and undignified employment.

Then almost instantly both she and Wayne knew what the boys intended to do, for they were shouting now at the top of their lungs:

"Come on, Miss Bypath; you're just in time. We'll take you down the next trip. The hill's fine and you'll have the time of your life. Just stand right still, and we'll put you on——"

"Oh, Wayne, don't let them!" exclaimed Miss Gracen. "They mustn't. They would frighten her to death. Go. Stop them!"

She took her hand from his strong arm, and pushed him forward; and Wayne, with a back glance of assurance at her, took long strides upward, shouting at the very top of his strong lungs:

"Cut that out, boys! Cut it out!" Though of course in the clamor his words were not heard.

Miss Bypath stood her ground in snow nearly a foot deep, and frowned ominously at the oncoming boys. At first she did not understand them; and then her ire rose with increased force at the indignity put upon her, a respectable woman. She did not think it worth while to answer them. She would crush them by ignoring them. But, when they made toward her with that fragile sled, and declared their intention of putting her on it and sending her down that fearful declivity, with its bumps and curves, and glistening, winding, ribbony track, panic seized upon her.

"Don't you dare to lay a finger upon me, you—you——" she screamed, and stamped her foot in its squashy arctic ineffectually in the deep, powdery snow.

Then to her excited imagination it seemed that Victoria Gracen was laughing at her, and that she had sent another boy to help them on in their disgraceful attempt to put her on the sled and ride her down that hill,—probably just so that Victoria might have company in her own disgrace.

If those four boys had been four fiends rushing on to drag her down to the bottomless pit, Lydia Bypath could not have picked up her respectable skirts with more expedition, nor made her thin ankles fly faster through the impeding snow. On she went, faster and faster, her breath growing shorter, her eyes blinded with the flopping veil which descended over her face, her arctics getting heavier and heavier, until, just as she was almost to the pasture fence where the bars were let down, she caught her foot against a bowlder that lay hidden under the blanket of snow, and went down full length, with her nose in the cold, cold snow: with snow up her nose, and snow in her eyes, and snow in her ears, and even, when she gave an involuntary cry, snow in her respectable, back-biting mouth. It was a terrible fall for both her pride and her body; and she lay there for a whole second, dazed and floundering, until the snow up her sleeves made itself felt, and she was impelled to rise.

The boys stood bent double, laughing at the grotesque figure as it fled across the snowy pasture; and even Miss Gracen had to smile at the precipitate flight of their guest when offered the entertainment of the occasion, albeit her smile had a shade of trouble in its wavering.

She arrived at the top just before Miss Bypath's downfall and just in time to hear Tom's disrespectfully expressed wish that he could wash her little, mean face for her in the snow.

"O, Tom," she said sorrowfully, "O Tom, that isn't right. You must not speak so about her."

"Aw, Miss Vic," said Tom, his face as red as his hair because he had been overheard, "I didn't know you were there; but indeed, Miss Vic, I can't bear that woman. You don't know all she's done to me all my life. Why, one time I was with some boys that stole her apples. I hadn't touched one. I was too little; I was just a real small kid; and she caught 'em at it, and chased 'em, and they got away; and so she grabbed me. I told her I hadn't touched her old apples, but she wouldn't believe me. She said I'd told a lie and she was going to punish me for it; so she took me into her kitchen, and got some soft soap and hot water, and washed my mouth out, for a lie she knew I hadn't told. I hadn't an apple, nor hadn't had, and *she knew it*. She's the meanest old thing alive."

"But she's a woman, Tom; and, O, see, she's fallen down! I'm afraid she's badly hurt."

It was Wayne who went with long, swift strides through the snow to her assistance, and went before there had been time to ask him to do it.

Lydia Bypath lifted her head fearfully from her cold,

feathery plunge, and gazed about her, gasping, brushing the snow from her eyes; and there close at hand was one of those terrible boys coming rapidly on.

Floundering and almost hysterical, she scuttled to her feet, and turning to face him, her frightened eyes flashing blue sparks, her shaking voice calling out:

"Don't you come another step toward me! Don't you dare to lay a finger on me! You bad, *bad* boy!"

"I was only coming to help you up," said Wayne haughtily, stopping at once. "Are you hurt?"

"Help me up? Yes, help me up! I understand what kind of help you would give me. I know who you are. Your father is in prison for committing a crime, and you'll be there some day yourself. You are a wicked boy. Don't you dare come another step!"

Wayne stood, tall, broad-shouldered, fine and handsome, facing her as she hurled the hideous words at him; and his face grew white with wrath. He clinched his fists hard inside his sweater pockets. If she had been a man, it would have gone hard with her that day; but she was only a foolish, cranky woman, and he was a gentleman; so he stood, and answered her not a word, with his hands held hard in his pockets, his chin held haughtily like a young king, his fine eyes looking steadily, blackly into hers. Something in their look warned her that she had said enough, for she turned shakily, and began to wabble and wallow her way out through the pasture to the road.

Wayne stood and watched her until she crept through the fence and made her way to a cleared path; then he turned, with darkness in his face and a tumult in his shadowed heart, and came back to the waiting group.

"She's a mutt!" he said, frowning, and that was all he said; but Miss Gracen knew that something very great had troubled the soul of her boy, and she set about thinking how she might heal the hurt.

They went on coasting, but Wayne laughed aloud in free enjoyment no more. He took his place solemnly, went silently down with the rest; was kinder and more thoughtful to Miss Gracen than ever, seeming to antici-

pate every little need and prepare for it; but he said
nothing, and at last Tom blurted out:

"What's the matter, Forrie? Where'd you get the
grouch? Lost your heart to Bydia Pylath?"

But Wayne only frowned, and did not answer.

Meantime, Nemesis, trembling, but still determined,
made her slow and tortuous way to the street and to her
own home. She was much shaken by her fright and falls,
and she was still trembling with anger; but she meant
now to let nothing stand in the way of her vengeance.
Those boys should meet with the punishment they deserved, and Victoria Gracen would have to take her disgrace along with them. She would hide Victoria's de-
grading "goings-on" no longer. They should come to
light and have the judgment of public opinion upon
them. Only public opinion could now save Victoria
Gracen from utter wreck and ruin.

She stole to her home, set the key in her lock, and
went in to put on some dry gloves and remove the extra
snow from her wrists and ankles. It took half an hour
to dry the inside of her arctics by the kitchen fire and
get on a set of dry sleeves throughout; then, fortified
by a cup of strong tea, the little vixen girded herself
up once more, and set out on her self-appointed mis-
sion down the street to the parsonage gate.

Now it happened that the minister had just returned,
cold and weary, from a far funeral in the country. He
had driven in the teeth of the wind twenty miles, over
roads that were still unbroken, and where sometimes
the only way to get on was to follow the tops of the
fences and get out and help the horse wallow through
the drifts. The harrowing scenes through which he had
passed at the house of mourning, and the long, hard
drive back, had taken his strength. His wife had just
brought him a cup of tea and a plate of delicious but-
tered toast made by her own hands, with a soft-boiled
egg invitingly dropped on the toast, when the door-bell
rang and Lydia Bypath entered.

The minister's slippered feet were slowly thawing in
front of the study fire, and he had taken but one bite

of the toast and one life-giving swallow of that tea; but the blundering maid, a farmer's daughter who was cheap and self-sufficient, ushered Miss Bypath into the sacred precincts of the study because the wily visitor had asked whether she might go right in where the minister was, as she had some very private business with him.

The minister was taken at a disadvantage. He saw in his visitor's eye keen disapproval of a mid-afternoon meal for a man who had a large parish and should have been at work. At a single glance she took in the dressing-gown and the slippered feet, the bright fire, and easy chair, and with a tone of implication said:

"Oh, I didn't know that you were ill, Mr. Atterbury."

"Not ill, Miss Bypath," said the minister with as good a grace as he could command, getting to his feet with the plate and cup in his hands. "I'm getting a bite after a long, dinnerless day. I've just returned from a funeral over at West Forks."

"Oh," perked Miss Bypath, ready for a bit of gossip before she opened up her budget, and quite prepared to study the contents of the minister's plate and report to the congregation how his wife fed him.

But the minister had no mind to eat his lunch under inspection, and with a courteous "You will excuse me for just a moment, Miss Bypath," he carried his comfortable lunch into the cold dining-room, gulped his cup of tea, took one bite of the delicately browned toast, and with a lingering, wistful glance at the rest went back to his caller. There had been that in Lydia Bypath's manner and eyes that indicated an unpleasant interview ahead, and he wanted to get it over as soon as possible.

He had, however, made nothing by carrying his plate away from her gaze, for she always doubled her animosity when people tried to escape her vigilance. Moreover, he had given her time to gather her shaken forces and prepare her initial remarks. She opened up fire even before the minister sat down, and her tone caused him to choose a stiff, hard chair by his desk rather than the comfortable seat in front of the fire. He would have need of his utmost dignity, he knew; for he had experienced calls like this from her before.

"Mr. Atterbury, the time has come for something to be done, and done quickly," she announced with righteous vehemence; "and, as your own eldest-born is involved in the disgraceful case, I thought it best to come straight to you with the matter."

This was the way she had begun on several former occasions when Tom had been supposed to have been stealing apples, smashing street-lights, or breaking windows with his ever-blameful ball.

The minister started, and sighed. He had been a little more comfortable about Tom lately, for no one had complained of him for six whole months. He had hoped the boy was beginning to grow up and leave behind some of his youthful sins and follies.

"I am very sorry to hear that my son has been getting into trouble again," said the minister gravely. "What is the charge you have to bring against him?"

"It is a most painful matter," wept Lydia Bypath, getting out her handkerchief and allowing the copious drops to trickle down her thin cheeks; "but I always do my duty by my friends, and I felt you must know at once——"

"Yes?" said the minister, preparing himself for the worst. He knew one could not hurry Miss Bypath in her preamble.

There was silence in the study, broken only by dramatic sniffs for a minute; then the caller raised her vindictive little eyes and in a half whisper that reminded the minister of a serpent's hiss, she told him.

Chapter XVII

"I HAVE been grossly insulted and ill-treated, Mr. Atterbury, this very afternoon, and by your son, in company with a lot of other good-for-nothing ruffians, —ruffians—it is the only word I can use to fully express what they are,—one of them the son of a common thief. I have only escaped as by a miracle from an actual assault, and I am so much shaken that I can scarcely tell the story calmly."

"You cannot mean that my son insulted you, Miss Bypath. I am sure there must be some mistake. Tom has been rather a mischievous boy, but I am sure he has always shown respect to ladies."

Miss Bypath lifted her tear-stained face impressively.

"Did you ever know me to tell a falsehood, Mr. Atterbury? You know that I am speaking the truth, and I am not mistaken. It was your son who started the whole thing, and who put the other—ruffians—up to giving me chase. I will tell you just how it happened, that you may understand the case; but you won't mind my breaking down, for I have been through a great deal, and am scarcely able to sit up." She eyed the big chair by the fire; but the minister sat up very straight, and took no hints. He wanted to hear the story to its finish now, and she was forced to go on.

"I have been very much troubled for weeks about my *dear* friend Victoria Gracen, and the disgraceful way in which she is going on. Of course, it is an infatuation, and at her time of life it is all the more pitiable. Mr. Atterbury, you have no idea to what lengths she goes. Why, the sounds that proceed from her house at all hours of the day and night whenever those wild, ungoverned creatures are let loose there are unbelievable! And Sundays! *Sun*days! Just think of it. They have regular feasts, I am told. Think of the old Gracen mansion harboring an orgy of wild, disreputable, *bad* boys on the Sabbath! And the respectable servants are obliged, I am told, to work harder on the Sabbath than on any other day to provide feasts for all this mob. I wonder they don't leave, I certainly do. Poor Victoria has no more idea than a babe in arms what she has brought upon herself, for the whole town is talking about her. They are using very severe expressions indeed; in fact, they are using words about her that are not at all nice" She lowered her voice to the hissing whisper again. "Obsession," she hissed; "that was the

word they used. They said she was *obsessed* with
boys. I wouldn't mention it if it weren't important that
you should know, being a minister of the gospel; and
of course you'll understand. I know, of course, that
some of the modern women are using it in their club
papers just to be fashionable; but I don't think it is at
all a pleasant word to use, and it breaks my heart to
have it used about my d-e-a-r—o-l-d—f-r-r-i-e-n-d."

Here she sobbed tenderly.

"But," raising her head and going at her duty again,
she went on, "you'll quite understand how I hated to
tell her; and I put it off, and put it off, hearing as I do
from my near vicinity the awful sounds almost every
night of the week, *not excepting the Sabbath*. They tell
me it is the kind of music used in saloons called 'the
rag.' I'm sure I can't understand how Victoria, being a
musician, ever brought herself to endure it. It drives
me into a sick-headache three doors away. Well, as I
was saying, I made up my mind to go and tell her all
this very afternoon; and I took my life in my hand, and
went through this light snow, and me with the lumbago
and neuralgia. But, when I got to her house, I found
her out. And *where* do you think she was? Why, Mr.
Atterbury, I couldn't have believed it. Even her faithful, old, man-servant was embarrassed, and wouldn't
tell me till I guessed and made him own up. *She was out
behind the house with a whole mob of boys sliding
down hill!* At her age, *sliding down hill!* Her hair was
all mussed up; and she had on a cap and mittens, just
like a giddy girl; and those boys were *helping her up the
hill as fine as you please,* just exactly as if she were one
of them; and she didn't seem to mind a bit! I tell you
this that you may see that she really needs somebody
to talk to her and make her understand. She's—I beg
your pardon—she's *obsessed;* that's what she really is."

She paused for appropriate shock to appear in the
minister's face; but instead a kind of sympathetic
gleam came into his eyes, and his face wore an inscru-
table expression, an unbiased watcher might even
have thought it a look of satisfaction. But the story
went on before he had opportunity to say anything.

"I saw her go sliding down that awful abyss." Miss Bypath had learned many hymns as a child, and occasionally utilized some of their vocabulary in her conversation. "I saw her with my own eyes, though I could scarcely believe my senses; and then, when she came back up the hill, those awful boys came ahead of her; and your son was ahead of them all. When he saw me, I grieve to say, he gave a shout of wicked glee, and ran at me with all his might, calling to me in the most insolent way, that now he was going to give me a ride, and threatening if I refused he would put me on his sled in spite of myself. Think of the outrage of even suggesting such a thing to a respectable woman like myself." Here the tears flowed freely. "And the worst of it was," she said, sobbing now with an "et-tu-Brute" manner, "that—my—dear—old—friend, who used to sit in the same seat in school with me, and give me apples and cake out of her lunch-basket, not only didn't stop them, but actually sent another boy, that son—of —a—forger, to chase me; and I'm sure she was laughing at my dis-dis-dis-comfiture."

Here her feelings completely got the better of her, and she sobbed outright.

The minister, who was having all he could do to control his facial muscles, attempted to interrupt with an "O, no, Miss Bypath, you're mistaken. Miss Gracen would never do that."

But she put in fiercely once more:

"No, you wouldn't think she would; but I tell you she's utterly changed. Utterly! Why, the other night I was there, and asked to see her alone; and she as good as told me that whatever I had to say I must say before that whole mob of *boys!* And your son, I regret to say, was present on that occasion also, and got off a very insulting remark about wish-bones to me. I have put up with a great deal from that boy through the years, but I felt that the time had come to make all known to his father——"

"But Miss Bypath," began the minister.

"Kindly let me finish my story," she went on with dignity, "and then I will leave the matter in your hands. They insulted me, as I was saying; and, when they found I resented their insolent language, they came at me to put me bodily on that awful sled of theirs! But for a miracle I might even now be lying, a ghastly spectacle, scattered in the valley by the creek."

It was not from his gentle mother's side of the family that Tom Atterbury had inherited his keen sense of the ridiculous, and there suddenly came over the minister such a strong desire to throw his head back and laugh that for an instant he felt it impossible to control it. The vision of severe, little Miss Bypath flying down the long Gracen hill and lying scattered over the snowy valley in many fragments seemed a possibility so grotesque that he was about to beat a hasty retreat from the room until he could bring his face into order again; but just then Miss Bypath terminated her effective pause, and began again.

"Now, it is not for myself that I have come to you; it is for the salvation of your son. When I remember Eli's sons, and the bears that ate the forty and four thousand children, I feel that I should be unpardonable if I did not bring this to your knowledge; and I know you will be grateful. It seems to me that the first thing you should do would be to stop your son's going to Miss Gracen's, and forbid his having anything more to do with those evil companions of his. A Sabbath-breaking crowd is no fit place for a minister's son, and I have been surprised at you for allowing him to go out on the Sabbath, though, of course, I suppose you did not know what he was doing."

It was not the first time since Mr. Atterbury had been pastor in Roslyn that Miss Lydia Bypath had attempted to teach him how to bring up his children. He had the meek and quiet spirit which knew how to take the thing sweetly and go on doing as he thought best in spite of it, but the warning she gave this time touched an uneasy spot in the minister's mind. He had never been satisfied about those companions of Tom's, nor quite happy about his going out every Sunday evening for supper. Several times he had questioned Tom, but always to have his worst fears allayed, and a shadow of hope for his boy's future raised in its place. Now, however, the vague uneasiness returned.

"Miss Bypath," he said kindly, when he saw she had quite finished, "I am sorry, indeed, that my boy has distressed and frightened you in any way. I shall talk with him about it as soon as he returns home, and I feel convinced that he will be able to explain his side of the matter so that the affair will be proved to be nothing worse than a mistaken attempt at fun. Tom has no unkindly feeling toward you. He is a kindhearted boy——"

"We do not always see into the hearts of those with whom we live the closest; the human heart is deceitful and desperately wicked," quoted the visitor righteously.

"And as for Miss Gracen's Sabbath afternoons," went on the minister ignoring her implication, "I have been given to understand that they are most orderly affairs. Miss Gracen reads to the boys, and they sing hymns; the feasts, I am told, are simple,—sandwiches and cookies and the like. I have really felt that Miss Gracen was most kind to try to help the boys in this way."

"*You have been given to understand,*" repeated Miss Bypath ominously. "May I ask *who* gave you to understand?" She faced the minister unflinchingly with her keen, little eyes, and read her answer in his guilty brown ones so like his son's.

"*Your son* gave you to understand, didn't he? Of course. Where else could you find out? And I am grieved to tell you that he has probably told you his own version of what goes on. Naturally he wants to keep up his Sabbath-breaking, and he knows he can't if you find it out. But let alone the question of whether you want your son to be a Sabbath-breaker or not, Mr. Atterbury; you surely don't want the whole town talking about you because you let your son take part in disorderly gatherings on Sunday. Mr. Atterbury, if those afternoons of Miss Gracen's are all right, why doesn't she invite *you* to come and speak to the boys? What right has she to set up a meeting in her house as if she were an opposition church? I should think you as her pastor would think it your duty to investigate, and I have come here this afternoon to demand as a member of your flock that you exercise your official duty over my friend Victoria Gracen, and go and find out what she is doing on Sunday afternoon."

"I have no doubt Miss Gracen would be quite glad to have me come in on one of her meetings if she were asked," risked the minister, trying to be evasive; but his caller caught him up quickly enough.

"Don't ask her for pity's sake," put in Lydia, the ferret; "just drop down upon her, and catch her in the midst of her folly. Then you will be able to speak to her from what you have seen. If you tell her beforehand, like as not there won't be a boy there, and everything will be as staid as the meetinghouse. Just go in there to-morrow afternoon after they all get there, and see for yourself. Come over to my house, and you can watch till they all go by, and you hear them sing the first song; and then you can be sure they're well started."

Miss Bypath's eyes gleamed with the excitement of the chase, as the old Pharisees' eyes must have twinkled when they were pursuing the Christians. She honestly thought she was doing God service by exposing Victoria Gracen's follies to the minister, who had a right to upbraid her and show her the error of her ways.

The minister sat calmly facing her, wondering how best and most quickly to send her on her way. At last he said gravely, quietly,

"Very well, Miss Bypath; I will do as you have suggested to-morrow afternoon, on one condition; and that is that you do not open your mouth on this subject to a living soul until I give you permission." He looked at her kindly but firmly, and she drew her breath in a quick gasp of disappointment.

She opened her mouth to speak, and shut it with a snap. Then she opened it again.

"But——"

The minister raised his hand.

"Miss Bypath, you have put this matter in my hands for investigation; and, if I am to deal with it, I want it absolutely left with me. I cannot consent to do anything about it unless you will be absolutely silent about the matter to every one."

"Do you mean that I mustn't mention the indignities that were put upon me by those evil boys, either?"

"I do."

"But isn't it right that people should know how bad they are?"

"I don't see what is to be gained by it."

"Don't you believe in punishing sinners?"

"Yes, but not necessarily in publishing their faults."

"But I tell you I had a bad fall, and got all wet with snow; and I expect I shall be very sick. I feel as though it were coming on now. I shall have to call in the doctor. I suppose you've no objection to my telling him."

"I must insist that you mention the matter to no one."

"What will the doctor think? I'll have to tell him something."

"Tell him you had a bad fall in the snow, and were frightened. He doesn't need to know anything else."

"But isn't that deception?" asked the little woman sharply.

"Not to tell him a lot of details that are not his business? No."

"You talk very heartlessly," sniffed Lydia; "but I suppose I don't understand the heart of a parent."

"Probably not, Miss Bypath. However, on this occasion I am not thinking so much of my son's reputation as of Miss Gracen's and I must insist on having this kept absolutely between us for the present."

With much dissatisfaction Miss Bypath arose to take her leave. She had not started the tremendous rumpus that she had expected, and it was quite flat to go home and keep still until to-morrow afternoon. Her heart burned hotly against her one-time friend and against those horrid boys who dared to ridicule her. To see them set up in high places where she would fain have been herself was more than she could bear. And yet, if

she would have her way and let the minister investigate,
she must do as he had bidden.

In silent but submissive wrath she went her grim way
home. Her thin limbs trembled more than when she
came, and her whole being was utterly used up. She
wanted nothing so much as to lie down and rest. The
tears weakly trickled down her faded cheeks, and yet
they were mad tears. She was outraged to the depths of
her respectable, embittered nature; and her hurt pride
demanded redress. She wanted with all her heart to
have Victoria Gracen suffer for it, suffer for the mortification she herself had passed through when she fled
through the snow and lay in a heap at the mercy of the
village boys, the echo of their ridiculing laughter ringing all about her.

So she crept to her home and her bed; and, as there
was no satisfaction in sending for a doctor who couldn't
be told the cause of her disaffection, she made some
herb tea and drank it, rubbed herself well with arnica,
and went to bed. Albeit the next morning, stiff and sore
though she was, she could not refrain from gathering
herself together and going to church just to see whether
Victoria Gracen would be there, and hear whether the
sermon would contain some covert hit at her goings-on.

The minister did not need to put his son through an
inquisitorial process to get his side of the story that
evening; he gave it freely and with many amusing vari-
ations at the supper-table.

"We offered her a ride, father," he said, his eyes
twinkling with the memory; "and you just ought to
have seen her beat it. I don't guess she'll chase Miss Vic
out to the meadow again in a hurry."

Plainly Tom had nothing to hide, and had apparently
told the whole story. The minister hesitated on the edge
of a reproof, and scarcely knew what to say, there were
so many subtle shades of difference between Tom's
story and Miss Bypath's.

Moreover, he did not at present wish to let the boy
know that Miss Bypath had been complaining to him.

"Were you entirely respectful to Miss Bypath, my
son?" queried the minister with a troubled look.

"Why, yes, dad," responded Tom heartily. "We were real cordial, and offered her a ride the minute she appeared on the scene."

"Wasn't it rather impertinent in you to do that, son, when you knew she would not care for that sort of thing? Would she not take it as a sort of insult, an attempt to hold her up to ridicule?"

Tom's innocent brown eyes looked roundly into those of his father.

"Why, dad, there wasn't any reason for her to take it that way. We'd have taken her down in great shape if she'd let us. I even offered to put her on the sled comfortably. Of course, she's no old sport like Miss Vic, but she might have been polite. We meant to show her a good time for once; we really did. Say, dad, wouldn't it have been great to see Miss Bypath sailing down the long hill? I bet it would have got into her blood after she once tried it, and you'd have seen her out on the sly, moonlight nights, sliding by herself. Miss Vic enjoyed every minute of the afternoon, and didn't mind a tumble any more than us fellows, though, of course, we didn't let her tumble much."

The minister suddenly asked a question which appeared to his son entirely irrelevant.

"What kind of a boy is Wayne Forrest?"

"He's all white, father. You'd like him; you really would," said Tom eagerly. "Miss Vic thinks he's great. She raves over his voice, and I certainly do like to hear him sing. He's polite and all that. You and mother would think he was *some*. He *thinks* to do all the little things you are always talking about, taking off hats and helping people. Why, he even ran ahead to try and pick up Miss Bypath when she fell over in the snow after she had been so impolite as to run away from us and call us names. Forrie was as mad as anybody at the way she acted, but he went and tried to pick her up; and then she wouldn't let him. She just reared up when he came near her, like a fishing-worm, and began to rave at him, till he got his chin up in the air, and stood back and let her get up herself. She told him not to dare to touch her, and she called him the son of a thief. He didn't know I heard her, and he never said a word about it when he came back; but we all heard enough to know she was reminding him of his father's disgrace. I tell you it was pretty tough on Forrie, but he came back and never said a word about it, just looked dark and had a grouch on the rest of the afternoon. Even Miss Vic couldn't bring him out of it, and he wouldn't hear to staying to supper, though she asked us. He went home and so we all did. He's an all-right fellow, dad. He seems to like to come to church now, too."

The minister walked his study that night for a long time, trying to make up his mind what to say to his son about apologizing to Miss Bypath, and finally decided to wait until the next day. He did not want to reprove him for nothing, neither did he want to do any half-way business if the boy really was to blame. He decided to investigate a little further, and perhaps have a conference with Miss Gracen before moving in the matter. It was his ability to look on the other side of a question which made some of his flock feel that he hadn't any backbone when certain pet hobbies of theirs were at stake. However, late that night, when he heard Tom starting up-stairs to bed after an evening of really hard study, he called to him.

"Tom, I feel troubled about your conduct toward Miss Bypath. I would like you to go to her sometime to-morrow and explain that you meant no discourtesy in offering her a ride on your sled."

Tom's face grew blank. "Oh, dad!" he protested. "She'll just flare up some more."

"Never mind; you will have done your duty. I shall feel concerned about the matter until you have made it right. Will you attend to it to-morrow?"

"Sure," said Tom, his ready cheerfulness coming uppermost. After all, he bore Miss Bypath no ill-will, and she had given them a good laugh. Why should he not explain if it pleased his father? He supposed it was pretty tough on her, getting all that snow up her sleeves and falling down, though she had no business to speak to Wayne Forrest that way; and his heart burned hot with wrath as he mounted the stairs to his room, pondering in his boy-way whether he could not work in a little reproof to her along with his own apology and explanation, and kill two birds with one stone. If his father could have known his thoughts, he might not have sat down to his belated sermon with quite so easy a mind. However, Tom was not all bad, and he really meant to make it right with Lydia Bypath, even if he did intend to give her a few facts concerning her own conduct which he felt she ought to know.

The household slept. The minister finished his sermon, and knelt to pray for a blessing on his work of the morrow, and to plead that the task of investigating the matter of Miss Gracen's boys might not be so difficult as it seemed at present; then he went up-stairs to his well-earned rest.

Two miles out on a lonely, country road in the little, cold attic chamber a strong boy tossed on his bed, and his heart burned hot within him over the words of shame that had been flung at him by a woman's lips that afternoon. In the darkness hot, scorching tears burned their way into his eyes. His father! Oh, his father! Why had he sinned and left such a heritage of shame for his son and daughter when he went to pay his penalty by a living death? Was there a God, as Miss Gracen had almost made him believe? And, if there was, why did He let such things happen to people who were not in the least to blame?

Chapter XVIII

Miss Gracen was in her place in church that morning, with the boy Richard by her side; and a few minutes later, just as the first hymn was being announced, Harold Constable came hurriedly up the aisle as if he were being waited for, and, slipping past Dick and Miss Gracen, sat down on the other side of her. It was the first time he had been to church in the morning, and Miss Gracen gave him a radiant smile in welcome. Ly-

dia Bypath took that smile as a personal insult. Next
to the minister's son and the forger's son she hated this
child of a wealthy and snobbish mother who never
recognized her on the street, nor asked her to any of
her teas, though they had been members of the same
club for five years or more.

The minister from his seat in the pulpit noted the
look of devotion on the boy's face, and knew without
being told that he had come to church to please Miss
Gracen. Involuntarily Mr. Atterbury glanced toward
Miss Bypath to see whether she had noticed; and he
caught the gleam of hatred in her face, and sighed as
his Lord might have done over the Pharisees, who
paid their tithe of mint, anise, and cumin.

When service was out, he took special pains to shake
hands with Harold Constable. Something in the hearty
grasp of the lad's hand as he said in his easy way,
"Good-morning, Mr. Atterbury; thank you; I enjoyed
being here," gave him a thrill of new hope for his
ministry. What if such young fellows as this would give
their lives to Christ and come into the church and
serve the Kingdom? How wonderful it would be! What
if his own Tom would some day love and serve the
Lord?

He smiled understandingly at Miss Gracen as she
murmured her pleasant "Good-morning," and knew
that the joy in her eyes was because the Constable boy
had been in the morning service.

"I'm glad you preached just that sermon this special
morning," she murmured in a low voice as she passed
him; and her eyes sought significantly the handsome,
curly head just in front of them.

The minister had asked for light about the investigation he was to make that afternoon, and it would seem
as if the heavenly Father were answering his prayer in a
very special way that day. As he walked slowly and
thoughtfully from the church study, where he had been
detained by one of his elders in a few minutes' conversation, he came up with Mr. Constable, who in high silk
hat and Prince Albert coat, with a long cigar, a white
bulldog, and a quaintly gnarled cane for company,

was taking a Sunday stroll. Indeed, it seemed that Mr. Constable actually halted, and turned to wait for the minister, instead of hurrying by and ignoring him, as was his custom. Mr. Constable had little use for churches and ministers in his life.

"Good-morning, Mr. Atterbury, good-morning," he greeted him. "Fine morning for the middle of winter, isn't it? Too bright to stay indoors. Had a big congregation this morning, didn't you? I think I saw my son coming out. Well, it can't hurt him. Pretty good place to pass away the time for a boy of that age. Since his mother's away I guess the boy does about as he pleases. But I'm glad to see he's taking an interest in church. I used to when I was a boy, myself; had to go, in fact, every Sunday, and got enough of it to last the rest of my life, ha, ha!" He laughed as if the joke were a good one. "But it's different when a boy goes of his own free will. I'm glad to see Harold taking an interest. That young Gracen's a nice sort; seems like his father before him. I remember what a good ball-player he was. Miss Gracen's got a lot of sense about boys. My boy's quite stuck on her. She makes her home very attractive for them. Harold thinks there's nobody like her. By the way, I want to make a contribution to the church if my son is to share in its benefits."

He put his hand into his pocket and drew out a long wallet, selecting two bills of large denomination and handing them to the bewildered Mr. Atterbury.

"Just take those, and use them where they're most needed, won't you? And, when you've any special call for more, just let me know. I'll be glad to contribute regularly. Good-morning. I'm glad my boy Harold is taking an interest in the church. I wish I'd done so myself when I was young."

And the portly gentleman touched his hat and turned down the avenue before the minister could recover from his surprise sufficiently to thank him.

It happened that the home-mission collection for that month had been very small indeed, and the minister had been troubled in his own heart about how he could afford to swell it to less mean proportions out of his own slender "tenth," which often stretched and stretched until it became more like a fifth than a tenth.

While he was eating dinner, there came a call for the minister to come at once to an old man who was dying just on the outskirts of the village; and whom should he meet as he came out of the house after his call was made but Wayne Forrest?

Wayne's brow was still dark and his eyes were burning unhappily. He had almost made up his mind—not quite—to stay away from Miss Gracen's house that afternoon, just from the memory of those awful words of Miss Bypath's. If he had known the minister was to open that door and come out to the road at the moment he was passing, he would have gone miles out of his way to avoid the meeting. He frowned now, and tried to hasten his steps, hoping the minister would not know him; but Mr. Atterbury held out his hand with a smile of greeting. Here was another answer to his prayer, another opportunity to find out about Miss Gracen's work among her boys.

"Well, Forrest, glad to see you," he said, grasping the reluctant hand the boy held out. "I've been hearing good things about you from my son. He is telling me what a fine voice you have. Going down to the village? That's good; then I shall have company."

Wayne's brows lowered. He did not want to walk with the minister, but there seemed no choice; yet, strange to say, they had not been walking together five minutes before he forgot his gloom, and was laughing. The minister had a way with him that reminded him of Tom, and Wayne was surprised out of himself.

When Mr. Atterbury referred to his singing again, the boy answered half shyly:

"Oh, my voice isn't much; it's only that Miss Gracen likes it, I guess. I just sing a little to please her. I never sing for any one else."

"She's a great little woman, isn't she?" said the minister leadingly; and before he knew it Wayne was telling some of the things she had done for him. She was helping him to keep up with the school studies, so that if opportunity offered he could go to college some day.

"Of course I can't ever go to college," added the boy as if it were a joke; "but it's rather interesting to get ready. I want to know all the things, anyway; and what's college, after all, if you know as much?"

"That's a sensible way to look at it," said the minister; "still, college is college, and there are ways to go, you know. Keep on getting ready. Maybe one will come your way."

"No chance of that ever for me," said the boy gruffly, kicking a block of frozen snow out of his way. "My life's cut out all the way ahead."

The minister, studying the fine, strong, sad face of the boy, was stirred as Miss Gracen had been, and decided that Tom had been right. He did like Wayne Forrest. His heart burned within him that Lydia Bypath had dared to hurt him by a reference to his father.

Mr. Atterbury linked his arm in the boy's as he might have done with his own son, and so walked into town with him; he might have preached at him, but he didn't. All he said was: "Maybe not, maybe not. We can't always see ahead;" and then he led him to talk of other things and of Miss Gracen's Sabbath afternoons until they reached the parsonage, and the boy's eyes lighted with pleasure in saying good-bye as the minister told him how glad he had been to see him in church, and how he should enjoy him all the better as a listener now that he knew him as a friend.

He had rather planned to stop at Miss Gracen's on the way home from his call, but it seemed unwise to do so in Wayne Forrest's company; moreover, Wayne had made no move to go into the Gracen gate himself. It was probably too early for the meeting to have begun. So Mr. Atterbury sat by his study window, watching behind the curtain until he saw Wayne Forrest return with Harold Constable and two other boys and whistle softly for Tom, who presently joined them. They went down the street together. Even then he paused, and waited a half-hour, kneeling by his old study-chair for guidance in this most delicate matter that he was about to undertake.

Out in the street again he perceived a large gray-haired man across the road, who took especial pains to bow to him, and finally, after hesitating, crossed over at the next corner and walked with him. He was a contractor, and anything but a religious man. He had never had much use for Mr. Atterbury before, and had always gruffly declined the various invitations to church the minister had given him; but now his ruddy countenance was beaming.

"Pleasant afternoon," he said, and adjusted his gait to the minister's.

Mr. Atterbury, much surprised, answered him affably, and wondered inwardly at the changed manner of his companion.

"Say, you got one member of your church that's an A No. 1 Christian all right," was his next remark.

"Is that so?" laughed the minister. "Which one is that?"

"Well, there ain't but one like her," said the man, "and from all I hear tell she's doin' fer your son same's she is fer mine; so I've no need to mention her name. I think you know who I mean."

The man's heart was so evidently overflowing with pride that his son should even be counted in the same category with the minister's that it was impossible to resent the implication of the words; besides, Mr. Atterbury knew that Tom's life had not been exemplary in all ways; so he responded most heartily:

"Oh, is your son one of those who go to Miss Gracen's house? She seems to be giving them delightful times there. Does he enjoy it?"

"Enjoy it! I should ruther guess he does," said the man heartily; "why, he can't talk of nothin' else from mornin' to night when he's home. It's, 'Ma, don't fergit to have me a clean shirt fer to-night, 'cause I hev to go to Miss Gracen's,' er, 'Ma, you'd jus' oughter make some cake oncet like Miss Gracen's Rebeccer made last week.' He's took to singin', too. I guess he ain't got much voice, but it sounds real cheerful round the house;

and he reads a lot. I don't think myself he keers much about books, but he'll do any old thing fer her. Why, he's even took to goin' to church nights. I guess you've noticed."

The minister remembered that this man's stolid, young son had been of the group that Miss Gracen marshalled into service last week.

"You see," he went on volubly, "he ain't much fer church, bein' as he never cared fer settin' still much; but he says it's only right he should do it when she asks. She don't just say they sha'n't come to Sunday meetin' else they do, but he says as how that's the only way they know they can sorter pay her back fer all she does fer 'em—that an' bringin' the other fellers. They seem to set a big store by that there Sunday meetin'. My son's just went. Well, so-long. Guess I turn off here."

The minister walked on more slowly toward the Gracen house.

When he opened the gate, a burst of song greeted him clear and strong from rich, deep, boy voices,

> O Love that wilt not let me go,
> I rest my weary soul on Thee;
> I give Thee back the life I owe,
> That in Thine ocean depths its flow
> May richer, fuller be.

He paused half-way up the walk, and caught his breath. There was something in the song that touched his soul—an appeal, a wonder, and a prayer. How they could sing! Surely no one could object to music like this on the Sabbath.

He looked cautiously up at the front windows, but saw no sign of any heads or eyes looking out. They were all engaged in singing. He stepped shyly up on the porch, and for the first time it struck him that his presence there at that hour might almost be regarded as an intrusion. His son would be likely to regard it as such, he was sure, and perhaps resent it.

This thought struck him as he placed his finger on the electric bell, and caused him to half withdraw it even as he heard the ringing of the bell in the distance. If he had not rung already, perhaps he would have turned and gone softly down the steps and out of the gate again without entering; but now he must at least wait until some one came, or he might be caught stealing away from the door.

The second verse of the song rolled on more distinctly now; for he was nearer, and he noticed that a window in the front was part way open.

He forgot to think what he should say when he got inside, for his mind was filled with the words of the song uttered with so much feeling from these unaccustomed voices. It made his heart thrill to think of such boys singing such words, and his son among the rest. He wished Miss Bypath could hear this singing. What could she have meant by her strange account? But then, of course, she was too far away to distinguish what songs they were singing. He glanced down the street at the old brick house, shabby and staid with its stiff, box-bordered path and its two silver poplar-trees rustling dismally in the clear winter air, and frowned at the thought that he had been obliged to come on this most unpleasant errand because of its owner's whim. He began to feel himself in an awkward position.

Then the front door opened silently. Hiram stood with question in his eyes, and the minister felt still more out of place.

"Is Miss Gracen in?" he asked, purely out of habit, for he had not thought what he would do.

"She's in, sir, yes, sir," murmured Hiram almost in a whisper, "but she's havin' her boys. I could call her?" He put the suggestion as though it were a precedent scarcely to be thought of.

"Don't call her, Hiram," said the minister, catching at the chance; "I won't disturb her now. I'll come in another time. It was just a little matter I wanted to speak to her about. I'll stand here a minute, and hear them sing; and then I'll go on——"

"Step inside, sir," said Hiram with pride. "You can sit in the dark of the alcove in the hall, sir, and never be seen. That singer fellow'll likely be having a solo in a minute or so. I'll put a chair in the shadow, and you can set as long as you like, and slip out when you get tired, without their ever knowing you're here."

Hiram set the chair with absolute silence, and the minister like a culprit in a crime slipped into it and kept silence, listening to song after song that rang full and strong from the chorus. They were grouped around the piano, he could see from his sheltered alcove; and his own son stood in their midst, with an arm over Dick's shoulder on the right and another over Harold's on the left. Then Wayne Forrest, standing close to the piano, sang alone; and the minister's heart stood still for a moment with the wonderful thrill of the voice in its plaintive appeal from the depths of a soul that had suffered. Where had the boy gained the sympathetic tone and clearness of expression that sent every word he sang home to the heart of the hearer?

> O Jesus, Thou art standing,
>   Outside the fast-closed door
> In lowly patience waiting
>   To pass the threshold o'er.

There was that in the song that held the little company perfectly quiet as they sank into the chairs around the room, and a hush settled over them. When the song was finished, to the minister's surprise, there followed a prayer.

"Dear Father, be in our midst this afternoon, and show us how to find Thee. Let the songs we sing be acceptable praise, and open our hearts to hear whatever message Thy word shall bring us. May we none of us be left out in the blessing Thou hast for us. In Jesus' name we ask it. Amen."

It startled him to hear Miss Gracen's voice. She had always begged to be excused from taking part in public meetings, though he knew she sometimes led in prayer at the women's missionary meetings; but here in her home, among these strange boys, whom no one else

seemed able to reach, and whom no one cared to
try to, she spoke to God as a man speaketh to his friend,
face to face. He glanced across the hall and into the
room where the light of the afternoon flooded the scene
and showed the bowed heads and closed eyes. Not a
boy was staring about. All was quiet and reverent.

They sang again, lustily, and then there came the
Bible reading. Tom had never divulged the fact that
the word of God was a part of their afternoon reading.
The minister sat astonished, and listened while the
leader read the story of Elisha at Dothan with his
frightened servant who reported the surrounding of the
city by the Syrian host, and of the opening of his eyes
to see the hosts of God with their chariots and horses
of fire in a multitude upon the mountain, ready to de-
liver them. A few illuminating explanations were given
as she went on with the reading, but most of the explanation and vividness of the story was due to the
remarkable reading it received. The reader then turned
to the story of the blind man healed, as told by John,
and read it as though it had been a drama, until the
Pharisees, the neighbors, the father, the mother, and
the blind man lived and moved and spoke before the
audience. There was a tense stillness in the room when
the Pharisees had cast the man out and Jesus came and
found him.

Miss Gracen closed her book, and said just a few
words about three kinds of blindness in the chapter they
had read—a blind follower of God who couldn't see
God's help all about, ready to sustain him; a blind soul
who had never known the light and could not understand what he was missing; blind Pharisees who had
every reason to see aright, yet chose to be blind. There
was no preaching about her words, but the minister felt
that each boy listening knew he was included somewhere in that list of blind people who might receive
sight.

It was a strange study to watch those boys through
the wide-open doorway, as they sat about the room absolutely quiet, either watching their leader intently, or
gazing off thoughtfully through the window, or sitting

with closed eyes. The boy Wayne was exactly opposite the door, and his keen eyes were fixed upon the reader as though he might miss a word if he took them off; and all the sorrow, anguish and disappointment of his life, with all the hopeless longing, seemed to come and sit in his face unrebuked as he listened. It was as if he had caught a glimpse of the light somewhere, and had forgotten himself.

As the afternoon waned, the hall grew darker; and the minister in his quiet corner dared watch the interesting group. Harold silently arose to turn on the electric light, while Dick touched a match to the fire laid in the fireplace; and firelight and electricity made visible all the little audience to the interested watcher in the hall.

There was a stir in the other room as Miss Gracen closed her book and went to the piano. They were going to sing again. But Tom Atterbury's voice broke in, and hushed them to stillness.

"Miss Gracen, you said the other day when you were reading about Saul that everybody sometime in his life got a vision of Christ, or a call to serve Him. I'd like to ask you if you think they have to wait for that, and how do you think it comes? Does everybody know it? Is it always something big and startling like lightning, or is it sometimes just a kind of conviction?"

Something strange and queer gripped the minister by the throat. He didn't sense the answer that was given, except to know afterwards that it had been all that it should have been. He only felt the voice of his dear, mischievous, hard-to-manage eldest son, whose life was entwined about his heartstrings in a more than common love. His boy, his bad boy, was asking a question like that, and asking it as if he really cared about the answer! Oh, had his boy heard any slightest call, seen any glimpse whatever of the light that shines in the face of Jesus Christ?

He did not know it; but he sat all during the hymn that followed with tears streaming down his face, sat in the dark alcove weeping and praying for his boy, and for these other boys; and for this woman who was so quietly and wonderfully ministering to them all.

After the song they all settled down in their chairs again, and Miss Gracen read several chapters in Elizabeth Stuart Phelps Ward's remarkable story, "A Singular Life." It appeared that they had all heard the beginning and were deeply interested in the story, and it also appeared that the reader had selected her chapters, and was sketching what came in between with remarkable skill, omitting some parts that might have been merely worldly, or touching lightly upon them, but gathering up the thread of the story in such a way that the one central figure of the man, the "Christman," of the story stood out before them.

It occurred to the minister that he ought to get away before he was discovered; but this was no time to make his escape, for the room was so quiet that any sound from the hall would attract attention. He must wait until they sang again, and were all standing around the piano with their backs to the door. So he heard the story too, and saw the tray approaching at last, with Hiram carrying it as though it were a sacrament; although he did not know that the old servant had sat just within the back-hall door with it open a crack, and enjoyed the whole service as much as any of the boys.

He made his escape out into the clear winter dusk with the tears still wet upon his cheeks, and a song of thanksgiving within his heart which rivalled the song, "It is well with my soul," that rang out from the lighted parlor as the meeting came to its close. A moment he lingered outside the window, and, watching, saw his son among the rest; saw him courteously handing a cup of something steaming hot to his hostess and smiling adoringly down upon her in her cushioned chair by the window. Then he turned and hurried home to tell the boy's mother what he had seen and heard.

And Lydia Bypath, watching, ferret-like at her front window, after her long afternoon's vigil, saw with mortification that he was not coming in to report to her!

Chapter XIX

THE minister entered the pulpit that evening with a glorified expression on his worn face that made him almost look young again. He glanced down at the double row of boys surrounding Miss Gracen and saw their faces in the light of the afternoon's revelation. Heretofore he had looked upon most of them as so many hindrances in the way of his son's living a right life; now he saw them as immortal souls awakening to the call of the Christ, and his heart was filled with a great desire to say some word, leave some thought, which would help them to make the great decision.

Wayne Forrest looked up, and caught his eye, with a gleam of recognition; and the minister smiled slightly, with just a suggestion of a nod. Lydia Bypath, stiff and sore, sitting erect in her pew, saw it all, and fairly glared. If the boys had seen her, they would have said, "She certainly has it in for the minister." But fortunately the boys did not see her. They sat quietly, reverently, joining in the hymns with a vigor that made the dear, old senior elder turn and look at them approvingly more than once; and the only disturbance that arose in their company was the silent scuffle that went on over every hymn, each boy trying to be the first to give Miss Gracen the book with the place found. This explained the few quick smiles and nudges and winks that Lydia Bypath rolled as a sweet morsel under her tongue as she sat by, looking on. Oh, she certainly "had it in" for that minister!

The sermon that evening was short and plain, with two or three brief illustrations that had come to the minister during his two hours' reflection in Victoria Gracen's hall alcove,—striking stories in themselves and leading up to the great thought of self-surrender. They caught and held the boys' attention, and deepened the impression made by the afternoon meeting. When ser-

vice was over, the boys went down the aisle more slowly
than usual, and gathered affably about the minister at
the door, perhaps because Wayne stood talking easily
to him as if he had been an old friend. There was a new
look of friendliness about the minister that the boys
were quick to appreciate and expand under.

But behind them, grim, forbidding, with pursed lips
and snapping eyes, stood Lydia Bypath awaiting her
turn; and every word the minister spoke to every boy
was an offence in her eyes, because she knew he saw
her standing there waiting, and he ought to have sent
them off instead of smiling at them in that ridiculous
way, "encouraging them in their conceit," she called it.

But at last Miss Gracen and her escort moved out of
the church door; and Mrs. Atterbury, turning from her
kindly inquiry about the janitor's baby, saw Miss Bypath approaching her husband, and knew they were in
for another half-hour at least.

"You have something to tell me, Mr. Atterbury," she
challenged, as the minister closed the outer door and
turned back to his study to get his coat and hat.

"Oh, why, good evening, Miss Bypath," said the
minister cordially, yet fencing for time. "Let me see,
you wanted to know about the boys' meetings, didn't
you? Yes, well, suppose you come into the study,
where it is a little warmer. It makes this room cool
off quite suddenly to have both those doors wide open
on such a sharp night, doesn't it?"

The minister led the way up the aisle to the study
back of the pulpit, and motioned to his wife to come
with him.

Miss Bypath followed perforce, remarking that some
people kept the door open unnecessarily long, it
seemed, on Sunday night. They might do their visiting
and laughing on another evening, to her way of thinking. It dispelled the solemn influence of the service to
allow a lot of gossip after it was over. For her part——

But the minister broke in upon her reflections with a
cordial "Sit down, Miss Bypath. Here's Mrs. Atterbury. She's interested, too. I've just been telling her be-

fore service what a wonderful time I have had this afternoon. I really can't thank you enough for leading me to make this investigation."

For an instant Miss Bypath's firm jaw relaxed in pleased surprise, and she straightened herself proudly, and flashed an "I-told-you-so" gleam into her eyes; but the minister hastened on quickly.

"I must tell you that you have been entirely mistaken regarding the gatherings held at Miss Gracen's. There is nothing whatever objectionable about them; and on the contrary, the work that Miss Gracen is so quietly doing is led, I believe, by the Holy Spirit, and is being greatly blessed. I am glad to be able to tell you that there is a most reverent attitude among the boys and that some of them are really in earnest in trying to live better lives."

"Who told you this?" burst forth Miss Bypath with flashing eyes.

"No one told me; I heard and saw for myself, and the sight was one I shall never forget. I do not feel at liberty to tell more about it, Miss Bypath, save to say that you, as a member of this church, have reason to kneel and thank our heavenly Father that He has put it into the heart of Victoria Gracen to give her time and thought to work for these boys. I believe our church and our town will be the better in the years to come for what she is doing; and, if more people could devote their time to cultivating the young human souls all about them, the world would be a better place in which to live. I think it would be well, Miss Bypath, for you to say nothing further to any one about this matter."

"Indeed," said Miss Bypath, rising with offended dignity, "I shall do my duty, whatever anybody else does. I suppose that because your son goes there he has been able to pull the wool over your eyes and make you think black is white; but, Mr. Atterbury, there are people who know; and this is a serious matter. I do not intend to be insulted by your son or any other boy, and keep perfectly quiet. If you will not do something about it, I will; and as for Victoria Gracen, she is making herself simply ridiculous, and I do not feel that it is my duty to shield her any longer. It is time such doings were shown up. If your eyes are blinded, too, it is all the more necessary that some one speaks."

Then up spoke little, quiet Mrs. Atterbury.

"Miss Bypath, our son Thomas had no idea that he was insulting you yesterday. He asked you to ride in genuine earnest, because he says he wished to be polite to you and give you as pleasant a time as the boys were giving to Miss Gracen."

It is possible that even Tom himself would have opened his wide brown eyes in surprise over his mild, credulous little mother's faith in him; but there would have been a tender gleam in them for her for taking his part, and there is this to be said: Tom's mother always believed the very best of him, and she honestly thought that what she was saying about her son was true. His father saw through many of his pranks and pretenses, but his mother never did. Perhaps this was one reason why Tom had found it so exceedingly easy to tread the downward path of mischief and madness, because his mother believed in him, whatever he did, and never saw any harm in him.

But Lydia Bypath was not one to allow any illusions to remain if she could help it. She turned upon the small, meek woman, like the little fighter that she was, and fairly spluttered in her rage:

"Polite! Trying to be polite! Now, Mrs. Atterbury, don't you know any better than that?" she screamed. "That boy wouldn't be polite to anybody in the world, and he just hates me because he knows that I won't stand his nonsense. There's none so blind as those that will not see. As for you, Mr. Atterbury,"—she turned to the minister with a withering glance,—"as for you, I'm compelled to believe that you are as bad as Victoria Gracen yourself. I think you have become *obsessed*."

Miss Bypath drew her small figure to its greatest height, and sailed out of the minister's study. The minister turned troubled eyes to his wife, who was quietly weeping into her handkerchief.

"Never mind, dear," he said gently, putting his hand tenderly on her shoulder. "It really doesn't matter what she says. Let us be glad over the change that is coming to our boy. Come; we will go home, and I will tell you all about that wonderful meeting. Do you think I ought to confess to Miss Gracen how I sat in her hall and looked and listened this afternoon?"

And so he comforted his timid wife, and soon had her smiling again.

Mrs. Atterbury went up-stairs to see whether the younger children were tucked safely into bed; and the minister went to his study window, and stood looking out on the moonlit snow and thinking of the earnest boy faces he had seen that afternoon. A great longing for his own boy filled his heart.

And just then he saw them come up the street, Tom, Harold and Wayne, whistling in soft, clear harmonies the song they had sung that afternoon for closing, "It is well with my soul."

Tom turned in to his own home, and the other two went on, calling, "Good-night" in joyous, care-free tones. Was it imagination, or did the minister catch a note in their voices of better intent than had sounded there at other times when he had heard them thus?

Tom came into the house still whistling softly, and, glancing into the study saw his father by the window.

"Hello, dad!" he called, and there was a ring of genuine pleasure in his voice.

"Hello, son," said the father, turning toward him quickly and smiling.

"Say, dad, that was a real good spiel you had to-night. The fellows liked it."

"Thank you, son," said the minister, almost choking with sudden emotion, and throwing his arm across the boy's shoulders lovingly.

The boy stood thus for a moment, half shyly, as if there was something he would like to say, but could not. At last he drew his father up to the window again, and they stood together looking out. It touched the minister beyond anything the boy had ever done before since he was a little fellow. For of late Tom had rather avoided his father's company, having always some escapade to hide or some delinquency to cover. But to-night he seemed to like just to stand there quietly with the man's arm around his shoulders.

"Dad," said Tom almost inaudibly, "when's the next communion?"

The father almost started with the joy and the hope in his heart.

"Six weeks from this morning," he answered, and tried not to show his agitation. "Why?"

"Oh, I don't know," said the boy evasively, "I was just thinking." He paused, and the silence was deep between them as they gazed out into the moonlight. Then the boy's voice in slow, hesitating drawl took up the sentence again. "I was just thinking—Miss Gracen's been reading us a lot of things—I was just wondering—if maybe I wouldn't like to join church sometime——"

The father's arm tightened about his shoulders.

"Son, you know what it would mean?"

"I think—I—do," came the slow answer.

"You know it would mean making your life fit your profession."

"Yes, sir; that's where the rub comes in. I'm not sure I could do it."

"You'd not have to do it alone."

"I know," said the boy seriously, and then after a pause, "I know," and breathed it reverently.

"Oh, my dear son," said the father deeply, tenderly; and then they stood a long time together silently. At last the boy turned to go up-stairs.

"I don't know, dad," said the boy shyly; "I haven't got it all doped out yet. But I'm thinking about it. I thought I'd better tell you."

"My son, you know this has been my wish, my prayer for years, your mother's and mine."

"Yes, I know, dad. Good-night."

The boy caught his father's hand, and pressed it hard; then, flinging it from him, hurried up the stairs, whistling again and breaking softly into the words,

My sin—O, the bliss of this glorious thought—
    My sin, not in part, but the whole,
Is nailed to His cross, and I bear it no more,
    Praise the Lord, praise the Lord, O my soul.

The father could hear him moving around in his
room above and singing the chorus.

It is well, it is well with my soul.

And this was the boy that Lydia Bypath thought was
past all redemption!

Yet, when Tom Atterbury first sang that song at
Miss Gracen's house, he used to sing it with a twinkle
in his eyes, and come out loud and clear in the chorus
with his deep rumble of bass; and the words that he
sung were these:

It is *swell*, it is *swell* with my soul.

The change in the chorus had come to express the
change in the whole attitude of the boy.

By and by it was very quiet up in Tom's room. His
father was still standing by the study window, looking
out on the white moonlit world. He was thinking about
his son. Then again he heard the stir and moving about
up-stairs, and the soft echo of that chorus,

It is well, it is well with my soul.

as the boy threw up his window and jumped noisily
into bed. A startling thought came to his father. Had
the boy been praying during that silence overhead?
Something thrilled through his soul like unto no joy that
had ever come to him yet in his ministry. His own son
praying, trying in his awkward, boyish way to "dope"
out the matters of eternity, and to adjust his own shy,
fun-loving soul to God and the great plan of salvation.
Could it be?

The father stole softly up-stairs, and listened a moment by his son's door. Then, as he heard no sound,
he softly opened the door and slipped in, tip-toeing over

to the bed. The boy was asleep already, his happy, healthy body yielding quickly to the pillow and the darkness. And there in the quiet room, with the moonlight in a long pathway across the carpet at his feet, the minister knelt beside his eldest-born, with his hand upon the boy's head, and prayed as he had never prayed before for his son.

It was just a little more than three weeks from that time that Lydia Bypath broke her leg.

"Gee! Wasn't it lucky she didn't break it the day she did that sprinting stunt down in the meadow?" exclaimed Harold Constable when he heard of it. "We'd have been in wrong forever after, sure, if that had happened. Gee! I'm glad she waited three weeks. She'd have tried to blame us with it if it had happened the same week."

"I should worry," answered the others in chorus with that peculiar shrug that expresses so forcibly the self-centered life.

Only Wayne Forrest had stood still, frowning, and said nothing. For it all happened in this way.

Tom Atterbury on his way to attend the Friday-evening frolic at Miss Gracen's was called back by his mother to take a bundle of clothing for the missionary box which was being packed by Miss Bypath, who was in charge of the box work in the missionary society. The bundle contained a dozen pairs of new stockings for the missionary and his wife, sent by an absent church-member to the minister's wife to put into the box. Mrs. Atterbury was anxious to have it get to Miss Bypath that night before the box was nailed up, and so called Tom back, and gave him directions.

When Tom again reached the snowy street, he heard a peculiar whistle that caused him to halt and wait until a dark figure in the distance caught up with him. It was Wayne Forrest.

"Say, At, did you remember to call up Brownie and give him Miss Gracen's message about that lantern she wants to borrow for the pictures to-morrow night?" he asked as he came up.

"Great Scott! No, I didn't," said Tom. "Say, Forrie,

you just run back and phone from the drug-store for me, won't you? I've got to do an errand for mother before I can go to Miss Vic's."

"Not on your tintype, At," said the other boy darkly. "I'm in wrong with Brownie; it wouldn't do a bit of good for me to ask him. Better go yourself. What's your errand? Can't I do that for you?"

"Why, yes, I guess you can," said Tom, thrusting the bundle into his hands. "Just take this to Miss Bypath's, and tell her it's from old Mrs. Corson for the missionary box. She'll understand."

Wayne looked down at the bundle in dismay.

"Good-night! At, I can't go *there!*" he exclaimed.

"Oh, yes, you can," shouted Tom, who was already off toward "Brownie's." "You needn't go in; just hand her the package, and tell her it's for the missionary box. She won't know you from a bunch of beets."

By this time Tom was almost a block away and making good time toward his errand, for they both desired to be at Miss Gracen's early.

Wayne turned, frowning in the darkness. He had half a notion to put the bundle on the parsonage porch and tell Tom he could do his own errand, but a sense of honor made him finally turn and reluctantly walk toward Miss Bypath's house. After all, distasteful as it was for him to go near her again, he could probably get the errand over with a single sentence and hurry away before she had had time to recognize him.

He marched up to the front door, sent the bell pealing viciously through the house, and waited impatiently for the door to be opened. He even wondered whether it would do to leave the bundle on the steps and retreat, but decided that wouldn't be quite the square thing. She might think it was a joke or a personal donation, and make all kinds of trouble for Tom's mother or the missionary box, though why he should care he didn't know.

But no one came to the door, and he rang again. Still no answer when even a third ring clanged through the empty hall. He stepped back and down the path to survey the dwelling. Surely he had seen a light. Ah!

yes, there it was at the back. She was out in the kitchen, likely; but why hadn't she heard the bell? She didn't seem to be deaf the last time he saw her. He had never heard that she was. Well, he wouldn't have done his duty, and he couldn't get rid of that package, until he tried everything; so he took his way around to the back door.

Chapter XX

Ten minutes before, Lydia Bypath had stepped out of her back door wrathfully to search for the broom. She had given it to the plumber to brush the snow from his feet, when he came to fix a leak in the water pipes, and of course he had not put it back in its place. The broom was just outside the door, leaning against the wall in the darkness; and the light that streamed across the back porch wickedly left the broom in the deepest shadow at one side.

Miss Bypath stepped out on the brick pavement to see whether he had thrown the broom down in the snow, and her foot slipped on an icy brick. She put out her hand to catch hold of the porch pillar, but missed it and fell, her feet twisted under her, and her head striking the edge of the porch. It was a most humiliating position, as well as uncomfortable, and her wrath at the plumber and the lost broom increased. Both bare hands were reaching vainly for something to catch hold of; and she felt a strange, sickening pain in her leg just above the knee. The wind was sharply cold, too; and she had come out now without even her little shoulder-shawl, a carelessness of which she was seldom guilty.

She tried to rise quickly, but that strange, sick pain caught her, and held her fast when she even attempted to move; and once the sickness overcame her, and the starry sky overhead seemed to darken and lift far away into eternity. Something was the matter with her leg. What could it be? That was ridiculous. She must get into the house. She made another frantic attempt to rise,

and succeeded in getting to a sitting posture only to
fall back with a groan, this time her head and shoulders
in the snow.

It was the cold that finally brought her out of her
faintness, and that made her call aloud for help, little
realizing how short a distance her little thin, inadequate
voice would carry.

When she had called until she was weak, and the
cold had seemed to chill her through and through,
she lay and wondered how long she would stay there
before some one found her and helped her in.

What could be the matter with her leg, anyway? Was
it broken? Horrible thought. Perhaps she would lie
there all night, and freeze to death; or, if not that, at
least she would suffer terribly, and perhaps lose a
chance of having the fracture set, if it was a fracture.

Thus in sad plight she lay and began to think the
day of judgment had arrived for her at last, when suddenly she heard steps in the distance crunching cheerfully down the street, and a clear, sweet whistle. Rag-
time, and she hated it! It was some wicked boy, of
course. How terrible if they should see her here and
gather around to point a finger of scorn! Her brain
was already hazy with pain and anxiety, and in imagination she could see a set of village boys dancing about
her and loudly rejoicing over her downfall. It seemed
to her upset mind that she must keep very still until
this boy had passed.

But the steps came nearer, and she heard her own
door-bell. Instinctively she roused herself to one more
effort to get up and answer her bell. It seemed that her
house was undefended against an enemy; but she could
not rise, and only a low moan escaped her white lips.

It was thus that Wayne came upon her in the broad
belt of light that streamed from the kitchen door and
lay across the fallen victim in the snowy path. With an
exclamation of surprise he stopped and looked down
upon her. Lydia Bypath, her old nature still vivid within
her, opened her eyes and saw the boy upon whom she
had uttered an anathema a short few days before.

"What business have you here in my back yard?"

she snapped, and then closed her eyes because of the pain a sudden movement had brought.

Wayne's face darkened, and he would have turned away but that he saw by her attitude and expression she was in pain.

"I've brought a package from the parsonage for the missionary box," he said; "but I won't trouble you if you feel that way about it."

Then, as he turned, something of Miss Gracen's recent talk about the good Samaritan flashed into his mind, and he swung back again.

"Is there anything I can do for you? Shall I help you up?" he asked.

"Well, you can help me up, I suppose," she said ungraciously. "I seem to have twisted my leg."

Like a flash it went through his mind that here was a good opportunity for revenge, but with the thought came flocking the word-pictures Miss Gracen had made the Sabbath before of the soul in the sight of God when harboring hate. A wistful tenderness that hovered around her mouth and eyes as she had talked about loving people, even loving enemies, seemed to appeal to him now and his hatred melted within him.

He stooped, gathered her in his strong, young arms, and tried to lift her upon her feet; but a cry burst from her white lips, and she fell back unconscious. Then more swiftly he gathered her up again, and carried her into the house; through the kitchen, on into her sitting-room, where he laid her down upon the couch, and stood back, wondering what to do next.

His mother's long invalidism had made him gentle and helpful. He stooped over her and arranged under her head a hard little pillow embroidered with stiff lilies. He went out to the kitchen, brought some water, and bathed her head and face with a towel that he had found hanging by the sink.

Presently he saw a quiver in her face, and her eyes opened; but she began at once to groan with the pain, and he thought by her ashen look that she would faint again. He saw she was in no condition to be questioned, and he looked about frantically for a telephone, but, discovering none, concluded perhaps she couldn't afford one. Then he made a dart out of the back door and around the house to the front. Putting his fingers to his lips, he sent a long, shrill, double whistle into the crisp night air, waited a moment, and repeated it; then faintly from the distance came an answering echo.

Tom had heard. He whistled a bird-call signal that only the favored few of the boys understood, and received an immediate answer; sent a "Hurry up" after it; and this time the answer was near at hand, and he could hear Tom's flying footsteps.

"Get a doctor, At," he called as soon as he felt his words could be heard. "And go get your mother or somebody quick! Miss Bypath's fallen down and got badly hurt. Beat it! I'll stay here till you come back. I think you'd better get the doctor first."

Tom turned without a word. These boys were accustomed to obeying orders from each other when given in that tone of voice, and asking questions afterward; it was a part of their code, a bit of the loyalty to one another that kept them all such fast friends.

Tom simply flew to the doctor's office, and caught him just before his office-hours were over. But it was not his mother he went after, for she was almost sick in bed with grippe; but he hurried down the street to tell Miss Gracen. She would know just what ought to be done.

Ten minutes later Miss Gracen entered Lydia Bypath's sitting-room in time to see Wayne bending over his patient and trying to adjust the pillow and cover her with a thick, plaid shawl according to her querulous directions, given in a strained, shrill tone between groans.

A second later the doctor came in and set them all to work at once; but it was that first glimpse of Wayne, with his face all gentle and pitying, trying to do his awkward best at nursing the cross, suffering creature who cried out upon him at every move he made, that filled Miss Gracen's heart with a great joy.

She had seen the dark look on his face when this same woman had turned upon him and had sent to his soul those deadly words about his father, and she knew from some hesitating questions he had asked that forgiving was not an easy thing for this boy. She had half suspected that this was one thing that held him away from God. Yet here he was, gentle as if the cross old woman upon the couch had been dear to him.

Tom, with Dick and Harold, who had been at the Gracen home when the summons came for Miss Gracen, entered the house a second later, and, standing in the open kitchen door, looked on with a kind of admiring dismay at their comrade.

"Gee!" said Tom, looking at Harold.

"*Good*-night!" responded Harold under his breath.

"Some situation for Forrie," appreciated Dick, turning away to hide the emotion that suddenly threatened to show itself in his eyes.

Then they proceeded quietly and swiftly to obey the orders given by the doctor.

A broken leg was the verdict of the doctor, and the patient must be got to bed at once.

Tom was sent for a nurse; Harold, to the doctor's office for a certain roll of bandages which had been forgotten in the hurry; and Dick and Wayne were ordered to prepare the way to carry the patient to her bed in the adjoining room. But just the second before they left on their various errands, while they stood in a huddled group by the kitchen door attentive to the doctor's directions, Lydia Bypath opened her ferret eyes, and for the first time in her pain seemed to recognize her enemies.

"What on earth are those wicked boys doing out there in my nice, clean kitchen? Won't somebody put them out? The idea of their taking advantage of my helplessness in this way! You see, Victoria Gracen, just what they are——" and her weak voice trailed off into silence, for she had fainted again.

"The poor stew!" said Harold as he started out with Tom. "Hasn't she any sense at all? If Forrie hadn't found her out there in the snow, very probably she'd have been lying there yet."

"She doesn't deserve anything," answered Tom indignantly; "but we've got to do it for Miss Vic's sake." He paused, and a sudden thought came to them both. They each knew that Miss Gracen would say, "Do it for Christ's sake;" and in the silence the two boys looked up to the stars shyly, without a word, while each in his heart offered his service in a queer, half-questioning, boy way; and wondered whether, with all the childhood years of boyish dislike back of it, it would be accepted or not; each wistfully hoping it would, but neither daring to tell the other. Perhaps each understood how it was with his fellow, and respected the silence. It was a part of their code again.

The evening was over at last. They got poor Lydia Bypath into her bed, and quiet under an opiate while the bone was set; they established a good nurse by her side and a strong woman in the kitchen to look after the house; and then, after having worn themselves out to make her as comfortable as they could, they all went home.

"It's too late now for our programme," said Harold wistfully.

"But you'll all come in and have the refreshments," said Miss Gracen smiling. "You've worked hard, and deserve a bite to eat; and the things are all ready. Rebecca will be disappointed if they are not eaten. Then you can have one song before you go home."

"Sure! We're in for the eats every time," responded Tom heartily; and into the house they all trooped, Wayne as usual, lingering gallantly to help Miss Gracen up the steps.

"My dear boy," she said in a low tone, her hand on his arm as they stopped a second by the door, "I want to tell you how deeply touched I am by all that you have done to-night."

"It was nothing," said Wayne embarrassedly.

"Yes, it was something. It was a great deal," breathed Miss Gracen softly. "Do you think I don't know how you feel toward that woman? Do you think that I didn't hear what she said to you the other day when she fell in the snow and you went to pick her up,—my dear, great-hearted, splendid boy?"

The rich waves of red rolled over Wayne's fine face, and a flood of gladness came into his handsome eyes. There was a mingling of rage and love in his face; rage toward the woman who had spoken those awful words about his father; love for this woman who could appreciate how he had felt.

"I did it for your sake," he said, looking his gratitude into her eyes in one quick flash, and then dropping his gaze to the floor.

Her eyes flashed back their love and appreciation, and she took his hand in a warm, quick grasp.

"Thank you, my dear boy," she said earnestly, "and—you did it for Christ's sake, too, didn't you? Am I right, Wayne?"

He returned her hand-clasp, and, looking down upon her tenderly, said, in tones that were half ashamed for their admission:

"Mebbe," and smiling, turned away. It was a great deal for him to admit, but she knew it meant far more than he had said.

She went smiling and happy in to meet the rest of the boys, who had awaited her return in the big parlor, which had gradually changed its stately aspect and became their regular meeting-place.

The frail furniture of delicate workmanship had retired to a small reception-room on the other side of the hall; and had been replaced by plenty of big, easy chairs of heavier build and comfortable aspect, and a big table of dimensions suitable for evenings of study or almost any kind of a game. The piano and the rich Oriental rugs alone remained, and seemed to blend and harmonize entirely with the new surroundings. There were still some fine old paintings on the walls, but even some of those had been replaced with modern pictures, etchings and photogravures of notable men and places about which the boys had been studying.

The whole aspect of the room had changed so entirely that Mrs. Elihu Brown, calling one afternoon to

adjure Miss Gracen concerning some club duty, and
letting herself by habit into the big room on the right
instead of the small room on the left, where Hiram was
timidly endeavoring to escort her, paused in utter dismay on the threshold. She put up her lorgnette, survey-
ing the place as though it had been the ruin of some
treasure-city lying waste and desolate, then turned and
fled to the shelter of the confines of refinement within
the smaller room that Hiram, with his silver card-re-
ceiver, was indicating. Here, poised upon the edge of a
Chippendale chair, she identified one by one the Gracen
articles of vertu, recalled others missing, which had
been relegated to the attic on account of lack of room,
and marvelled at the extremity of Miss Gracen's obsession. To give up her drawing-room! That seemed to a
club woman the height of all possible fanaticism. To
give up her great, beautiful drawing-room to a pack of
ill-mannered boys! Where now could she hold receptions? No place for bridge-whist parties! What a calam-
ity!

"And you don't mean to tell me that you really serve
refreshments to those young boors in your exquisite
priceless china?" asked the caller a few minutes later,
when in response to her voluble questions Miss Gracen
took her eagerly about the reconstructed parlor, and
showed her all the devices for giving a good time to
the boys, pointing to the little tea table with its delicate
cups and silver fittings as ready as when the room
had been for her lady friends. "And you let them use
your silver spoons! Do you think it's quite right to put
temptation in their way like that? They tell me one of
the boys who comes here has a father in jail for stealing.
Did you know it?"

"Wayne Forrest is my dear and trusted friend," responded the hostess with quiet dignity. "There is no
more conscientious boy in town, and he would protect
me and all that belongs to me with his life."

"H'm!" The caller turned her lorgnette upon her
hostess curiously with the air that in a boy would have
meant, "Well, you have got it bad;" but she only replied:

"Well, you always were good. I hope you won't be disappointed in your paragons, but I must say it's more than I would do. I can't see, myself, why ironstone china wouldn't do for them to eat from. It's likely all the most of them have at home, and boys could hardly appreciate Dresden china and antique silver."

Then she turned back to the more congenial atmosphere of the small reception-room and her club business.

Miss Gracen thought of it now as she stood in the doorway and watched her boys handle the delicate cups and plates and deftly pass the spoons. They knew her silver spoons now almost as well as she did herself, and often helped pick them up and count them at the close of an evening, when all hands pitched in and helped to save the servants from extra work. She smiled to remember that not a single cup or fragile plate had been broken yet in all the handling back and forth that had been done that winter; and she believed in her heart that her boys did know the difference between them and the ironstone china, and that her dishes were a part of the refining influence that they needed in their lives.

Not that these things were, of course, essentials. If she had had nothing but ironstone china in which to serve her simple refreshments, she would not have been greatly troubled about it; but, as she had these, why should they not be consecrated, and set to work their charm of beauty, and give the uplift that all rare and lovely things can give?

Now and then she had given a word, a hint, a story, that helped them to be interested in rare things. Did they know how cloisonné was made? Naturally they studied it with new wonder and interest as she showed them the delicate metal tracery, and spoke of the wonderful effects achieved by the patient workmanship and rare colorings. Those two cups were two hundred years old! They looked at them with awe, and handled them with infinite pains, speaking of their cups out of which they drank as individuals. They grew to respect the fine, old, costly cups even more than the modern hand-painted ones, beautiful as they might be; and so the spoons, some of them, came to have stories connected with them, for Miss Gracen had told about her funny experiences at the Chicago Fair and her ride in the first Ferris wheel, as she showed the tiny spoon, half gold and half silver, with Columbus on the handle and the city of Chicago on the bowl. They knew the story of the spoons that came from Paris, and were fond of holding up the little gold ones to look through the Russian enamel set in the filigreed handles.

In fact, each beautiful adornment or elegant furnishing of her house had come to mean to these boys a part of their education; for she had told them wonderful stories of other lands, and hung them for memory on the pegs of pictures, vases and books.

It was when the changes were being made in parlor and reception-room that they learned to tell Chippendale furniture, and Sheraton, and began to take an interest in Oriental rugs, to hear how many hand-tied knots each had to the square inch, and to know that there was a lore connected with them, and an infinite variety of story and patient wonder in their weaving as well as in their strange, fantastic names. And it was so, without any word being said about carefulness or manners, that they grew to have respect for things in her house, while incidentally adding to their own stores of knowledge.

She stood looking at her boys as they ate, joked and laughed. Especially did her eyes linger on her own boy and Wayne; for of late they had been growing into close friendship, and she found herself glad. Wayne was developing in many ways, and not the least of all signs of his fine character was the way he had waited on the crabbed woman whom he had just cause to dislike. If he could forgive like that, she felt he was near to the Kingdom; for she knew by this time his hot, fiery temper and his keen sensitiveness.

Before they broke up for the night Miss Gracen stepped into their midst, and, raising her hands for silence, spoke to them in a tender, gracious tone.

"I'm as sorry as I can be, boys, that your evening was spoiled; but do you know I'm glad in a way, too, because it has given me a glimpse of the true kindliness and gentlemanliness you have in hiding in your hearts. I want to thank you for the way you have taken your disappointment, and for the beautiful way in which some of you have helped to-night, and shown real love in spite of your dislikes; and"—she paused and looked around on the group hesitatingly; then her face broke into one of its beautiful young smiles that they loved— "it is my Dick's birthday next Friday,—I wonder how you would like to go as my guests to the city, take dinner there, and attend the Symphony concert? There's a wonderful singer, John McCormack, as the soloist, and I thought you would like to hear him."

There was dead silence for a second, and then there arose a shout of joy from the group, which gathered strength and threatened to raise the roof before it was finished.

It is true that more than half the boys had only a vague idea what a "Symphony" concert might be and would have been far more attracted by a lively vaudeville or a good, stirring "movie," but whatever Miss Gracen wanted was the thing, and a jolly time together on the train, with dinner at some swell hotel, was good enough for anybody. They could stand a little dry music in between, if that was her whim. They never suspected that she had been studying the prospectus of the winter's amusements ahead for weeks with a view to selecting just the evening's programme that would elevate and awaken the latent tastes in their various natures. She thought she had detected a love of music in some; and while it was crude and largely confined to the better "rags," still, it was stirring; and she wanted to see the effect of a great orchestra on them. Even the most stupid of them would like the novelty of watching the different instruments played, and this might be the opening wedge for something more another time. She felt sure they would all enjoy the sweet singer whose Irish melodies would touch and hold them from the first note; and so she smiled in anticipation of her little experiment, while they cheered and rejoiced, and made the night air ring as they hurried down the snowy path.

But just as they reached the gate Tom and Harold and Wayne turned back to the door, which still stood wide open, where Dick and his aunt stood watching their departing guests.

It was Wayne who spoke, evidently voicing the sentiments of the three.

"Miss Gracen, we thought maybe there was something else we could do over there, to-morrow or some-time. Won't Miss Bypath need things? Walks shovelled if it snows—it's beginning a little now—furnace tended to, and errands? I could look after the furnace evenings when I come from the train, before I go home to supper. The other fellows could see to it mornings."

"Yes," said Harold, eagerly drawing his fur-lined gloves over his white hands not worn with work, "I'll do the furnace mornings, and empty the ashes. I don't have to go to school. Then Tom can look after the walks after school, and run any errands——"

The tears sprang unbidden to Miss Gracen's eyes, and she put out her hands in an involuntary gesture of blessing.

"Oh, you dear boys!" she said. "You dear, dear boys! That will be beautiful! Do you know, I think you are all trying to please Him?"

They laughed a soft, conscious laugh, and called, "Good-night" as they sped down the path; and Miss Gracen turned to see the tender look of her own eyes reflected in Dick's.

"They're great, aren't they, Aunt Vic?" he said, and then after a second: "What could I do, Aunt Vic? She's an awful boob, but I want to do something, too."

Miss Gracen closed the door quickly, and, turning, folded her own boy in her arms, much to his delighted embarrassment.

"Oh, Dick, dear. You too! Oh, I am so happy! You are all so dear!"

"Well, you see, Aunt Vic," said Dick, struggling hard to explain in a matter-of-fact tone, "we had to be because you are."

Chapter XXI

THE winter days had lengthened into spring promise, and still Miss Bypath lay and suffered—and made others suffer. Her system was in bad condition, and the bone knit very slowly, making it necessary for the cast to remain on a long time; but the rest and the forced cessation from both privation and hard work to keep up appearances were doing her good in many other ways. Her mind was more vigorous than ever, and she led the trained nurse a life of it, ordering her about from early morning till late at night, being determined, as she told her friends, to "get the worth of her money out of her," although the truth of the matter was that it was not Lydia Bypath's money that paid her—for she had no money—but Victoria Gracen's.

Faithfully all the long days had the boys taken turns in tending the furnace, emptying ashes, shovelling snow, and running errands, until they too had begun to seem to the bedridden woman like a part of her establishment, and it was nothing more than her due that they should attend to matters thoroughly.

The nurse, poor, long-suffering woman, was an imported affair from the city hospital, and knew nothing about the free gift of their service by these boys. She supposed they were paid for their work; and therefore, when Lydia Bypath sent her down with a message to them she made it fully as disagreeable as it had been originally, and even added a word or a tone now and then for the scornful silence in which her directions were always received. She had to bear such words continually from her patient, and it seemed no more than right that she should pass them on to others. Who so thick-skinned, and withal so needing them, of course, as boys? She believed that boys in general were all wrong, and that they needed constant discipline; so she gave it in full measure, as it had been measured out to her.

"Miss Bypath wishes you to be more careful about letting the ashes come up through the house in that wild fashion," she announced to Harold Constable, standing crisp and starched in her white garments on the cellar stairs, and letting her imperious eyes run over him disapprovingly, as with his brand-new blue overalls and his curly hair powdered with ashes he essayed to clean out the furnace for the first time. He looked up, his eyes dancing with fun, and, touching his plaid cap politely, said:

"Yes, ma'am, I thank you," and went cheerfully on with his work.

"He's impudent, and good-for-nothing, I think," she told Miss Bypath up-stairs, and knew not that she had been ordering about the son of the richest man in Roslyn.

Harold sinned in other ways besides sending a cloud of ashes up the registers every time he manipulated the furnace; he *would* whistle and sing. His high tenor floated up to the sick-room in distinct words something like these:

> I never-heard-of-anybody-dying
> From kissing, did-you?

for Harold continued to love rag-time for some occasions despite the fact that he enjoyed Miss Gracen's rendering of a Chopin Nocturne with as keen a delight as a musician might. Besides, rag-time just fitted emptying ashes. It suited its rhythm to the motion of the shovel excellently. So he sang. Another choice selection which came distinctly to the bed-ridden woman was:

> Do-you-take-this-woman for-your-lawful-wife?
> I do. I do.

"Indecent and irreverent songs!" Miss Bypath declared, and sent her white starched nurse flying down the cellar stairs with the admonition that he should be discharged at once if he didn't stop, whereat Harold sat himself down on the potato-bin and laughed loud and long till the echo reached up through the pipes of the register to the indignant old lady's ears.

"All right," he declared merrily; "you may discharge me if you like, but I'm afraid you won't be able to find another as good."

However, he tried to remember not to sing when he was in the house, and succeeded in forgetting only a few times. Nevertheless, in one way or another, Miss Bypath kept her hand and her tongue on matters below stairs, and made it lively indeed for the people who were trying their best to do for her.

At last, one Saturday morning in March,—the birds were out in excited groups hunting flats for the summer, and there was a smell of spring in the air,—a load of wood arrived. Miss Gracen had sent it to be used in the fireplace. It would do to supplement the furnace heat morning and evening, when they wanted to keep the furnace low on account of the mildness of the middle of the day; and it would make a cheerful blaze for Miss Bypath to look at, now that she was able to sit up a little while each day. Miss Gracen sent word that some one would come that afternoon to saw and split it, and pile it ready for use.

When the wood came, it was dumped in the wrong place, of course; but it was done, and the man drove off whistling merrily, leaving Miss Bypath raging angrily at her nurse about the inadequacy of all mankind ever to do the right thing.

Immediately after lunch the boys arrived, and the sawing and splitting began. Lulled by the dreary monotony of the sawing under her window, Miss Bypath fell asleep for a few moments, but awoke to sudden alert action at the sound of sticks of wood being laid with a ringing clang one on the top of another, their ends thumping gayly against the side of the old house.

She called fretfully to her nurse, and declared that the wood must all be carried around to the other side of the house immediately and piled over again, so as to be nearer to the back stairs, so they wouldn't have to track through her nice, clean kitchen every time they wanted a stick, and wear out her kitchen oilcloth.

The nurse descended, gave her command, and there ensued an altercation. The boys were in a hurry, and were due at a basketball game at three o'clock. It would take too long to carry the wood around the house and pile it over again. The nurse went up-stairs with the report, only to return with more forcible commands. The boys were standing directly under Miss Bypath's window, and every word that was said could be distinctly heard by her. Miss Bypath listened like a bird in ambush as the nurse delivered her ultimatum, turned with her rattley skirts clattering around her, and shut the door. She desired no further impudent words from those boys.

The boys stood in silent disgust, facing one another for a full minute, Wayne with his old frown growing upon his brows.

"Isn't she the limit?" drawled Tom.

"She's an old boob, that's what she is," said Harold fiercely. "I'm about sick of this."

Then Wayne, with a sudden lighting of his eyes and a comical lifting of his eyebrows:

"The poor stew doesn't know we're not paid for it, perhaps. Anyhow, what's the difference? We're not doing it for her. We're doing it for Miss Gracen and for —something else," he added softly. "Come on, here goes, boys. It won't take much longer if we hurry."

"Yes," drawled Tom as he rose with his arms full of wood. "You know Miss Gracen said last Sunday we'd got to love one another, or nothing else we do would go down. I s'pose we've got to love this guy, even if we *don't* like her. Gee! if she was like Miss Vic, we could love her all right, but Bydia Pylath is another kind of a proposition. Well, here goes; only I kind of wish Miss Vic could know what we're up against. It might count for more."

"It strikes me she generally knows, even if nobody tells her," declared Wayne as he picked up a great pile of wood and strode off around the back of the house.

They worked silently and swiftly, and in a short time had their work done, and departed whistling cheerily down the street, light-hearted because they had conquered.

But somehow Lydia Bypath did not feel quite comfortable in her mind, and when an hour later Miss Gracen came in to bring her a new book, and see how she was feeling, she burst out with:

"Victoria Gracen, who were those workmen you sent here to saw that wood? Were they any of those ridiculous, bad boys of yours?"

Miss Gracen's cheeks grew rosy, but she looked at the poor, little, sharp creature on the bed steadily.

"Yes, they are some of my boys," she said gently; "they offered to do it for you."

"They *offered* to do it *for me!*" said the invalid sharply. "That's a very likely story. How much do you pay them for doing it?"

"Oh, I don't pay them anything. They offered to do anything they could for you while you were laid up. They suggested it themselves. Harold Constable has been attending to your furnace mornings and Wayne Forrest evenings. Tom Atterbury did the walks and the errands, and sawed wood. They were all here this afternoon piling the wood, I think. They have been very thoughtful about you, asking me almost every day if I knew of anything else you needed."

"Harold Constable attending to my furnace! That stuck-up, stylish, Constable woman's son emptying my ashes! Victoria Gracen, I never knew you to tell lies; but really I can't believe that."

"It's quite true," said Miss Gracen gently. She wasn't sure how the irascible little creature would take the news; for there was fire of some kind in her voice, and two bright red spots had come out on her cheeks; but, when she came back from lowering the window-shade to shut out a sunbeam that was dancing daringly on Miss Bypath's counterpane, she saw that there were tears slowly running down the sharp little face.

"Why, what's the matter, Lydia, dear?" she asked tenderly.

But Lydia Bypath was weeping excitedly into her handkerchief.

"They called me a booby," she sobbed; "right under my own window they called me a booby! I used to go to parties in my young days, and I always got the booby prize in any game I ever played. Oh, I know very well what they meant. And they called me something else, too. They called me a poor s-s-st-*ew!*"

The words came out with a jerk and the poor, upset suffering woman turned her wrinkled face to the pillow, and sobbed aloud.

Victoria Gracen, as she leaned over to try and comfort her, could not refrain from a smile and a merry glinting of her eyes, as she instantly knew just how those boyish young voices of disgust had sounded; but she struggled to control her own voice.

"They didn't mean anything wrong by it, Lydia; indeed, they didn't. They are dear boys. They didn't like the way the nurse spoke to them; that was all."

"Oh, I'm not blaming them," blurted out Lydia. "I s'pose I deserved it. I sent a lot of disagreeable messages down to them. I never knew that they were doing it for nothing."

"Well, never mind," said Victoria, smoothing out the crumpled pillow. "I'll tell them you didn't know they were doing it for you."

"They weren't," snapped Lydia in much her accustomed way. "They were doing it for you! They said so. They said it didn't matter what I said, so they pleased you. They called me an old guy, too; and then they called me Bydia Pylath! Oh, they didn't do it for me in the least, but I don't know as they had any reason to, either. I guess I've been all wrong;" and she wiped her eyes, and blew her sharp, red nose, and looked pitifully repentant for such a respectable, little, old fighter as she had always been.

"Well, I guess I've wronged you too, Victoria," she snapped out, again emerging from her sopping handkerchief. "I hope you'll forgive me. I guess my nerves are pretty well upset by this nasty broken leg of mine. I don't feel very pleased with what those boys said about me, but I s'pose you can tell them I'm obliged."

It was, indeed, grudging thanks, but it was almost as hard for Lydia Bypath to thank or to praise anybody as it is for a boy to tell the tender thoughts that come into his heart, and Miss Gracen had acquired much wisdom in dealing with human hearts during her winter's work; so now she only smiled and, pressing her friend's hand understandingly, said gently:

"I'll tell them," and went away singing a song of triumph in her heart. She would tell her boys. Oh, wouldn't she tell them?

And when she did, putting the grudging words through the lovely spectrum of her own imagination, or perhaps, more strictly speaking, through the clear analysis of what she knew to be Lydia Bypath's true meaning, the boys stood back astonished, awed, and slightly incredulous, it must be owned, among themselves.

"She never said it like that," said Harold, "not on your life! She couldn't! But Miss Gracen saw that in it, and that's what she wants us to see. Gee! you could almost love her if you could see her through Miss Gracen's eyes every day."

There came a day in early June when Lydia Bypath went to church.

It was communion Sabbath, and the windows were all wide open, letting in the breath of the June roses that garlanded the parsonage in lavish display, and the song of ravished birds as they exulted in the day.

Lydia came in a wheeled chair, and it was Wayne Forrest who wheeled it and who helped her up the steps and down the aisle to her seat, and then went on to Miss Gracen's seat; for Wayne and Dick and Tom and Harold were to unite with the church that day, and Miss Gracen wanted them all to be together.

Mrs. Constable was there, having arrived home the night before, and sailed into the church with smiling condescension, attended by her portly husband, a look of unusual interest on his florid countenance. He had never expected Harold to do anything so altogether respectable as to unite with the church, and he was openly pleased. Not that he knew much about religion himself; but he felt that a connection with a church would keep a boy from doing anything that was really out-and-out disreputable.

Mrs. Atterbury was there with all the little Atterburys, and turned a loving smile toward Tom, well content that he should be with his friends on this day of all days. Just before the service began Miss Gracen's carriage drew up before the side door of the church, and there slipped out of it and into the back seat of the church a quiet little woman in black with a long, thick veil, who was attended by a handsome blue-eyed girl with thick, yellow hair and an extremely simple white dress and a small straw hat. Few saw them come in, and they went before anybody had an opportunity to speak to them. They were Wayne Forrest's invalid mother and his sister, and Wayne did not know until he reached home that day that they had been there.

The solemn, simple service was wonderfully impressive. It seemed as though the coming of these four strong young men into the church had stirred the hearts of all present; and, when they marched quietly, embarrassedly up together to the front, and stood with bowed heads and earnest mien, more than one handkerchief was hastily taken out to dry a furtive, unexpected tear. And "Isn't it wonderful!" one whispered. "That Wayne Forrest! I always thought he looked as if he had a great deal of character." They had never said anything in favor of his character before. "And that handsome Harold Constable! I heard he was real wild. I wonder if it will last. And Tom Atterbury! Mrs. Atterbury looks too happy to live. I'm sure I hope it's genuine. He does seem to have changed a great deal this winter. I wonder how Miss Gracen did it. That nephew of hers is a fine-looking fellow. It must have been his influence."

And so went the comments softly, or flashing from mind to mind, and finding their way eventually to the dinner-tables of the town. There were a few whose hearts were stirred with a deep, glad joy, knowing the work of the Holy Spirit, by the power of prayer, to change lives; and knowing the drawing power of the Lord Jesus Christ. These believed in the young converts, and had faith that they would conquer temptations through Him who is able to keep such from falling and to present them to His Father blameless at the last day.

Among these sat Victoria Gracen, too filled with deep joy to do aught but smile and thank her heavenly Father; for she had learned to love every one of these four boys as if he had been her very own.

Sitting with her four boys later, during the communion service, Victoria Gracen beheld as it were the gate of heaven opened, and caught a glimpse of her Saviour's face. There were others present of the boys who frequented her house; but they had not presumed to sit with her that day, not counting themselves to have yet attained to the privilege, but sitting thoughtful, wistful, half decided; trying to make out what had come over their comrades to make them willing to surrender their lives, their fun, their liberty, everything, thus, before the world, to an idea. They had not as yet seen the whole vision.

When church was over, and the boys went solemnly, shyly down the aisle, it was Lydia Bypath's hand that came out to greet them first, to welcome them into the wonderful new life; and her sharp little face was wet with tears and much softened with smiles.

"I haven't been much of a Christian, I know you think," she said softly; "but I'm glad you've started, and I want to ask you,"—turning to Wayne,—"to forgive me for the mean things I said to you that day on the hill."

And Wayne, the hardness and blackness all gone out of his fine face, stooped and took her hand, and in giving his hand forgave forever the thing he had struggled to forgive, and thought he never could.

Standing on the church steps with the minister, the senior elder watched Miss Gracen going down the street with her escort, following closely behind the wheeled chair containing Miss Bypath.

"It is wonderful, wonderful!" said the senior elder,

brushing a film from his eyes and clearing his throat. "How did she do it?"

"She did it by giving *herself*," said the minister softly. "She never saved herself for anything else but those boys. They said she was 'obsessed' by boys." He smiled reflectively; he had never told of Lydia Bypath's visit except to his wife. "They said she was 'obsessed by boys,' and do you know I've been thinking that, if the whole church could have such an obsession, we should be able to gather them all into the Kingdom?"

"Amen," said the senior elder, and went reverently, thoughtfully down the street behind the little procession.

Novels of Enduring Romance and Inspiration by

GRACE LIVINGSTON HILL

☐	11762	**TOMORROW ABOUT THIS TIME**	$1.50
☐	11506	**THROUGH THESE FIRES**	$1.50
☐	12846	**BEAUTY FOR ASHES**	$1.75
☐	10891	**THE ENCHANTED BARN**	$1.50
☐	10947	**THE FINDING OF JASPER HOLT**	$1.50
☐	2916	**AMORELLE**	$1.50
☐	2985	**THE STREET OF THE CITY**	$1.50
☐	10766	**THE BELOVED STRANGER**	$1.50
☐	10792	**WHERE TWO WAYS MET**	$1.50
☐	10826	**THE BEST MAN**	$1.50
☐	10909	**DAPHNE DEANE**	$1.50
☐	11005	**STRANGER WITHIN THE GATES**	$1.50
☐	11020	**SPICE BOX**	$1.50
☐	11836	**JOB'S NIECE**	$1.75
☐	11329	**DAWN OF THE MORNING**	$1.50
☐	11167	**THE RED SIGNAL**	$1.50

Buy them at your local bookstore or use this handy coupon for ordering:

Bantam Books, Inc., Dept., GLH, 414 East Golf Road, Des Plaines, Ill. 60016

Please send me the books I have checked above. I am enclosing $_____ (please add 75¢ to cover postage and handling). Send check or money order —no cash or C.O.D.'s please.

Mr/Mrs/Miss_____

Address_____

City_____State/Zip_____

GLH—2/79

Please allow four weeks for delivery. This offer expires 8/79.

BRING ROMANCE INTO YOUR LIFE

With these bestsellers from your favorite Bantam authors

Barbara Cartland

☐	11372	LOVE AND THE LOATHSOME LEOPARD	$1.50
☐	10712	LOVE LOCKED IN	$1.50
☐	11270	THE LOVE PIRATE	$1.50
☐	11271	THE TEMPTATION OF TORILLA	$1.50

Catherine Cookson

☐	10355	THE DWELLING PLACE	$1.50
☐	10358	THE GLASS VIRGIN	$1.50
☐	10516	THE TIDE OF LIFE	$1.75

Georgette Heyer

☐	02263	THE BLACK MOTH	$1.50
☐	10322	BLACK SHEEP	$1.50
☐	02210	FARO'S DAUGHTER	$1.50

Emilie Loring

☐	02382	FORSAKING ALL OTHERS	$1.25
☐	02237	LOVE WITH HONOR	$1.25
☐	11228	IN TIMES LIKE THESE	$1.50
☐	10846	STARS IN YOUR EYES	$1.50

Eugenia Price

☐	12712	BELOVED INVADER	$1.95
☐	12717	LIGHTHOUSE	$1.95
☐	12835	NEW MOON RISING	$1.95

Buy them at your local bookstore or use this handy coupon for ordering:

Bantam Books, Inc., Dept. RO, 414 East Golf Road, Des Plaines, Ill. 60016

Please send me the books I have checked above. I am enclosing $_____
(please add 75¢ to cover postage and handling). Send check or money order
—no cash or C.O.D.'s please.

Mr/Mrs/Miss_____

Address_____

City_____State/Zip_____

RO—2/79

Please allow four weeks for delivery. This offer expires 8/79.

Barbara Cartland's Library of Love

The World's Great Stories of Romance Specially Abridged by Barbara Cartland For Today's Readers.

☐	11487	**THE SEQUENCE** by Elinor Glyn	$1.50
☐	11468	**THE BROAD HIGHWAY** by Jeffrey Farnol	$1.50
☐	10927	**THE WAY OF AN EAGLE** by Ethel M. Dell	$1.50
☐	10926	**THE REASON WHY** by Elinor Glyn	$1.50
☐	10527	**THE KNAVE OF DIAMONDS** by Ethel M. Dell	$1.50
☐	10506	**A SAFETY MATCH** by Ian Hay	$1.50
☐	11465	**GREATHEART** by Ethel M. Dell	$1.50
☐	11048	**THE VICISSITUDES OF EVANGELINE** by Elinor Glyn	$1.50 $1.50
☐	11369	**THE BARS OF IRON** by Ethel M. Dell	$1.50
☐	11370	**MAN AND MAID** by Elinor Glyn	$1.50
☐	11391	**THE SONS OF THE SHEIK** by E. M. Hull	$1.50
☐	11376	**SIX DAYS** by Elinor Glyn	$1.50
☐	11467	**THE GREAT MOMENT** by Elinor Glyn	$1.50
☐	11560	**CHARLES REX** by Ethel M. Dell	$1.50
☐	11816	**THE PRICE OF THINGS** by Elinor Glyn	$1.50
☐	11821	**TETHERSTONES** by Ethel M. Dell	$1.50

Buy them at your local bookstore or use this handy coupon for ordering:

Bantam Book Catalog

Here's your up-to-the-minute listing of over 1,400 titles by your favorite authors.

This illustrated, large format catalog gives a description of each title. For your convenience, it is divided into categories in fiction and non-fiction——gothics, science fiction, westerns, mysteries, cookbooks, mysticism and occult, biographies, history, family living, health, psychology, art.

So don't delay—take advantage of this special opportunity to increase your reading pleasure.

Just send us your name and address and 50¢ (to help defray postage and handling costs).